Lea Sherwood, ebullient chef-owner of San Francisco's newest restaurant, Panache, is the toast of the city—until a controversial Silicon Valley CEO dies of poisoning at her table. Branded a suspect in the murder of her old flame, Lea soon resolves to investigate on her own. Her pursuit of the killer pits her against rogue executives, wannabe millionaires, and cocky software wizards. It also leads her into a treacherous underworld of the Valley, where industrial espionage and financial fraud flourish, and greed reigns. As her life spins out of control, Lea risks all to confront the killer—and the dark side of the human heart.

PATTERNS IN SILICON

PATTERNS IN SILICON

Published by Drake Valley Press
Clinton, Mississippi, USA 39060
1-866-442-4990
www.drakevalleypress.com

This novel is a work of fiction. Any resemblance to actual persons, living or dead, is entirely coincidental. The characters, names, plots and incidents are the product of the author's imagination. References to actual events, public figures, locales or businesses are included only to give this work of fiction a sense of reality.

Cover art by Bonnie Watson. Copyright © 2004, Drake Valley Press.

ISBN 0-9728186-4-2 (Trade Paper)

Library of Congress Cataloging-in-Publication Data applied for

Printed in the United States of America

10 9 8 7 6 5 4 3 2

Author's website: www.maureenrobb.com

Dedication

In memory of my aunt, Marguerite Surry,
who introduced me to the joy of reading

Acknowledgments

Many thanks to the talented chefs who allowed me to observe behind-the-scenes at their San Francisco restaurants: Michael Mina of Aqua; Anne Gingrass and David Gingrass of Hawthorne Lane; and Sylvain Portay of The Dining Room at The Ritz-Carlton. They and their staffs generously took the time to answer my many questions.

Thanks also to my friends and sources in Silicon Valley who offered their expertise—and who in no way are to be associated with the chicanery depicted in this book!

I am also indebted to Boyd E. Lasater, Contra Costa County forensic toxicologist; Lt. Craig Zamolo of the Walnut Creek Police Department; staff of the San Francisco Police Department; and to so many members of the Mystery Writers of America and Sisters in Crime for their unstinting support and advice. I'd particularly like to thank Steve Hamilton, for his excellent comments on an early first chapter, and Roberta Isleib, golfer and writer *nonpareil*.

Finally, I thank my husband John for all his encouragement and help in making this book possible.

1

"You've certainly got a nerve," marveled Lea Sherwood. Keith Whitten laughed as if she'd paid him a compliment and attempted to kiss her on the cheek.

Lea sidestepped Keith adroitly and looked him in the eye. He was the last man she wanted to see in her restaurant that night, but she had to seat him. She had no choice. Both the law and her pocketbook dictated that she serve all paying guests.

Keith unbuttoned his jacket and brushed a speck of lint from the lapel of his double-breasted Italian suit. In the past year he had brazenly embraced the role of Silicon Valley CEO. His once unruly fair hair was now fastidiously trimmed, and his innate enthusiasm was muted, tinged with a self-conscious patina of sophistication. Keith's thin lips curled into a slight smile. Earlier that day he had achieved a coup— the takeover of Decision Ace, Inc. Apparently he had come to gloat.

Lea led Keith and the two men who accompanied him to an alcove table by a window. Outside, the cobblestones of San Francisco's old Barbary Coast glistened in the early June fog.

She took their drink order, dropped it off at the bar, and made her way to the kitchen.

Sydney Toth, Lea's no-nonsense *sous-chef*, accosted her as soon as she entered. "One of the servers said Keith Whitten is here."

"He is indeed," Lea said.

Sydney grimaced and with a linen towel hastily blotted flecks of sauce defacing the otherwise pristine rims of two gold, white, and crimson dinner plates. "For Table 8," she said.

Lea, who was short two servers that night, took the plates and maneuvered through the crowded kitchen. An oven door slammed as one of the cooks retrieved a leek tart. Veal scallops sizzled on a burner, and the aroma of mussel bisque vied with the woodsy incense of roasted chanterelles. Lea glanced at her six young line cooks in their starched white jackets and black-and-white, hounds-tooth checked pants. They spun intently between the stainless-steel work counters and the long gas range against the wall, jostling one another as they jiggled sauté pans over spurting blue flames. Sydney, ever alert, paced before the overlooking counter, shouting an occasional question and monitoring the progress of each dish.

Back in the dining room, Lea presented the plates with a flourish to Justine and Peter Brill, self-proclaimed foodies and two of her best customers.

Justine brushed back a lock of her honey-blond hair and took a bite of grilled sea bass with red pepper mousse, yellow tomatoes, and arugula. "Oh, Lea, this is scrumptious!" Justine exclaimed.

Peter smoothed his graying moustache with his forefinger and grunted his satisfaction as he speared a second forkful of fresh Indiana Culver Duck.

"There's just one thing we've been wondering, Lea," Justine said.

"What's that?" Lea asked. She smiled broadly, pleased to see them enjoying their dinners.

"We've been admiring your new painting." Justine gestured at an abstract canvas done in bold strokes of scarlet and black. "But whatever is it supposed to be?"

"It's called *My Inamorata*, and it's by Sejei Hirai, the Japanese artist who lives on a houseboat in Sausalito," Lea said with a mischievous air. "Actually, I use it as a kind of Rorschach test of my customers. Tell me what it suggests to you."

Justine pursed her lips. "I'd say it does remind me of love."

Peter sniggered. "It reminds me of madness."

Lea burst out laughing. "Well, some say there's a fine line between the two!" With that, she left the couple to their dinners.

When she returned to Keith's table with champagne flutes and the reserve *Blanc de Blancs* the men had ordered, Keith introduced her to his companions. Both were executives of Whitten Systems Corp., Keith's software firm.

"Lea's an old friend," Keith said as he appraised the dining room, with its soaring ceiling and eclectic crowd. "She's done a great job here with Panache. It's my favorite San Francisco restaurant," he said proprietarily.

"Mine too," Lea thought. She popped the cork.

As she poured the wine, the boyish-faced man who'd been introduced as Randy Derrough spoke up. "Congratulations, Keith," he said. "I've got to confess—I was skeptical when you began making overtures to Decision Ace. And after they gagged at your initial offer, I never thought you'd pull off a merger. Now I see that this could be the first in a string of acquisitions for us."

"There's just one thing I don't understand," said Marshall Schroth, a well-built man with a receding hairline. He and Randy were seated across from Keith. "The takeover went through smoothly—so why did you call an emergency board meeting for tomorrow morning? No one's been able to tell me. Why all the secrecy?"

Keith stiffened. "How did you hear about it?"

Lea placed a standing silver ice bucket near Keith's elbow and nestled the remaining wine in a cocoon of ice. She turned from the table and began to walk through the dining room, pausing here and there to exchange pleasantries with her diners.

As she skirted Table 23, she noticed that Marvis Choate, a regular patron, had hardly touched her food. Lea stopped and laid a hand on the elderly woman's shoulder. "Is something wrong?"

"Oh, I don't know, my dear," Marvis said apologetically. "I ordered the chicken with tarragon cream because I enjoyed a dish by that name last year in Talloires. This is interesting, but it doesn't taste the same."

Lea whisked the plate away and promised to bring a substitute.

As she headed for the kitchen, Lea sighed. There were as many interpretations of each classic recipe as there were chefs. And Lea had won raves for this particular dish. But the customer was always right. Especially in San Francisco, where dining out was a religious experience. The city led the nation in restaurants per capita, the markets catered to exotic foodie trends, and the media raptly chronicled the peregrinations of celebrity chefs.

San Francisco was, however, the riskiest dining market in the country. Of the city's 3,000 restaurants, a third failed in their first year. Two out of three didn't make it to the end of their second. Competition was brutal, and only the nimble and well-capitalized survived.

Nevertheless, Lea had opened Panache five months ago, and so far, the critics had been kind. Lea smiled as she walked past a framed copy of *Bon Vivant's* review, which she'd hung in the hallway leading to the kitchen. She knew one passage by heart: "The ebullient Lea Sherwood, veteran of three-star kitchens in the south of France and Brussels, has created a stylish oasis of civilized dining in the financial center of San Francisco. The modern space is stunning, and Sherwood's luscious plates have nuance and verve. Each night she creates smart, contemporary classics of California-French cuisine. This 33-year-old chef-owner has a bright future ahead of her!"

The accompanying photograph showed Lea celebrating with her staff on opening night. She glanced now at her image: playful hazel eyes under strong brows, her oval face framed by auburn, shoulder-length hair and her slender figure sheathed in the gold silk dress she often wore to greet dinner guests.

So she had passed a milestone—reviews and word of mouth had built an initial clientele—but ultimate survival was far from certain. San Francisco diners were notoriously fickle in their allegiance.

As Lea re-entered the kitchen, Sydney called out. "Where is that Robert? His order for Table 31 is ready."

"He's busy with a party of six," Lea said. "Give it to me. I can take it." Instantly, she realized with a pang that the table was Keith Whitten's.

Sydney arranged three plates on a tray, which she thrust at Lea.

Keith was boasting about his prowess as a CEO when Lea got to his table, and again she marveled at his behavior. She'd never seen him so feisty and voluble. Either his success—or the *Blanc de Blancs*—had gone to his head.

Lea served the men and handed her tray off to Robert.

As she strolled through the dining room, Lea tuned into the buzz—an almost palpable energy that animated the room. Snatches of conversation came her way:

— "Kristin doesn't begin to understand why I'm dissatisfied. She says I'm successful because I'm an attorney. But hell, everybody I know is an attorney."

— "My English teacher once said there are three classes of people. Those who talk about other people, those who talk about things, and those who talk about ideas. I've always remembered that."

— "I had to laugh when I finally saw the Rosetta stone. Human nature hasn't changed in 2000 years. It's a decree from Ptolemy V granting economic favors to the temple priests. In return for their political support!"

At Table 14, Lea stopped to help Robert extract the corks from three consecutive vintages of Caymus Cabernet.

Robert, an acting student with leading man good looks, brought a theatrical air to Panache and was popular with guests. He and Lea gently decanted the shimmering mauve liquid and poured it into flights for a vertical tasting.

The host of the table, an avuncular man sporting an olive green silk cravat, beamed with *bonhomie* and raised his glass. "If I may quote Alexandre Dumas: 'Wine is the intellectual part of a meal.' "

Suddenly Lea was startled by a commotion and whirled to see Keith, torso contorted, slumped over the table. He was gasping for air and trying to loosen his tie. In an instant his entire body was racked by a spasm.

"He's having a seizure. Call a doctor!" someone cried.

Lea dashed to the phone and dialed 911. An almost tangible anxiety rippled through the dining room.

Keith's eyelids were fluttering and he appeared barely conscious when paramedics burst through the front door six minutes later. Lea averted her gaze as Keith was hoisted onto a stretcher. Marshall Schroth and Randy Derrough shrank back into their chairs.

"He was fine when we came in," Randy asserted, apropos of nothing. "It must have been something he ate."

A stunned silence prevailed as the medics wended their way through the dining room, past the peach and ecru walls, the custom-designed table lamps, the multimedia artwork, and the *outré* art glass. Finally Keith was conveyed across the intricate black, white, and coral mosaic-tile walkway that snaked through the foyer.

As the stretcher cleared the front door, the room erupted. Lea nervously caught shrill snippets of conversation. Apparently word was circulating about who Keith was.

Lea's distress deepened as the evening dragged on, and her staff, sensitive to her mood, grew fretful and tense. Sydney, who virtually never made an error, sent four meat plates to a vegetarian table. Robert spilled coffee on the lap of a bank vice president, and Ernesto, the good-natured dishwasher, dropped a rack of cordial glasses and brandy snifters. Lea thought the night would never end.

At 11:30 Lea gratefully bolted the front door and collapsed into a seat in the foyer. She'd been on her feet since dawn, walking the equivalent of at least eight miles. Tonight, if she were lucky, she might be able to stretch her usual five and a half hours of sleep into six.

Insistent knocks on the front door brought her abruptly to her feet. Lea peered out the plate-glass window onto fog-shrouded Jackson Street and saw two middle-aged men in sport coats and slacks. One of them flashed a metal badge.

Startled, Lea went to the door and eased it open.

"Miss Sherwood?" inquired the taller man, who wore a bow tie. He extended an identification card. Lea glanced at it and barely caught his name—Dante Talifano—and the fact that he was an inspector for the SFPD. Talifano then introduced his companion, a stout Japanese-American man, as Inspector George Fukuhara.

"What can I do for you?" Lea asked.

"We'd like to talk to you about Keith Whitten. We understand he had dinner here tonight."

Lea shifted uneasily and opened the door wider to admit them. She led the way to seats in the dining room as the servers cleared tables and pretended that nothing was happening.

"How is Keith?" Lea asked, her heart thudding. He had been on her mind all night.

The two men exchanged a pregnant glance. "He died almost two hours ago," Talifano said.

Lea gasped, then shuddered. The notion of Keith dying seemed utterly improbable. "How did it happen?" she stammered.

"We don't have the particulars yet, but indications are that it may not have been a natural death," Talifano replied. "We'll do an autopsy in the morning."

Fukuhara regarded her stonily.

"Now, Miss Sherwood," Talifano continued. "Tell us everything that occurred from the time Mr. Whitten arrived. His companions are adamant that he was fine before they got here."

Lea complied, struggling to control the tremor in her voice.

"And you personally served their dinner? Isn't that unusual?"

She explained that she'd been shorthanded that night.

The two homicide inspectors exchanged another glance.

"We understand that you and Mr. Whitten were once good friends," Talifano stated.

"Ah, we did go out for a few months last year." As she often had, Lea berated herself for not having been a better judge of character when she had met Keith. If only she'd been more observant.

"And yet you are now seeing a Mr. Paul Boyd. We're told that Mr. Boyd's software company has just been acquired by Mr. Whitten's. Apparently the takeover was acrimonious."

Lea thought back over recent months. Just as she and Paul had grown close, Keith had launched his drive to buy Paul's firm. The pain and frustration she'd felt, unable to help as Paul fought desperately to save his company, swept over her again now.

She tried to explain to Talifano that Paul had not wanted to sell his start-up but had been outvoted by his venture capital partners, who held the majority of the stock. "It wasn't a hostile takeover in the strictest sense," she said. She neglected to mention that by all accounts, prior to the buyout, Keith had developed a personal vendetta against Paul, and that she felt responsible.

Talifano referred to his notepad. "We're told that Mr. Whitten's firm specializes in general business applications software—accounting and cost-control systems, inventory management—that type of thing." He glanced up at Lea.

"And Mr. Boyd, we're told, has developed a decision-support software package that's catching on. Apparently it's a sophisticated product that helps companies automate certain aspects of management decision making."

Lea nodded slowly. It felt bizarre to hear him discuss Paul's firm under these circumstances.

"So, Mr. Boyd didn't want to sell his company. Particularly to Keith Whitten." Talifano stated it as fact. "Under the circumstances, it's only natural that you'd resent Mr. Whitten. Who could blame you?"

Lea stifled a sudden impulse to laugh, and she flushed at her near loss of control. *Just relax*, she told herself as she struggled to stay calm.

"Is that a rhetorical question?" she asked.

Fukuhara coughed as though something had caught in his throat. His eyes darted to Talifano, who continued on, unperturbed. "When did Mr. Whitten make his reservation for tonight?"

"He didn't," Lea said. "I had no idea he was coming."

She was met by silence and wondered if this was a ploy to increase her discomfort and induce her to say something incriminating.

Talifano held her gaze, assessing her. "Do you mind if we question your staff, Miss Sherwood?"

"Of course not. Speak to anyone you wish."

As the cooks and dishwashers awaited their turn in the kitchen, Talifano and Fukuhara began with the servers. One by one they were summoned: Dominique, a coltish young Australian who hoped to become a professional cello player; Stephen, a physics major putting himself through college who worked at soup kitchens on weekends; Josh, a rakish writer who had a way with the ladies; Pierce, an affable Brit, who, in the European style, planned a career as a server; and finally, Robert.

Lea retreated to a far corner of the dining room and curled up in a chair, crossing her arms tightly against her chest. A curious ache welled up, and her mind raced. She strained to remember every word and nuance of Keith's conversation that night. But as her staff trickled out and 2:00 A.M. approached, she was stymied by one inescapable question. Why would anyone want to kill Keith Whitten, aging whiz kid and Silicon Valley CEO?

2

The closing swell of an organ fugue subsided, and a hush fell over St. Andrew's Church of the Peninsula. Werner Sewell, the silver-haired chairman of Byteron, the San Jose database software firm, strode to the rose marble podium. He would be the first to deliver a eulogy. Sewell stood erect beneath a stained-glass panel of incandescent blue and gold, solemnly surveying the congregation. The elite of Silicon Valley had come to pay their last respects to Keith Whitten.

Sewell's voice crackled over the microphone in staccato bursts. "Ladies and Gentlemen, we are here today to honor one of our best, who, inexplicably, was cut down in his prime. Keith Whitten was an exemplar in an industry known for its brilliant performers and avid dreamers. And yet Keith did more than take a private vision and make it a reality. He was driven by more than a passion to create. Keith Whitten above all had a burning desire to make a difference." Sewell's voice, now resonant and tinged with regret, carried to the far corners of the church.

Lea stirred against the blond oak pew. She and Paul Boyd were seated in the fourth row, near the casket. It was late morning on Tuesday, five days after Keith's death. Lea's palms were moist, and the jacket of her fitted black suit was damp against her back as the rays of the sun streamed through the church windows. Since entering St. Andrew's, Lea had been jittery and restless.

Paul reached over and squeezed her hand. Lea turned to him and smiled faintly. She knew that the last few days had been difficult for him too.

"Although he died tragically, at the young age of 38, Keith Whitten lived his life intensely," Sewell was saying. "He truly lived for the creator's elation at the moment of technological breakthrough. And his passion above all else was to explore his limits."

Sewell paused to take a breath, and Lea heard a chuckle from the pew behind her. "Werner obviously didn't know Keith very well," a male voice said. "The theme of his life was success at any cost. All Keith lived to prove was how big an egotistical bastard he could be."

Another man replied, "I think Werner and Keith had lunch together maybe three times."

Sewell concluded his remarks and stepped down from the podium. He was followed by three other Valley titans of industry, two of whom appeared to be under 30. Each spoke in a similar vein. Lea wondered how well any of them had known Keith.

As the penultimate speaker took his seat, Lea consulted her program. The last to pay his respects would be Bennett Alston, vice president and general counsel of Whitten Systems. How odd to hear from only one person who had actually worked with Keith.

Alston, a tall, gaunt man in his late 50s with a mournful expression, took his place before them. The well-heeled crowd stirred but maintained a respectful silence. Alston spoke at length of his collaboration with Keith, and Lea was relieved when he finally prepared to close.

"I think I speak for all of us here when I say that Keith Whitten will be sorely missed," the attorney intoned. "Keith was not only a visionary in our great industry, he was a personal friend. The others have spoken eloquently of his legacy. But I can attest that Keith will also be remembered by those whose lives he touched. Speaking on behalf of his colleagues, I can say unequivocally that the purity of Keith Whitten's vision was surpassed only by his integrity."

Suddenly Lea was startled by a gasp. She glanced at the woman to her immediate left. Francine Reese, vice president and chief financial officer of Whitten Systems, had been fidgeting throughout the service. Francine now tossed back her blond curls and stared wide-eyed at Bennett Alston. A corner of her mouth curled in derision. "Hypocrite!" she hissed.

After the funeral, Lea and Paul mingled with the others in the lush church courtyard. Oleanders bloomed, palm trees swayed, and the air was steeped in the fragrance of jasmine. Lea looked on sadly as former mourners talked shop and exchanged business cards. Keith Whitten, *wunderkind*, was already forgotten.

At noon they said their good-byes and walked in silence to Paul's white Mazda. As Lea settled into her seat, she wanted to pinch herself to make sure she wasn't dreaming. Not only was she trying to come to terms with Keith's death, but, in a bizarre twist of fate, Paul had been recruited to take over as president and CEO of Keith's firm.

Carter Weberling, the venture capitalist whose partnership had backed Paul's start-up, and who was now a director of Whitten Systems, had argued that Paul uniquely possessed the technical expertise to integrate the two merged companies. And Whitten's board, reluctant to launch a lengthy executive search, had been persuaded to accept Paul. Still, it had been a hard sell on Carter's part. The board's attitude was clearly, "Show me."

Lea glanced over at Paul as he started the car. He was just under six feet and slim, with an angular face, deep-set blue eyes, and tousled dark hair that brushed his ears. At 34, he usually had energy to spare, but as they headed next for Whitten Systems, he seemed tired and preoccupied.

Paul sensed Lea's glance and turned to her, rousing himself from his reverie. "Are you all right?" he asked. "You seemed kind of shaky during the service."

"I know. I'm not sure why Keith's death has hit me so hard. Maybe because he was so young. He had so much of his life ahead of him."

Paul didn't reply, and Lea wondered if he was thinking about his father, a brilliant engineer, who had also died young—in a car crash when Paul was 15. Paul still missed him.

"Are you thinking about your dad?" she asked softly.

Paul nodded, and a muscle twitched in his jaw. "My mother's never gotten over the accident, and I suppose I never have either. My dad had so much he wanted to accomplish, and he wanted to see me go to college and get established in life. Then there are all the things we'd planned to do together. Go back to his family home in Scotland to look up long-lost relatives. Go backpacking in the Sierras. Maybe even start a company together."

"You never really recover from that kind of loss," Lea said.

"No, you don't." Paul paused and appeared to make a decision. "But dwelling on what you *don't* have is a sure path to misery. You can make the most of what you have, and I intend to. I count myself extremely lucky to have you." They were at a stop light, and Paul leaned over and kissed her. "In fact I hope to make up for lost time."

Lea caught her breath. The tension that had been building in her all morning began to melt away. She smiled invitingly. "Do you really mean that? Will we get to spend more time together?"

Paul raised an eyebrow. "Do I detect a note of doubt? Just you wait and see." He clapped his hand to his heart. "I hereby do pledge to lavish you with the attention you deserve. I look forward to morning walks with you by the ocean, afternoons hiking on Mount Tam, and evenings by the fire gazing soulfully into your eyes."

"Ummm," Lea said silkily. "I like this conversation." For the first time that day, she felt carefree. "Do you solemnly swear?"

Paul gave her a look that was at once amused and promising. "Absolutely," he said, raising her hand to his lips.

When they arrived at Whitten Systems, Paul parked and pulled a small, leather-bound book from his jacket pocket. "I brought something for you," he said. "I found my grandmother's diary last night when I was looking through my father's things." He smiled and handed it to her. "I'd like you to have this."

Lea flushed with pleasure and gingerly opened the yellowed pages. The entry that appeared in a garlanded handwriting was dated August 5. "Yesterday was a glorious day," she read. "Bill and I drove to the coast and had a long picnic lunch. Wild pink roses grew by the rocky shoreline, and loons flew overhead." Lea stopped reading and gently cradled the book. "Bill was your grandfather, wasn't he?"

Paul nodded. "This covers the year she met him and got engaged. She writes about the self-doubts she had growing up, the struggle to be dutiful to her family and yet try to live her own life, and the intense feelings of falling in love. She describes how she came to know that my grandfather was the man for her."

Lea looked up at him with shining eyes. "I don't know what to say."

"You don't have to say anything." Paul reached over to touch her hair. "She would have liked you."

They got out of the car and crossed the parking lot, passing a vintage Toyota MR2 whose license plate border caught Lea's eye. "Real Programmers Do It in C++," it asserted. She pointed it out to Paul, and they laughed. "Only in Silicon Valley do people define themselves in terms of their ideal computer language," Lea said.

Whitten Systems was headquartered in one of the Valley's ubiquitous industrial parks. Norfolk pines and lush landscaping framed acres of two-story, modern buildings, each vying to make its own architectural statement. The reflected rays from a looming bank of aqua-tinted glass momentarily blinded Lea.

They took a winding walkway that led to the company's entrance. A lean runner sprinted across their path on his way to the jogging trails, and a group of young Chinese men in T-shirts and jeans sauntered by—laminated identification badges flopping against their front pants pockets. A Sikh in a turban stopped and politely congratulated Paul on his new job.

"I understand you're going to pick up where you left off with your own decision-support system," he said.

"Yes," Paul replied, his eyes lighting up. "I'm really looking forward to it. Thank you for asking," he added, shaking the man's hand.

"How is it going?" Lea asked as they moved on.

Paul beamed. "I had an idea the other day on how to step up to the next level. If it works, it'll be *terrific*."

"You're really excited, aren't you?" Lea asked happily. It was so good to see him like this again.

"Honestly?" He grinned. "It could be the best idea I've ever come up with. I can't wait to get into it. It's a redesign of the original package—with new features, but simpler and far more elegant. It'd eliminate several steps and run *much* faster." He spread his arms wide. "I'm not claiming it will save the world, but I hope it can make it better."

Lea smiled delightedly. "It sounds fantastic!"

They entered the Whitten Systems lobby, and Paul stopped at the reception desk to get Lea a visitor's badge. He then pulled out his own electronic badge with his name and photo, waved it over a waist-high sensor, and led the way through the heavy glass security doors separating the lobby from the company's inner sanctum.

When they reached Paul's corner office on the second floor, Lea caught her breath. She hadn't realized he'd be working in Keith's former lair, and she squirmed at the sight of Keith's blatant trophy photo gallery. Frame after frame lined the walls. Keith with the heads of Fortune 500 companies and national sports-franchise owners. Keith with two governors of California.

"There was no other empty office," Paul said in answer to her unspoken question.

He went to his rosewood desk and sank into his high-backed leather chair. He nodded at the stacks of documents that covered virtually every inch of the desk's surface. "Will you look at all this?" he said. "As much as I'm dying to start on my own redesign, first I've got to take care of Keith's unfinished business."

Since entering the office, Paul had become subdued, and Lea sensed that something was troubling him.

"Is anything wrong?" she asked as she took one of two armchairs across from his desk.

He ran a hand through his hair, tousling it further. "I'm not sure," he said. "This is the first chance I've had to look at the books, and frankly, I don't like what I see."

"What do you mean?" Lea moved to the edge of her chair.

"I don't want to be an alarmist, but I have a funny feeling about the first quarter's earnings report. I stayed up last night reading it."

"And?"

"It looks to me like earnings may have been substantially overstated."

"What?" Lea groaned. "You can't be serious! Didn't Carter's auditors check the books?"

"Not since Whitten Systems was acquiring us outright. Also, Carter and his venture partners got cash, not stock. They didn't have a compelling reason to question recent earnings."

Lea took a deep breath. "What makes you suspect Keith might have inflated profits?" she asked incredulously.

Paul shook his head. "Let's just say you get a sixth sense in this business about what's legitimate and what's not. After all, it wouldn't be the first time someone tried to conceal financial problems with creative accounting. At some firms, stretching the rules is a hallowed art form." He hesitated. "Or, it could be something worse."

"Do you think money could be missing?" Lea stared at him.

"It's hard to tell what's going on at this point. Let me put it another way. Nowhere in its financial statements does Whitten Systems define how it calculates revenue. It makes me wonder how Keith valued his shipments to distributors. And whether his sales were overstated because he improperly booked shipments as sales." Paul glanced out the window, where a mockingbird on a pine bough was flexing its wings. "See, distributors usually have the right to send back any unsold products. That's why a lot of firms won't book shipments as revenue until goods are actually sold. Others set up reserves against potential returns. But if you aggressively push your products on distributors and then count them as sold, you can significantly distort earnings. You can claim you made millions on products that may in fact never sell."

"Is that illegal?"

Paul gestured carelessly. "No, but you can see the potential for trouble. And investors and securities analysts get very upset if they think they've been hoodwinked."

"So how do you tell Whitten shareholders that you may or may not have a problem?"

"Exactly. How do I?" A corner of Paul's mouth twitched.

"You're afraid this is serious."

He nodded. "I also learned that Keith was deferring vendor payments by about 90 days. The industry average is 30 to 45. It could be a sign he was strapped for cash."

"Do you think he got in over his head by buying you out?"

"I don't know. Keith was a peculiar guy." Paul sighed. "Just look at the way he did business. He was a master at touting vaporware. You know, products that don't yet exist. That way his customers were afraid to buy from competitors until they could see what rabbit he'd pull out of his hat."

"I would think that could backfire," Lea said sharply.

"Sure. In the long run, it can definitely hurt you." Paul considered this. "Maybe Keith's tricks finally caught up with him."

"But what does Francine Reese say? Isn't she your chief financial officer?" Lea recalled the woman's strange outburst at the funeral.

"Francine?" Paul laughed shortly. "I haven't talked to her about this yet. I need to discuss it first with Carter. He can tell me how best to approach her."

"You don't think she...."

"I don't know what to think at the moment," Paul said evenly. "But it wouldn't be the first time a finance executive juggled the books. And if she *was* concealing a cash flow problem—or maybe even embezzling—I'd better watch my step."

Lea shivered. "What if Keith suspected Francine was stealing from him?"

"I'd say it was an excellent motive for murder."

Lea shifted uncomfortably. From the start, she'd had mixed feelings about Paul's accepting this job. To assume responsibility for Keith's company was a leap into the unknown. And Paul might be working with a killer. Her heart flip-flopped.

Paul seemed to read her mind. "Don't worry," he said warmly. "I can handle the situation."

Lea managed a taut smile and said nothing. It would only distract Paul to voice her misgivings. She only hoped that for his sake, he'd made the right choice. He had already suffered the blow of losing his company after risking everything on it. And, although he hadn't explicitly said so, Paul apparently felt betrayed by Carter Weberling, who had been both his friend and mentor. Instead of continuing their support of Paul's firm, Carter and his venture partners had cashed in their shares by selling his company to Keith.

"All my life I've tried to build things," Paul had once told her. "You might call it my passion. As a kid I built model trains, ships, and cars. Then I assembled computers, and wrote my own programs. By starting my company, I was doing all the things I'd ever loved."

Paradoxically, by accepting the Whitten Systems job, Paul could salvage his previous work. But Lea was keenly aware of Paul's aversion to corporate politics. He had little tolerance for office turf wars. Instead he lived for intellectual challenges, and to make full use of his mind. Lea thought of his ability to penetrate to the heart of an issue and to draw his own conclusions. It was this ability to think for himself that had initially attracted her.

Paul, however, was clearly in the eye of a gathering storm. Whitten Systems' stock had plummeted 18 points the day after Keith's death, and the buzz was that it could go into free-fall. Paul's mandate was to restore confidence— immediately.

And now this. As Lea hoped for an innocent explanation to Paul's suspicions, she felt a burst of anger toward Keith. It was only when Paul looked pointedly at her hands that she realized she was clenching them.

She was trying to stay calm when the detectives who'd questioned her the night Keith died suddenly appeared at Paul's door. Inspector Talifano curtly addressed Paul. "Mr. Boyd, can you meet with us now?"

Paul frowned and glanced at Lea. "I suppose so," he said reluctantly.

With a renewed sense of dread, Lea got up and nodded at the men as she walked out of Paul's office. Talifano inclined his head in response.

She shut Paul's door behind her and turned to see Joy Nugent, Keith's former secretary, seated at her desk. Paul had asked her to stay on to help ease the transition.

Joy, who had worked with Keith for two years, evidently didn't believe in dressing down for funerals. In church she'd been resplendent in a vivid orange coat-dress, red lipstick, and perilously high, black sling-back heels. At 24, she wore her raven hair bobbed at chin length and exuded the type of glamour Lea associated with Nick and Nora Charles in *The Thin Man*.

Lea perched on Joy's desk in the shadow of a glossy Ficus tree. "I can't imagine why the police are back," Lea said. "They've already questioned Paul twice." The fact nagged at her.

Joy sighed profoundly. "Who knows? They've taken over the office. Our board room is now their command post." Joy crossed her eyes and feigned a zombie-like expression. "Last night they interrogated me until 11:00. I was bleary-eyed driving home."

The phone rang, and Joy lifted the receiver with a slender manicured hand. She shrugged apologetically to Lea.

Lea rose and went to the credenza perpendicular to Joy's desk. She picked up the day's *San Francisco Herald,* and the headline struck her like a blow. *No Leads in Restaurant Poisoning of CEO.* Lea felt the blood rise to her face. Why did the press keep implicating Panache in Keith's death?

She gazed blankly at the *Herald* and thought back to the time she had spent with Keith. They had met almost a year ago at a charity event. She had donated food; he software. Keith had been easy to like at first. He was smart, with an irreverent sense of humor. And he was a mine of offbeat information. Conversations with him were quirky and unpredictable.

Given their hectic schedules, they saw each other once a week for about three months. But Lea soon saw that beneath the glittering patter, Keith insisted on being the center of attention. At first she accepted this. Most people prefer talking to listening. And few make the effort to understand others who are different from them. But Keith, she eventually realized, was also disdainful of anyone who wasn't on top. He taunted his staff with threats or rewards. Clearly, he judged himself in terms of the power he wielded.

Still he remained in many ways the boy wonder, resting on the laurels of his early success. When competitors began to overtake him, he grew desperate to secure his personal niche. In fact his buyout of Paul's firm was a bid to acquire quality software that he simply couldn't produce himself. Keith, so cocky about his high IQ, never understood that it was only a tool at his disposal. Without integrity—or sustained hard work—he could never hope to stay on top.

Unfortunately, Keith had been the one to introduce Lea to Paul, at Panache, where Keith had made his first overture to buy Paul's firm. It was after she had stopped seeing him, but Keith had still been piqued that Lea preferred Paul. She supposed Keith never realized that Paul had the convictions he lacked. It had been just like Keith to celebrate his victory dinner at Panache.

Joy was now on a second call, and a catch in her voice roused Lea.

"I'm sorry, Dr. Pruett. It is true," Joy said. "We just got back from Keith's funeral." She listened for a moment. "Please, don't worry. I'm sure Keith kept your report confidential. What? Yes. I certainly will." Joy hung up and made a quick note to herself.

"Who was that?" Lea couldn't help but ask.

Joy glanced around to be sure they were alone. She lowered her voice. "A Dr. Anderson Pruett. He's a specialist on Asian economies for a management consulting firm here on the Peninsula. In fact he was calling from Taipei. He heard a rumor that Keith had been killed and he couldn't believe it." Joy frowned. "Funny, he seemed quite upset."

"It can be a shock to hear that someone you know is dead."

"No, it was more than that. It's almost as though he was afraid. Not at all like the time he called before."

"How so?"

"Oh, Keith had consulted him last month, and he called back to report the day before Keith died. I remembered him because his firm has such a difficult name—Kincaid Jenkins & Moore International. Also he made a nuisance of himself. He insisted I drag Keith out of a meeting."

Lea thought back to the night Keith had been killed, and the conversation she'd overheard. It had been bothering her. "Do you know why Keith called an emergency board meeting for the morning after the merger?" she asked.

Joy shook her head. "All I know is he asked me to set it up. He wouldn't say why. It *was* odd, now that you mention it. I got a lot of flak from the directors. One of them even refused to come unless I could give him an agenda. Then when Keith died ... well, I'd almost forgotten about the meeting."

"You said the police questioned you last night. What about?"

"The usual. Whether Keith had any enemies." Joy bristled. "Keith was so busy he didn't have any *friends*. I think Georgeanne Hughes was the only person he ever saw outside the office."

"You mean romantically?"

Joy nodded. "You probably saw her this morning. In the front pew, next to Keith's mother. She'd been seeing Keith since January."

Lea remembered the young woman, who to the best of her knowledge had not spoken to anyone but Mrs. Whitten at the funeral. "Does she work near here?"

"No. She's with Lollypalooza, one of those World Wide Web firms in the city. In the SoMa district, actually. Georgeanne designs corporate Web sites." Joy started to say more, but the door to Paul's office opened, and the two detectives came out, followed by Paul.

"We'll be in touch, Mr. Boyd," Inspector Talifano said.

Joy waited until the police were out of earshot and then handed Paul several messages. "Randy Derrough has called twice in the last hour," she said. "I don't know how much longer I can head him off."

"That's right, and my patience is wearing thin," said a voice from the hallway.

Lea turned and recognized the boyish-faced Randy. She took in his wide eyes, generous chin, and thick sandy hair. He was natty in a herringbone suit; a peach silk handkerchief peeked from his top pocket, and monogrammed gold cufflinks glinted against his starched white cuffs. He was stocky, however, and barely Lea's height of 5'7. Lea wondered if the sartorial splendor was an attempt to compensate for his height.

"Randy, let's do this later," Paul said wearily. "I don't have time now."

Paul turned towards his office, but Randy, face flushed, planted himself between Paul and the door.

"I don't appreciate what you did yesterday," he said. "You called me a liar to a client."

"Randy, not in front of the others." Paul tried to move past him, but Randy grabbed his arm.

"I'm not leaving until I get an apology and a promise that you'll let me run my department. I can't do my job as sales manager if you go behind my back."

A muscle twitched in Paul's cheek and he shook his arm free. "And I can't let you make false promises to customers. What's the idea of telling the folks at Billerica Discs that we're going to release our new software a month early? You know that's impossible. We'll be lucky to get it out on time."

"I said that because otherwise we'd have lost $35,000 in orders. You know Everhard is due out with their software six weeks before we are. Besides, I talked to our development guys. They said there's a good chance we'll make the early date."

"I can't believe our systems designers told you that! No way."

Randy squared his shoulders defiantly. "I am so sick of you technical guys with your holier-than-thou attitude. Who says a product has to be a piece of art? There's no law that you have to find every bug so that on February 29 a user in Dubuque won't lose a paragraph of data. Just make the damn thing work most of the time. That's all." Randy glared at Lea. Her presence seemed to further irritate him.

"Developing software is a bit more complicated than that," Paul said through clenched teeth. "But that's not the point. Since when is the sales department setting company policy? You can't decide on your own to revise our development timetable."

"Keith approved the idea," Randy asserted.

Paul's jaw dropped.

"Really. We discussed it a few days before he died. He didn't want it to come officially from his office. He wanted me to tell the clients one on one."

Paul stared at Randy in disbelief. "Let's get one thing straight," he said. "We're not going to win any business by lying to our customers."

Randy threw up his hands. "So that's how it is! Now I can see you've got your own agenda, Boyd. Don't even pretend you're acting for the benefit of this company. It's obvious you're out to make a name for yourself—and you don't care if it's at my expense." He paused significantly. "Whatever happens, I'll remember that."

Lea backed away hastily as Randy swept by, grazing her shoulder. He was almost to the hall when he stopped suddenly, pivoted, and met her eyes. His look chilled her.

"As for you, Ms. Sherwood, I hope you don't assume that you're in the clear," Randy snapped. "Don't forget, I was at your restaurant the night Keith died. And believe me, I was watching you."

3

Lea hung up the phone in disgust. It was barely 9:30 A.M., and already she'd had eight cancellations for lunch and dinner. Not that she could blame her customers. Of course they were leery of eating in a restaurant linked to a poisoning.

She rubbed her eyes, gritty from lack of sleep. She'd been up till almost 2:00 the night before, attempting to soothe her anxious investors. Since Keith's death, she'd spoken to all 28 of them, attempting to assure them—and herself— that her sudden notoriety would soon fade. At about midnight last night, her words had begun to sound hollow.

Memories of her struggle to open Panache leapt to mind. After Brussels, she'd returned to San Francisco to take a job as a bistro *sous-chef* and to line up investors. She'd called all the diners who'd ever gushed, "Remember me when you decide to go out on your own...." Most had stammered excuses and apologies. Finally she'd secured the 28 as backers and added her own life savings to their $900,000. Half of that went to outfit the kitchen. Then she'd endured a year of permit hell over renovations and seismic retrofitting. Only then did she hand-pick her staff of 60—one person for every five served.

She thought of her decision to go to culinary school, after majoring in history at college. As a child she'd loved reading cookbooks and watching Julia Child on TV. One of her first, happy memories was of eating a juicy ripe peach in a cousin's orchard. As a teenager, she'd had fun cooking for her family and friends. Later, when she dared to create her own dishes, she'd been thrilled by the artistic challenge. After debating whether she had the talent or the stamina to be a chef, Lea had moved to upstate New York to attend the American Culinary Arts Academy, the *grande-dame* of cooking schools. By the end of the first month, she'd been hooked. Graduating two years later, she'd apprenticed in Boston and New York City and begun to work her way up the culinary ladder.

Her mother, an artist, had first encouraged her interest in cooking, telling her that the two professions had much in common. Both, she'd said, tap into your intuition and creativity—and require you to trust your instincts. They also call for a curious blend of spontaneity and discipline, and a balance of the left and right brains, so that you can alternate technical and creative skills. And they let you create a world of your own that you can share with others. She'd said chefs also have to be generous—since feeding people is about artistry *and* nurturing. "It's the opposite of accumulating," her mother had noted.

When Lea had asked how she could know if becoming a chef was right for her, her mother had laughed and replied, "The creative impulse is a happy mystery, my dear. Who knows why any one of us loves something?" When Lea had pursued the question, her mother had smiled enigmatically. "Follow your passion," she'd said, and given her a quick hug.

Now, as ever, Lea was excited by food and all its possibilities. Not only was it fun to cook the proverbial egg 100 different ways, but she loved exploring the roots of a cuisine, and the cultural and historical influences that had shaped it. The thrill of discovery was matched only by the intense, flow experience of cooking—of losing herself in her work for hours. This, she came to realize, she also shared with her mother.

At 33, however, Lea was still single; restaurant hours sharply curtailed a personal life. And on her one day off—Sunday, when Panache was closed—she tried to catch up on sleep and to plan the week ahead. She lived alone, in an apartment on Russian Hill.

She occasionally wondered if the satisfaction of creating the restaurant had been worth all the sacrifice, but she instinctively felt that few things in life could give her the pleasure she derived in having a restaurant all her own. She felt that she—and Panache—stood for something.

Lea fretted now in her tiny office across from the kitchen. Why weren't the police announcing the results of Keith's autopsy? Surely they knew by now that Keith hadn't died of food poisoning. Lea had been told by city attorney Dorothy Unger that the police had always suspected foul play. But anyone reading the daily press—which had been tantalizingly vague about what Keith had eaten—might legitimately wonder if they should chance a meal at Panache. Lea squirmed. Until the autopsy results were made public, a pall would hang over her restaurant. Cancellations since the murder had cut business by a third.

Then another thought unnerved her. What if the police were intentionally suppressing the cause of death? It was a murder case, after all. She could hardly expect them to trumpet their evidence. Lea shuddered as she grasped the implications. The SFPD might take months to solve the case. By then, her business would be ruined.

A lump formed in her throat. Her greatest fear was that Panache would fail.

Lea rapped her fingers on the edge of her desk and fought to stay calm. If only she could discover how Keith had been killed! She toyed with the idea of calling Keith's mother, to whom she'd spoken at the funeral yesterday. But Yvonne had said she'd be flying back home to Cincinnati this morning.

Then Lea recalled Keith's girlfriend, Georgeanne Hughes. From what Joy Nugent had said, Georgeanne would be the one most familiar with Keith's recent activities. Ignoring her natural reticence to intrude on a person's grief, Lea reached for the phone book.

She found the number of Lollypalooza, the Web-site design firm where Georgeanne worked. Of course, she was probably taking the day off. Lea dialed without much hope.

To her surprise, the company operator transferred the call, and Georgeanne answered it. She was polite, and her tone of voice was matter-of-fact. Lea explained her predicament, and Georgeanne agreed to meet in an hour to talk. Although she was grateful, Lea hoped the encounter would not prove to be too awkward. After all, she had rejected Keith right before he and Georgeanne had met.

On reflection, Lea wondered at Georgeanne's willingness to see her on such short notice. Still, she chided herself, when someone close to you died, it was only natural to want to talk about him.

She went to the kitchen to let her staff know she'd be out. Her pastry chef, Minette, a pixyish 5'2, brushed past her while hoisting a 25-pound sack of flour, while Todd and Nicholas, the two youngest line cooks, struggled to lift a 55-pound stock pot from the stove.

Watching them, Lea was reminded that becoming a chef was not for everyone. She flashed back to her own grueling 18-hour-day apprenticeship: a blur of months spent plucking ducks, gutting fish, and stirring 45 quarts of *béarnaise* sauce each morning by hand. It astonished her that culinary schools were now besieged by applicants who considered cooking to be glamorous. Even baby boomers in mid-life, fantasizing about creating signature dishes, were switching careers.

When Lea left Panache at 10:45, fog shrouded the financial district. It was one of those days when the fog might lift for only an hour—or not. The wind whipped her hair across her face, and Lea buttoned her navy blazer. She was glad she'd chosen to wear one of her turtleneck sweaters with her customary slacks that morning.

At the corner of Sansome and Pine, she passed three middle-aged smokers, banished from their high-rise offices, huddled in an alley and puffing away. At Mission Street, she swerved to avoid a woman in a white beret who burst out of an espresso shop. Farther south, Lea craned her neck to study a new building bedecked by copper pyramids—it was the third skyscraper with a pyramid motif she'd seen in a month. Whatever would future archaeologists think?

At 11:20, Lea took a creaky freight elevator up to Georgeanne Hughes' South of Market office. Lollypalooza was located on the third floor of a grimy pre-war, red-brick building that had once been a meat packing plant. So far, the ambience hadn't changed much.

Once the elevator groaned to a stop, however, Lea found herself transported to modern SoMa, a hive of Web software activity. Lea trekked down a corridor painted a fluorescent yellow with alternating black waves. Eventually she encountered a green door. There was no sign—presumably that would be too conventional.

She entered the office and edged her way past a rack of bicycles and skateboards. At the receptionist's desk sat a young man with a goatee whose blue T-shirt touted a message in Japanese. Beyond him, in a cavernous cyber-village, was a warren of cubicles; its Generation X occupants gazed, rapt, at glowing monitors. Most were dressed as though their good clothes were at the cleaners. As Lea asked for Georgeanne, a young man with bleached, asymmetrical shocks of hair roller-bladed across the room.

Georgeanne Hughes emerged presently and introduced herself. For a moment, Lea was startled by her youth—she judged Georgeanne to be in her mid-twenties—and by her appearance. At the funeral, her hair had been restrained in a sedate knot, her eyes shielded by wide, dark glasses. Now her strawberry-blond hair cascaded over her shoulders, the wisps around her crown suggesting a halo. Georgeanne had light, almond-shaped eyes, a delicate mouth, and translucent skin. She looked like a cross between a fairy-tale princess and a pre-Raphaelite Madonna.

As Georgeanne conferred with the receptionist, Lea studied her, intrigued. She exuded a mysterious aura. Although some might view Georgeanne as aloof, Lea was inclined to think her otherworldly. She gave the impression of being on another plane—of aspiring to an ideal inner state.

Her mode of dress, however, was quintessential SoMa. Georgeanne's birdlike frame was enveloped in a black jersey, fitted black blazer with gold lamé pocket protector, thin black stovepipe pants, and clunky black shoes with thick, crisscrossing straps. Three tiny pierced earrings protruded from one ear.

On first impression, Georgeanne Hughes, Web goddess, was far too exotic for Keith Whitten, corporate marauder. But then Lea had never understood the bromide that opposites attract. To live with someone diametrically opposed to your personality or values had always seemed to her the epitome of schizophrenia.

"It's been wild here lately," Georgeanne said, waving a hand to indicate the activity behind her. "Every company in America seems determined to get a Web site. We're charging clients a million bucks and up, and we still have to turn away business." She smiled and nudged Lea. "Come on. Let's get out of here."

Georgeanne led the way down a rear flight of stairs and through a narrow, foul-smelling alley flanked by metal garbage cans. As they emerged onto Harrison Street, Lea looked north to the sleek silver and black towers of the financial district. Only a few blocks away, but a world apart. In SoMa, gentrification was the rage. Neglected foundries, sawmills, and brick-works were rapidly being transformed into residential lofts and multimedia centers. By day, Generation Xers created text, sound, and graphics; by night they roamed hip clubs.

Lea, who had grown up in San Francisco, could hardly

believe this metamorphosis. "Where are we going?" she asked Georgeanne.

"Just around the corner, to a cyber café."

The Café Isis occupied a nondescript, two-story stucco building that belied the ambience within. Its decor melded pop art with industrial chic: silver track lighting snaked across the ceiling, illuminating rectangular black tables flanked by purple and red chairs. Funky paintings in primary colors lined the walls. Alternative rock music blared.

Lea noticed that at most tables, casually dressed young men and women were hunched over computer terminals. She flashed Georgeanne a questioning glance.

"A lot of the computers and software are donated," Georgeanne said. "That way the companies get exposure for their new products. But you can rent time too, if you want to check your e-mail or surf the Net."

Lea smiled. "It's funny. When I was a teenager, we'd sit in the cafés in North Beach and talk for hours. Everything was new to us then—poetry, music, philosophy." Lea felt a surge of the old excitement. "We took it for granted that you had to debate philosophy. How else were you going to define yourself in the world?" Lea nodded at the silent denizens of the Isis. "But hardly anybody here is having a conversation."

Georgeanne laughed as she surveyed the room. "If you think this is bad, you ought to come to one of our loft parties. Computers are scattered around the living areas, and people sit at opposite sides of the loft having virtual conversations."

"You mean when they could be talking face to face?" Lea wondered if Georgeanne was pulling her leg.

Georgeanne shrugged. "That was something my parents' generation did. Standing around with a cocktail, chattering about social trivia. When you talk in cyber-space, you get right down to basics. You select a challenging topic and distill your thoughts."

They ordered *caffé lattes* at the counter from a slight young blond man with closely cropped hair. Gold studs pierced his right eyebrow and chin. A muscular man with a black

Labrador dog edged into line behind Lea; she could feel the dog's hot breath on her leg.

As they waited, a young woman Georgeanne addressed as Suki stopped to say hello. She wore a long flowing dress, men's motorcycle boots, and distinctive earrings. Lea commented on them, and Suki laughed. "Oh, these? They're made out of old SIMMs. You know, single in-line memory modules." She tugged at her left ear. "The 256K chips aren't much use anymore, but they make cool earrings."

Lattes in hand, they bid Suki good-bye and found a table. Lea felt like an intruder in occupied techie territory. "Who are these people?" she asked, surprised to see the café crowded so late in the morning.

Georgeanne glanced around. "A lot of these guys work at cool SoMa companies, but they insist on setting their own hours, like noon to midnight. See Michael Cash over there?" She gestured at a lanky fellow in a brown leather motorcycle jacket. "He works in my office. He's a super designer, and he might go all out for 20 hours straight, but *do not* expect him to show up for a 9:00 A.M. meeting!"

Michael Cash was seated next to a muscular man with an elaborate gray and black tattoo that obscured the back of his neck. The pattern reminded Lea of an Escher drawing. Similar geometric tattoos encircled his calves, visible below black bicycle shorts. The lone woman at the table, a blond with a nose ring, appeared to be wearing an ankle bracelet, but on closer inspection, Lea realized that it too was artifice—a delicate daisy-chain tattoo.

Lea sipped her *latte* and wondered how to broach the subject of Keith's death. Georgeanne did not appear to be prostrate with grief, but Lea reasoned that we all mourn differently. Perhaps she was still in denial.

"First, let me offer my sympathy," Lea began uncomfortably. "I know how you must have cared for Keith."

Georgeanne caught her breath and began to titter. She seemed genuinely amused. "I'm sorry. It's just that everyone's been walking on eggshells around me, as though I might suddenly go into a swoon." Georgeanne flung the back of her hand against her forehead. "But I'm not as delicate as I look. And to tell the truth, Keith and I had been seeing less of each other lately. I knew our days were numbered. Not that I've told my father that," she added impishly.

"Your father?" Lea echoed.

"Stepfather, actually. The esteemed Bennett Alston. Distinguished legal counsel to Whitten Systems. You heard him uttering platitudes at the funeral yesterday." Georgeanne rolled her eyes. "I know, you thought they got along so well. And in public, they did keep up the facade. But in private my father despised Keith, and my relationship with him." A smile played around the corners of Georgeanne's mouth. "I think that was part of the attraction for each of us. It all felt slightly illicit. Of course I was attracted to Keith at the beginning. Who wouldn't be intrigued by a guy who'd built a super software firm? But apart from an interest in technology, we didn't have much in common."

"Why did your father object to your seeing Keith?" Lea felt she was one step behind.

"You mean besides the fact that he wasn't an attorney or an investment banker?" Georgeanne's expression suggested that her father would have her consort with three-toed, bug-eyed alien life forms. "I've asked myself that many times. I think it had to be a competitive thing. You know, because of the friction between the two of them."

Seeing Lea's blank look, Georgeanne elaborated. "They were having this war of wills. But first you have to understand about my father. He fancies himself to be an astute thinker, with a penetrating legal mind. In fact he's trying to carve out a niche for himself as a leader in intellectual property law. You probably know how hot the field is now. My father's specialty is software patents. He's been bringing test cases on behalf of Whitten Systems. Can you imagine? He's actually in the forefront of making patent law sexy."

Lea flashed a smile. "Did Keith resent his growing prominence?" Keith would never have tolerated being upstaged by an employee, however accomplished. He'd even become annoyed at a dinner where Lea had received an award, prompting an argument on the way home.

"Oh, no." Georgeanne licked *latte* foam from her lips. "Keith's ego was too vast for that. He saw himself as a technical wizard who was shaping the future—a leader of a Silicon Valley aristocracy of brilliant minds. To Keith, my father was merely part of the support staff to carry out his vision. A hired hand. In fact Keith loved to belittle my father. Make fun of his patrician airs and long-winded discourses. Snicker about his being born with a silver spoon in his mouth. You should have seen Keith ridicule him when he asked questions about technical matters. Keith was always impatient if you didn't grasp a concept right away."

"I remember," Lea said, with feeling. He had in fact succeeded several times in making her question her own acumen. And she hated to feel slow.

Georgeanne appeared startled. "Oh, that's right. I'd forgotten you knew him before I did."

Lea wondered if she really had forgotten. Georgeanne returned her gaze with an innocent expression and toyed with a lock of her strawberry blond hair.

They were silent for a moment.

"It's odd," Lea said. "A lot of people are arrogant about their work. They think their own field is the most important."

Georgeanne smirked. "I know. It's certainly true of my father. He considers himself to be of the cultural elite. In fact he's rather a snob." She sighed. "He's got a trigger-quick mind. But he doesn't examine things deeply. Ever since I was a kid, I've distrusted his brand of cleverness. Anyway, you can imagine how galling it was for him to report to Keith. To my father Keith was just a boorish techie. An *arriviste* who lacked pedigree."

"So they each felt superior to the other?" Lea laughed in spite of herself. She had often been struck by how many people imagined themselves to be better than others. In college, a roommate who tippled had felt superior to another who smoked—and both were condescending to a girl across the hall who was struggling to lose 60 pounds.

"There must have been a lot of tension between them," Lea said.

"Yes, but they each got something out of the relationship. They used each other. My father stayed with Keith because Whitten Systems was his vehicle for becoming a legal star. Until now, it's been a win-win situation. My father got the glory by winning cases, and Keith collected millions in damages."

"Until now?"

"I was thinking of my father's latest project. A patent infringement suit against CadSure. It's a start-up software firm. Keith was all for it when they filed the complaint last year, but since then he's gotten a tremendous amount of flak. He was even becoming an object of derision in the industry. Maybe you don't know this, but software patents are highly controversial. Many programmers think patents shouldn't even exist. Anyway, Keith got accused of filing a frivolous suit against CadSure—a Goliath going after a young David for profit. I believe John Schuster, the legal columnist for ValleyTalk.com, used the term 'rapacious.'"

Lea raised her eyebrows. Although Keith had always felt free to judge everyone, he couldn't accept criticism himself. Ironically, it had been a point of contention between them that Lea believed you could not—should not—try to mold someone into the person you wanted them to be. In love, what you see is what you get. But Keith had attempted to chip away at her, subtly pressuring her to think and act as he preferred. "How did Keith react?" she asked.

"He ordered my father to seek a settlement. To save face." Georgeanne frowned. "But my father kept dragging his heels. He gave Keith one excuse after another for why the settlement was taking so long. I know for a fact he told Keith that CadSure was haggling over money when numbers hadn't even been discussed." She leaned back and fiddled with a sugar packet. "My father personally has a lot at stake in this. He thinks *he'll* lose face with his peers if he backs down."

"Have you told this to the police?" Lea asked excitedly.

"Hardly. Not after the way they treated me." Georgeanne was aghast.

"What do you mean?"

Georgeanne hesitated. "They asked me not to talk about it, but it's bound to come out eventually. Besides, they were so insulting. They all but accused me of poisoning Keith."

Lea gaped. "You?"

"They found poison in some pills I gave him," Georgeanne said reluctantly. A flush crept across her delicate cheeks. "Not that they would tell me what it was."

"You gave him pills?" Lea couldn't believe her ears. She began to consider Georgeanne in a new light.

"Actually, they were smart drugs Keith liked."

"You mean like super-vitamins?" Lea had heard her servers discussing them once.

"They can be. But a lot of them are pharmaceuticals. Some are used to treat Alzheimer's, AIDS—different diseases. They're legal in the sense that you can get them from a doctor or overseas by mail order."

"Why would Keith fool around with drugs like that?"

Georgeanne shrugged. "They're supposed to enhance memory, and mental stamina. You know, make you smarter and increase productivity. Anyway, Keith swore by them. He said they made him think more quickly."

"Funny. He never mentioned them to me."

"It was a recent enthusiasm. Keith also liked to go to a smart bar two blocks from here." Georgeanne tossed her head. "Talk about atmosphere. We ordered 'smart drinks.' " She pantomimed quotation marks with her index fingers. "They're like smoothies—fruit juice blended with powdered vitamins and amino acids. They call the one I like Memory Mix. Anyway, Keith said that when the smart-drug scene first came over here from Europe, a lot of people who got into it were well-read and computer-oriented. Now they all feel like they're breaking ground. They say in the future everyone will start the day with smart drinks instead of coffee."

Lea tried in vain to suppress a smile. "I had no idea Keith was such a trend-setter."

Georgeanne laughed. "Keith told me once that before he hit it big, he used to worry that people considered him a nerd. But in the past year, he worried that he appeared too corporate. Especially in a social setting. Smart drugs made him feel cool."

Lea shook her head. Keith was more of a risk taker than she'd guessed. "What drugs was he taking exactly?"

"Piracetam was his favorite. It stimulates the central nervous system and is used in Europe to treat strokes and dyslexia. Keith got it over the Internet, but he ran out of his last batch the week before he died. That's when he asked me to give him a few capsules to tide him over."

Georgeanne was now openly defensive.

"Do you take them too?"

"Keith gave me some to try, but I don't like messing with chemicals. I gave him back the pills he'd given me."

Lea exhaled slowly. "Who knew Keith was taking piracetam? Anyone at the office?"

"It certainly wasn't a secret. He kept a bottle in his top desk drawer. I once saw him pop a pill with three people in the room."

"So basically you're saying that anyone at the company could have done it."

"Not quite," Georgeanne said cautiously. "Keith only had this particular batch of pills for a few hours before he was killed. We'd had dinner Wednesday night, and I gave him the pill box then. Keith took one capsule right away and put the rest in his coat pocket. Then he went home."

Georgeanne sighed. "He must have taken the pills to work Thursday morning and popped one more in the morning and another that night. I'd put seven capsules in the box when I gave it to him. Only four were left when the police searched his body Thursday night. Two of those were poisoned. I figure Keith left the pills in his desk Thursday morning and then put them back in his coat pocket when he left the office at noon."

"Why at noon?" Lea asked. She began to feel uneasy.

"That was the day of the merger, remember? After the press conference with Paul Boyd in the morning, Keith left for the city to meet with investment analysts. He went straight to your restaurant afterward and never went back to the office."

Lea thought back to the night Keith had died. He had arrived at Panache at 7:00 with Marshall Schroth and Randy Derrough in tow.

"I tell you," Georgeanne said. "The police have been driving me insane, asking intrusive questions. And of course they wanted to know who had access to my apartment." Georgeanne drained the last of her coffee and dropped her cup with a thud. "But I live alone, and I've only had two friends over since Keith gave me those damn pills. I told the police to look for the killer at Whitten Systems. Obviously it has to be someone who was in Keith's office that morning."

Georgeanne went on, but Lea was no longer listening. The morning of the merger. A shiver ran down her spine. Paul had told her he'd spent that morning at Whitten Systems. Meeting with Keith. And if the police didn't know it already, they were sure to find out.

4

Lea nosed her dark green Renault, a legacy from her year in France, onto Highway 101 en route to Whitten Systems. She had been fidgeting for hours, ever since leaving Georgeanne. Unable to reach Paul by phone, she had finally leapt at the chance to see him when Joy Nugent had predicted he'd be out of a board meeting by 4:00.

She merged into heavy traffic, slamming on her brakes as a white BMW convertible cut her off. Its license plate read "To D Top." Suddenly the convertible swerved, darting in front of a black Lexus with diplomatic plates. The ambushed driver held up a finger in a universal gesture of ill will. Lea shook her head and glanced at her watch—it was barely 3:00. Rush hour began earlier each time she left the city.

Traffic was stop-and-go all the way to Candlestick Park, and Lea squirmed impatiently as she kept hitting the brakes. Ahead of her, concrete overpasses crisscrossed eight lanes of gray roadway. Beyond the shoulder, dusty, stunted trees drooped. Finally the bay came into view as she approached the airport, and a robin's-egg-blue jumbo jet took off, sailed in an arc above her, and veered west toward the Orient.

Once past SFO, Lea appraised the old Burlingame frontage road. Gleaming new high-rise hotels dwarfed ranch-style motels frozen in the 1950s, and one cocktail lounge still advertised its wares with a pink neon martini-glass sign. Lea wondered how long it would be before all of Burlingame was annexed by Silicon Valley. The high-tech industry had already sprawled north to Redwood Shores and San Mateo, and the latter, a once-sleepy suburb now dubbed Games Gulch, had improbably become a hotbed of video game development employing 10,000 designers.

When she arrived at Whitten Systems, Lea parked in the company's lot and took the winding walkway to the front entrance. She skirted a man-made pond as mallard ducks, their emerald heads gleaming, honked and preened. Lea wondered if the landscape designers had built the pond to soften the austere impression created by the Whitten Systems' building. The two-story structure was paneled with black glass intersected by thin silver strips, and if a building could look inscrutable, it did.

In the lobby—an oasis of black leather couches and computer art—Lea obtained a badge and called Joy to escort her into the office.

She found Paul standing at his desk, and she went to him and slipped her arms around his waist. "I've missed you," she said.

He drew her close and kissed her.

"I've been thinking about you all day," he said softly. He held her for several moments and then released her.

She thought he was about to say something, but instead he turned and looked out the window. Shadows rimmed his eyes, merging into the creases above his cheekbones that seemed to lengthen each day. Lea also noticed that his blue dress shirt hung on his frame. In times of crisis, she knew, Paul often forgot to eat. Most troubling, however, was that his usual air of optimism had given way to a distracted expression.

"How are you, really?" she asked.

He turned to her and smiled halfheartedly. "I'm managing, I suppose. How about you?"

"About the same," she said. She told him about the cancellations at Panache, the worried calls from her investors, and her conversation with Georgeanne Hughes.

"So that's why the police kept harping on who was in here that morning," Paul said. "They never let on about the pills, though. Imagine that." His blue eyes were troubled. "Then the killer has to be someone who worked closely with Keith."

And who is now working with you, Lea thought. The fact gnawed at her.

"Do you have any idea who *was* in here that morning?"

"I know Carter Weberling and I were. In fact we waited for Keith here. We had to sign merger documents before the news conference, but Keith wasn't on time to meet us. Apparently he was with his public relations manager, preparing a statement for the press. I remember thinking it was arrogant of him to keep us waiting."

But typical, Lea thought. It still seemed incredible to her that Paul was now sitting behind Keith's desk. "How long did you and Carter stay in here?" she asked.

"Actually, I waited alone for about five minutes. Carter was so miffed that he left to find Keith. After all, Carter was pivotal in making the merger happen, and he was joining the board that day. He deserved to be treated better."

Lea felt a pang of worry. "Did anyone else stop by while you were here?"

"I don't think so. The police asked me that, but I just drew a blank."

"Randy Derrough was in here right before you came, Paul." Joy Nugent's silky voice projected from the doorway.

Startled, Lea glanced over her shoulder to see the secretary enter the room. How long had she been outside listening?

Joy sauntered over to Paul's desk and deposited a stack of telephone messages and inter-office mail. "I told the police, but Randy had the nerve to deny it," she said pointedly.

Lea and Paul stared at one another but remained silent until Joy had left the room. "It may not mean anything," Paul said. "Maybe he honestly forgot. It was a hectic morning."

Still, Lea couldn't help but remember Randy's excitability and evasiveness the other day. He didn't strike her as being a stickler for the truth.

"How are you getting along with Randy now?" she asked.

"He keeps resisting me—every step of the way." Paul sighed. "Randy's a strange guy. He's a good salesman, and I respect the part of him that's good at what he does...." Paul's voice trailed off.

"But?"

"But he defines his identity as being a good salesman, regardless of what he's selling. It doesn't matter to him whether our software is sensational or total schlock. He's selling himself. He believes customers buy from him because they like him. And his sense of self-worth depends on that."

"The two of you are completely different," Lea observed.

"I'll say. My biggest fear in life is that I won't achieve my potential—that I'll fail to make a difference. Since I was a kid, I've always wanted my life to count for something." Paul sighed again. "I've tried to point out the obvious to Randy. First you build a better mousetrap. Then people will buy it because it's better. But he insists that product quality is irrelevant. He says that in order to sell, you've got to read the customers. Adapt your personality and mannerisms to theirs. Understand their emotional needs. Are they insecure? Indecisive? If so, reassure them that everybody else is buying the product. That way they won't look like imbeciles if it doesn't work as promised. All that strikes me as manipulative."

Lea frowned. She had always been baffled by people who were indifferent to ability or performance, because she felt badly when she didn't try to do her best. She also lived with the recurring question: "Am I giving it my all?" How could others not feel the same?

"Okay," she said. "So Randy is crafty. How far do you think he'd go to get his own way?"

Paul shook his head. "I don't know. And I admit that I'm biased against him. It's the classic tension between sales and technical people. The sales guys goose us to get the product out bigger, faster. They don't begin to appreciate the technical problems we've got to solve. It also galls me to hear Randy stretch the truth. He has no compunction about promising a customer the moon." Paul waved a hand. "But that's beside the point. I've got more pressing problems at the moment."

"What do you mean?" Lea didn't like the look in his eyes.

He took a deep breath. "I've decided to call in a special audit team to go over the books. They're getting started today."

"You're doing an audit?" Nasty scenarios sprang to mind. "How long will it take?"

"Who knows? It could be weeks. They have to go back and verify all the numbers. Not to mention unearthing any omissions." Paul looked pale.

"Have you talked to Francine Reese yet?" Lea asked, almost afraid to hear the answer. She remembered that Paul had been unsure of how to approach her.

Paul set his jaw. "Yesterday I asked her to meet with me and the auditors first thing this morning. But last night she left me voice mail saying she'd been called out of town on a family emergency. Apparently her mother back in Baltimore had a heart attack."

"Francine is gone?" cried Lea. She pondered all the implications. "But you're in touch with her?"

"Hardly." Paul sighed in disgust. "She's not answering her cell phone."

The knot in Lea's stomach tightened. "Paul, I can't help but worry…"

"Oh, I didn't realize you were with someone," a voice interrupted.

Lea swiveled her head to see a woman she had never met peering at them from around the door.

"It's all right. Come on in," Paul beckoned. "I'd like you to meet Lea, in fact. Lea, this is Patrice Holbrook. She's heading up the auditing team."

Lea smiled as Patrice approached them. She had perfectly coiffed, medium-length blond hair and wore a white shell blouse and pearls with a tailored, navy-blue business suit. She appeared the consummate professional.

Patrice shook Lea's hand and then turned to Paul. "If you could set aside a half hour later today, I'd appreciate it. I've come across something we need to discuss."

Paul frowned. "What in particular?"

Patrice hesitated, glancing at Lea.

Was Lea imagining it, or was the auditor scrutinizing her?

"I'd prefer to tell you later."

"All right," Paul said warily. He scanned his day calendar. "How does 7:30 tonight sound? I should be out of my other meetings by then."

Patrice agreed and glanced again at Lea on her way out.

Lea began to ask Paul about Patrice when his phone rang. He took the call, listened for a moment, and then caught Lea's eye as he covered the receiver with his hand. "Lea, I'm really sorry. I know every time we start to talk, we get interrupted. But I've got to speak to this client. I'm afraid it'll be a while."

She nodded with disappointment. "I'll come back."

Joy was away from her desk, so Lea took stock of her options. She thought back to the night Keith had been killed, and the conversation she'd overheard. Had Randy Derrough or Marshall Schroth ever learned why Keith had called that emergency board meeting? They'd both been keen to find out. Lea didn't think she could pry much out of Randy, but she decided Schroth was worth a try.

Buzzing the switchboard operator, Lea asked for the location of Schroth's office: it wasn't far—just a few doors down. Lea also inquired about his title. The operator, obviously surprised that she had to ask, informed her in a reverent tone that Mr. Schroth was Whitten Systems' executive vice president of worldwide marketing and sales.

Marshall Schroth was sitting at his desk reading when Lea knocked on his open door. He looked up abruptly. Schroth appeared displeased to see her.

"Yes?" he said.

Lea approached and reminded Marshall of their recent acquaintance. He rose and reluctantly took her extended hand. Lea didn't know whether to be surprised or annoyed as he shook it limply, without conviction, eyes focused on a horizon past her shoulder. She thought of the days when you presumably could judge a man by the firmness of his grip. Yet today it was fashionable to insert your hand into another's as if it were an inert flounder.

"May I sit down?" Lea asked.

"If you must."

Marshall Schroth was tall, with a solid build and dark hair that had begun to recede at the temples. He had regular features in an unlined, broad face, with slightly hooded eyes. Lea guessed he was approaching 40. He wore an expensively tailored gray suit with a yellow and black silk tie. His carriage was ultra-erect, but it was his manner that most struck Lea. In the style affected by certain corporate executives, his expression was bland and hard to read; he seemed to cultivate an impassive veneer. Lea also thought she detected an overweening ego. She remembered Marshall's conversation at dinner. He had spoken in a low, modulated voice evidently calculated to convey that his words carried great import. By all accounts, Lincoln had been more modest while delivering the Gettysburg Address.

Lea took a seat across from Marshall. Like Paul, he had a rosewood desk and console, but the similarity in decor ended there. Lea saw at a glance that Schroth had exotic, and expensive, tastes. His sofa and chairs were upholstered in red and gold Oriental silk, and Japanese lithographs lined the walls. The balcony that ran the length of the office boasted exquisitely pruned bonsai trees.

As Lea met Marshall's eye, she was struck by his shrewd, appraising glance. She had the odd sensation that he was taking her measure—assessing her strengths as well as her vulnerabilities, and cataloguing them for future reference.

Before she could speak, however, Randy Derrough entered the room. The sales manager, surprised to encounter Lea, glanced uncertainly at Marshall. "I don't mean to interrupt anything," he said.

Marshall leaned back in his chair and smiled expansively. "Not at all," he pronounced with an air of noblesse oblige.

Randy's reciprocating smile, meant to be winsome, was obviously strained. "I just thought I'd stop by and touch base with you before I left for the night. Do you need anything before I go?"

Lea averted her eyes. She felt uncomfortably like a voyeur, witnessing one of the obligatory social rituals of advancing in a corporation. Randy obviously had no specific reason for being here.

Marshall, however, accepted the visit as his due. "Actually, I was wondering how the sales presentation for tomorrow is coming," he said.

"Just great," Randy replied heartily. "I'm going to polish it tonight. The script will be on your desk first thing in the morning."

"Fine. And what about the Archer account? I understand the Archer team still refuses to upgrade to our new software until we work out the bugs in the version they're now using."

"Unfortunately, that isn't easily resolved. I checked with our technical staff, and they maintain that Archer's problem isn't related to our software. They insist it's a user error."

Marshall raised an eyebrow. "That isn't satisfactory, Randy. Archer is a major account. We'll have to do better than that."

"Umm ... I can talk to our tech staff again, but they claim they're already up against the wall. Everybody's frantic trying to meet the deadline for our new release. Harry Coulter, the new software manager Paul brought in, told me he doesn't have any slack to hold a client's hand. And just between us, I do think the problem originates with Archer. The word on the street is Archer had trouble even before installing our software."

Marshall's annoyance had grown as Randy was speaking. Now he splayed his palms on his desk and fixed his gaze on Randy. "Listen to me. I have enough on my plate at the moment, and I certainly can't do everything around here. Nigel Armbruster in Hong Kong just wasted an hour of my time over a piddling problem he could have solved himself. You tell Coulter for me to do whatever it takes to keep Archer happy. If Coulter wants to remain here, he's simply going to have to be more flexible."

Lea suppressed a grimace. When someone advised you to be more flexible, what they really meant was to do it their way.

Randy bobbed his head. "Okay, Marshall. Right. You make an excellent point. I'll get on it immediately." Then, as if accepting an unspoken dismissal, he walked out the door.

"Poor Randy," drawled Schroth. "He outworks everyone. He outthinks no one."

Lea stared at Marshall in amazement. What breed of men were these?

"So, Miss Sherwood," Marshall said. "I must say I'm surprised to see you here. From what I read in the newspaper, I would think you'd be trying to salvage what's left of your restaurant."

"Unfortunately, Mr. Schroth, that's exactly what I'm trying to do. I'm here to get some answers. I thought perhaps you could help me."

Marshall observed her closely. "And how do you suggest I do that?" A wariness had crept into his voice.

"Did you ever find out why Keith called that emergency board meeting? I remember you were quite curious about it when you were having dinner with him and Randy."

Marshall grunted. "I fail to see that it's any of your business, but yes, I've satisfied myself as to what was on Keith's mind. He was concerned about a protracted legal matter that our counsel had embroiled us in. Although Keith initially endorsed the complaint, he became disillusioned about Bennett Alston's ability to see it through. Keith increasingly saw it as a liability to Whitten Systems and told Bennett to seek a settlement. I believe Keith was afraid the news would leak out and he wanted the board's advice on how to handle the ensuing publicity."

"Are you referring to the CadSure patent infringement dispute?"

"Yes." Marshall appeared surprised that Lea knew about it.

"But why wouldn't Keith have said so when you asked him about the meeting? It sounds like you were already in the information loop."

Marshall eyed her with condescension. "I can see that despite your prior friendship with Keith, you didn't begin to understand him. He was a complicated man, and he preferred to operate close to the vest."

Lea studied Marshall uneasily. His explanation was not entirely convincing.

She began to reply, but he cut her off. "I'm busy, Miss Sherwood, and I've given you all the time I can spare. I trust you can see yourself out?"

Lea got up, and Marshall resumed his reading.

Yet as she turned to leave, he cleared his throat and spoke again.

"As long as you're so intent on asking questions, Miss Sherwood, I would suggest you consult a more profitable source—your friend Paul Boyd. He knows more than you suspect. Ask him, for instance, what he discovered when he opened Keith's safe. And, while you're at it, find out why he's hiding its contents from the police."

5

Joy Nugent was standing at her desk when Lea returned. As usual, Joy was an oasis of style in a couture desert. She wore a fitted apricot suit, a pearl-gray scarf embossed with tiny crowns, and gold earrings in the shape of dolphins frolicking. Her spike heels were of the type that health magazines and podiatrists proselytize against. She was packing a cardboard box with awards, mementos, and the framed photographs from Keith's office.

A glance at Joy's phone console told Lea that Paul was still busy on his line.

"Do you know anything about Paul opening Keith's safe?" Lea asked hesitantly.

A queer expression flickered in Joy's eyes. "Where did you hear about that?"

"Marshall just mentioned it."

Joy appeared flustered. "I can't imagine how he found out. Paul hasn't wanted it to get around. The last thing we need is more gossip."

"The only thing Marshall didn't seem to know was what was in it."

"Thank heavens for that." Joy's voice dripped sarcasm. She glanced down the hall to make sure no one was coming and spoke *sotto voce*. "Actually, I can't tell you what Paul found either."

"When did he open the safe?"

"Just yesterday. I had to call a locksmith."

"But what did Paul say afterwards?"

"Nothing directly. But I was surprised at his reaction. It's the only time I've seen Paul lose his temper. Usually he's so composed. He called Bennett in, and they had a row. I couldn't hear exactly what they said, since the door was closed, but their voices were angry. They were at it for a good 10 minutes."

"Do you know if Paul told the police about the safe?" Lea asked, puzzled.

"That was the other funny thing. After Bennett left, Paul came over and asked me to consider the whole matter confidential."

Lea paused, unsure of how to probe further. She felt a prickle of guilt for discussing the safe with Joy, but she couldn't be sure when she'd get to talk to Paul. "I guess then we'll never know if something in Keith's safe pointed to his killer."

"Oh, I think I can tell you that," Joy said with a sigh. "Paul said it was his opinion that the safe's contents had nothing to do with Keith's death. Also that the fewer people who knew about the safe, the better. When I asked if that included the police, he said yes."

Lea frowned. When would Paul find the time to talk to her?

"Oh, you know what?" Joy rummaged in the cardboard box, rearranging a few photographs. "A friend of yours was asking about you. Did you know that Paul brought in Harry Coulter to head up our software development? He started a couple of days ago."

"Yes," Lea said. "I just heard." Lea was intrigued by the move. Harry had worked closely with Paul at Decision Ace, Paul's old firm. Theirs had been an amicable partnership until the past few months, when they had quarreled about the design of a major new program. She was glad they had put the lingering bitterness behind them.

Joy interrupted Lea's reverie. "You know, I can't believe it's been almost a week since Keith died. I still keep expecting to see him charge out of his office. I mean Paul's office." Joy faltered. "I even dreamt about him last night."

"What kills me is that the police don't seem to be getting anywhere," Lea said.

Joy laughed without amusement. "Ain't that the truth? From what I can tell, all they've accomplished here is to get everyone riled up. It's so perverse. Everybody's looking over their shoulder and acting with exaggerated courtesy. Even the guys who used to work until dawn are sneaking out at 6:00 P.M. You'd think someone was going to jump them in the parking lot after dark."

Lea made a wry face. "It doesn't make sense! Somebody must have seen or heard something unusual. Corporations are supposed to be hotbeds of gossip and intrigue. Why is everyone pleading ignorance?"

"There's a thriving rumor mill, all right," Joy said cautiously. "But since Keith died I've heard a lot more fiction than fact."

"Okay. What do *you* think happened? You worked with him. You were privy to who he met and why. Did anything unusual happen before he was killed? Did he act differently? Leave the office at strange times?"

Joy cocked her head and considered Lea's questions. "He was always in the office. It was his life. But now that you mention it, he was acting more furtive than usual. He'd close his office door and make long phone calls. And a couple of times he got calls that seemed to come from Antarctica— the connection was so bad. The man phoning wouldn't identify himself. He said Keith was expecting him to ring up." Joy raised a finger to her chin and looked thoughtful. "He had an Asian accent. Which nationality I couldn't say."

"He said he was ringing Keith up? That sounds like a

British expression. Maybe he lives or spends time in Hong Kong."

Joy shrugged helplessly. She reached for a photograph from the stack on her desk and picked it up, all the while staring at Keith's image. She traced a finger along the rim of the picture's silver frame. A sadness seemed to envelop her.

Lea felt a curious sensation. Had Joy been in love with Keith?

"What else struck you as unusual?" Lea asked after a respectful interval.

Joy glanced up, a faraway look in her eyes. "What? Oh, let me see." She put the picture down. "There was one other strange thing. One night I found Keith here alone. I had gone to a bluegrass concert at Skyline and got back to the office after midnight." Joy looked sheepish. "I was dumb enough to leave my house keys in my desk drawer. Anyway, when I came in, I saw Keith in Francine Reese's office, of all things. He was so involved that he didn't notice me, and naturally I didn't want to advertise the fact that I was here. But after I got my keys and was leaving, I saw he'd moved from Francine's office to Bennett Alston's. And I thought that was awfully strange, because Bennett has a taboo against anyone entering his office after hours, even Keith. Although who'd be interested in his legal mumbo-jumbo, I couldn't tell you."

"What was Keith doing?"

"The same thing he was doing in Francine's. Sitting at the computer. Calling up files, I would think. He didn't seem to be entering any data."

Lea wouldn't put it past Keith to have spied on his employees. But she didn't want to plant the idea in Joy's mind if it hadn't already occurred to her. "What did you make of it?" she asked lightly.

"I didn't know what to think at first. It was odd. But then I remembered that he had a powwow with securities analysts first thing in the morning, and I figured he was retrieving earnings reports, maybe summaries of legal cases—

that sort of thing. Afterwards, I just forgot about it. With the merger pending, a lot was going on."

"But wouldn't Keith have had his own copies of legal and financial reports? And if he'd misplaced them, wouldn't he have asked for new sets earlier in the day?"

"You would think so," Joy agreed. "But Keith was a little eccentric about time. As in losing track of it. Some days he'd get wrapped up in a project and forget about everything else. I've seen him try to reach department heads at 9:00 at night and be annoyed that they'd gone home for dinner." Joy paused. "I've noticed Paul is a bit that way, too. Maybe it comes with the territory."

Joy's phone rang, and she picked up the receiver and cradled it between her head and shoulder. A tiny gold dolphin bobbed up and down against the phone as Joy spoke.

"Gosh, I'm sorry, Lea," Joy said a minute later as she hung up. "Marshall wants to see me." Joy snatched a few papers from her desk and favored Lea with a dazzling smile. "Good luck catching Paul."

As Joy hurried off, Lea recalled her earlier remark about Harry Coulter. Maybe she should look him up—certainly he was never dull company. And it was possible that Harry had picked up scuttlebutt on Keith.

Lea headed for the stairs, stopping at the restroom along the way. She pushed open the door and noticed the auditor, Patrice Holbrook, applying red lipstick. Patrice was standing at the long marble sink opposite a wall-to-wall mirror. Suddenly she looked up, unguarded, and her reflected gaze caught Lea's eye. Instantly, Lea was on notice. Patrice, affable enough in Paul's office earlier, now looked wary, even hard.

Before Lea could speak, Patrice tucked the lipstick into her purse and with nimble fingers clicked the purse shut. As she did so, however, Lea caught a glimpse of solid, gleaming black metal. She could have sworn it was a gun.

———————

On the first floor, dozens of young software designers toiled within a maze of gray, shoulder-high cubicles. All was silent save for the hum of computers and the faint clicking of keyboards. Eerily, the blinds were drawn against the bright afternoon sun. Lea chuckled. Like gamblers and vampires, programmers appeared to shun the light of day.

She found Harry in an office across from the maze, and he smiled delightedly as he recognized her.

At 47, Harry Coulter was an *eminence grise* in an industry that fed on youth. His face was dominated by a shaggy, pepper-and-salt beard, and the paunch around his middle was the legacy of a lifetime spent assiduously avoiding exercise. Harry's pale complexion was also the product of years spent in the wan light of computer terminals—whether writing software or playing games far into the night. In crunch times, Harry was intense, focused on the problem at hand. His stamina and analytical abilities were legendary in an industry where 16-hour work days were the norm. In his social mode, however, he viewed the world with wry amusement. Now, as he grinned at Lea, he resembled a playful dancing bear.

"You are looking for me, I hope?"

Lea's smile was bemused as she nodded and entered Harry's office. Already he had managed to clutter his desk with memos and computer print-outs that overflowed onto a chair, the floor, and a credenza. A framed copy of Murphy's Law held pride of place on the wall above his desk.

"You've upgraded your wardrobe," Lea said in surprise. "I thought there was an unwritten law against programmers wearing ties." Harry wore a yellow dress shirt, a maroon-and-gray tie, and pressed gray slacks. The Harry she'd known was partial to plaid short-sleeved shirts and rumpled khakis.

Harry shook his head sadly. "Must dress the part— manager of software development." He brushed his tie distastefully. "Gotta be a role model for the great unwashed," he said, waving a hand to indicate the casually dressed programmers nearby. "Not to mention the fashion-challenged."

"Don't believe a word of it," said a young Chinese man with taped-together glasses who appeared at Harry's door. "He's still got his desk drawer stuffed with 'I Live to Hack' T-shirts. He's only presentable today because he sat in on a board meeting."

"My secrets exposed!" Harry hung his head.

The young man winked at Lea, who grinned in return.

"I just thought I'd let you know that it looks like another all-nighter," he told Harry. "I've been trying to merge our sections of code, but the program keeps blowing up. Too many coders with different styles."

"That's what's wrong with teamwork," Harry complained to Lea. "Ideally, every program should be written by one individual, to preserve its integrity. Instead we have to kludge together the aesthetics of 20 designers. It adds a tremendous amount of time and complexity to any project."

Harry turned back to the young man. "All right, Chunlai. But at least try to crash for an hour or two in the futon room."

The two exchanged glum looks, and the programmer pivoted in his high-top sneakers and headed back to his cubicle.

Harry sighed. "Some things never change." He flashed Lea an impish smile. "So, what brings you to the bowels of this august organization?"

Lea told him about her fear that the police weren't getting anywhere. "Why is it no one here will admit to having seen or heard anything suspicious?" she demanded. "We both know someone must have." The anxiety she'd felt earlier in Paul's office was back.

"Hmmm," Harry said. "From what I've heard, the troops are relieved that Keith's out of the way. He didn't exactly inspire loyalty." Harry appeared to be considering whether he should say more.

"What do you mean?" Lea prodded.

"I mean that no one here is eager to avenge Keith's death. And anyone who did have suspicions might be inclined to pooh-pooh them. Far easier to let things lie."

"You can't be serious!"

Harry shrugged. "It's not only that. Keith left behind huge problems. Everyone's worried and stressed out. Who has the luxury of second-guessing some tidbit of conversation they overheard? Look at poor Chunlai." Harry gestured toward the door, indicating the programmer who had just left. "He hasn't been home in three days. Mind you, he's extremely bright, but even he's stumped."

Lea felt a jolt of trepidation. Poor Paul. Now it was up to him. "What kind of problems?" she asked sharply.

"I don't like to speak ill of the dearly departed, but hell, you should see the code for the accounting software we're due to ship next month. We've still got 78 bugs. I tell you, it's scary." Harry picked up a can of Diet Coke from his desk, saw it was empty, and rose from his chair. "Join me?" he asked, holding the can aloft.

Lea followed Harry back the way she had come. In one cubicle, the turbaned Sikh was muttering furiously as lines of code zipped by on his computer screen. A tower of CDs teetered on the edge of his desk.

Harry pointed to another man of about his own age. His thinning hair was pulled back in a pony tail, and he wore a frayed blue denim work shirt and jeans. "That's Art Turino," Harry said. "A legend in his own time." Harry's eyes gleamed. "He's one of those crazy old hackers who used to break into the international telephone net—just for the fun of it. Claims he's reformed now. He's here as a consultant for a few days to help us out."

They reached an alcove beyond the cubicles that had a sink, a coffee-maker, and a mini-refrigerator. Harry opened the refrigerator door and plucked two cans of Diet Coke from the top shelf, handing one to Lea. He squinted at the caffeine-free label on his own, feigning disgust. "Look at me," he said. "In the old days, programmers were required to ingest vast quantities of pizza and caffeine. Now we know that pizza kills—all that cheese—and even caffeine is suspect." He shook his head mournfully, drained the can, and tossed it into the recycling bin.

Lea burst out laughing. "It's lucky you've made it this far!"

"Seriously, I'm getting too old for this business, Lea." Harry gazed out at the cubicles. "When you're young, this Valley is Mecca. It's totally exhilarating. You get so caught up in a project you hardly remember to eat or sleep. You're turned on by this incredible technology and what you can do with it. Or by the challenge of building a new system that millions will use." Harry spread his arms. "But you're also competing with all these brilliant people, and you're scared that you're not good enough. Every day, you have to prove yourself."

Harry's shoulders drooped, and he thrust his hands into his pockets. "Then there are the demands of the marketplace. It's all so incredibly fast-paced. Hell, new start-ups are launched all the time. Someone is always gaining on you, and there's always an urgent problem to be solved. You're constantly working against the clock to beat your competitors to market. Sixty days can mean the difference between getting a product out before they do. It can also mean the difference between getting rich or going broke. So it's no wonder everyone kills himself to get the job done.

"The kicker is when you're doomed before you start. I mean in terms of product quality. What drives the best programmers and engineers is the challenge to create the optimum system or device. To get things right. That's why people are willing to sacrifice their personal lives, even their health and marriages. But when you know from the start you've got no chance of succeeding, it eats you up inside."

"What are you getting at?" Lea asked. "And what, pray tell, does this have to do with Keith?"

Harry stroked his beard. "I was just thinking about Keith and how arrogant he was. His early success went to his head. He thought his competitors would never catch up to him. And when they did, he was stunned. But instead of hunkering down and developing better products, he tried to talk his way to profits. But he was only paying lip service to quality." Harry laughed shortly. "Keith loved to give interviews and pretend he was this technical guru. But Keith was no hacker. The hacker ethic is all about creating great code."

Lea eyed Harry quizzically. "So?"

"So most people in this business are driven by a dream to change the world. But Keith was into becoming a mogul. If he could accomplish that by selling mediocre products— so be it. He pushed sales over development. Sales at all costs. The bottom line was that he really didn't care if he released software with bugs that drove users crazy. And he didn't care if his technical people killed themselves trying to prevent it. One guy here told me he was so stressed he couldn't get his hands to stop shaking for two weeks." Harry grimaced. "We all know you have to accept tradeoffs between quality and getting the product out. But it was more than that with Keith."

"It didn't bother him to cut corners," Lea stated. She felt a flash of anger as she considered this in light of the firm's financial irregularities. "Just how far do you think Keith might have gone?"

Harry pursed his lips. "Maybe I've said enough already."

"What do you mean?"

Harry smiled enigmatically and said nothing.

Lea tried another tack. "Did you know Keith?"

Harry hesitated. "Uh, no. I didn't." He shrugged, as if to change the subject. "But hey. I'm not the best guy to comment on my fellow man. I'd rather be programming."

Lea smiled, recalling a night she and Paul had visited Harry in his Potrero Hill loft. It had been late, but Harry had acted like a mad scientist, determined to finish a program by daybreak. "I remember," Lea said.

Harry looked intent. "I swear, writing computer code can be absolutely addictive. It's a rush, solving all the problems almost as fast as they come up." Harry shook his head. "I used to drive my ex-wife crazy, though. She said any man who stays up all night writing code is in love with his machine, not her. She didn't understand me. She couldn't figure out how I could debug a program for hours on end when I didn't have the patience to stand in line at the bank. What she never grasped was that programming is a pleasurable challenge. You control your own destiny. What I need patience for is dealing with the outside world."

Lea's attention was diverted by a fellow in a black shirt and paisley tie who had joined them as Harry was speaking.

"Yeah, computers are fast, logical, and consistent," the man agreed. "Unlike people!"

Harry whooped and pumped the man's outstretched hand. He turned to Lea. "This is Dennis Zaslow, tech writer and editor *extraordinaire*. He produces our user manuals and spots all the inconsistencies in our systems."

"Pure hyperbole," Dennis protested to Lea. "Harry here is a giant among software developers. Now that he's on board, it's no longer a dysfunctional office."

"Suck-up," Harry said cheerfully, patting the man on the shoulder as Lea laughed. "Tell her about Keith," Harry prompted.

"Oh, Keith was the worst." Dennis crossed his eyes. "He rushed everything out the door so fast—there was never time to do a decent job on a manual. And if it wasn't clear whether our software was compatible with other products, Keith would insist that we obfuscate. I swear, some days I could have killed the guy."

Lea, startled, shot Harry a look as Dennis paused in mid-sentence, realizing his *faux pas*.

The tech writer fingered his shirt collar, cleared his throat, and glanced from Lea to Harry. "Naturally," he said, "I only meant that as a figure of speech."

6

Sous-chef Gerard Michaud was hunched over a crate of morel mushrooms muttering in French when Lea entered the kitchen the next morning.

"Is something wrong?" Lea asked. Gerard was unusually preoccupied.

Gerard scowled as he scrutinized and then sniffed a morel. "I do not know if Smitty was trying to pull a fast one, but the produce he sent us today is to laugh at. I refused to take his asparagus. It had no flavor, and the stalks were like wood. Now I have to find a substitute in the next hour."

As day *sous-chef*, Gerard was in charge of the kitchen from 5:15 A.M. through the lunch service. He supervised the morning prep work and personally inspected each delivery by the twenty-odd suppliers who streamed into the kitchen from dawn to mid-morning.

Lea had met Gerard when she was a *sous-chef* and he a line cook at Le Castel, the three-star restaurant in Brussels. Gerard had grown up in a family of restaurateurs in Alsace; he began his culinary career as a kitchen apprentice at age 12. While at college in Lyons, he had studied languages and philosophy and dreamed of living in the United States. He had an innate capacity to remain cool under pressure, and a mischievous sense of humor. At 28, he had light brown hair that was already growing sparse at the crown, and his lips were frequently drawn down in a wry smile. His round tortoise-shell glasses gave him an owlish appearance.

"Smitty's usually so reliable," Lea said in dismay.

"I know. But I wouldn't take his raspberries either. Luckily he had some Queen Annes to give me—after I twisted his arm. I'll use the cherries instead."

They were interrupted by the arrival of Ralph Stinson, a delivery man for Ferguson's, one of their five seafood suppliers. Ralph had graying, curly hair and biceps almost as big as Popeye's. He strode through the back door and placed two long, waxed cardboard boxes with the day's salmon catch on the counter. Ralph whistled as he hoisted a whole salmon from its bed of ice for their inspection.

"*Sacrebleu!*" Gerard swore.

Lea glanced at the salmon and shuddered. The skin of the 12-pound fish was dry and unappealing. Its eyes were dull. Quickly she checked the other box. Both carcasses deserved a speedy burial at sea.

"What on earth is going on?" she exclaimed.

Ralph peered at the salmon and flushed in embarrassment. "Gosh, I'm sorry, Miss Sherwood. I didn't pack your order myself this morning. I'm not sure what happened." Hastily he scooped up the boxes and backed out of the kitchen. "Let me check in the truck. I've got a few more orders to deliver. Maybe I can make a substitution."

He returned minutes later with two new specimens and pressed a forefinger to glistening flesh, which appropriately sprang back.

Gerard sighed in relief and initialed the invoice with a flourish.

Ralph turned to go. "Oh, I almost forgot," he said, extracting a crumpled envelope from the back pocket of his jeans. "From the boss." He handed the envelope to Lea.

As Ralph's truck rumbled off down the alley behind Panache, Lea extracted a single sheet of paper from the envelope. Gerard hovered by her side.

Lea read the message and looked up at Gerard. "It's no accident that we're suddenly getting the dregs," she said in a quavering voice. "Our credit line's been cut off, and from now on it's strictly cash on delivery." She balled up the paper and tossed it fiercely into the trash. "Damn! I suppose it's only a matter of time before our other suppliers follow suit!"

Gerard's eyes widened in chagrin. He moaned softly.

"Obviously the word on the street is that we're in *big* trouble," Lea said.

L ea went to her office and sat down at her desk to check the morning's mail. Zoe, her bookkeeper, had already sorted out the bills, leaving Lea a four-inch stack of correspondence. Several letters were hand-addressed to her personally.

She cringed as she opened the first. Freshly minted hate mail. She had started receiving it two days after Keith's murder. The prevalent theme of the writers was that Lea would soon get her due, and a few even went into lurid detail.

Lea pursed her mouth in disgust and vowed from now on only to open mail with return addresses. Zoe could screen the rest.

Next she scanned and discarded the usual sales pitches for kitchen devices and labor-saving processed foods. Last were the charity requests. Each pleaded with her to donate food and time to a worthy event. Lea received at least 15 such requests each week, and if she complied with even a quarter, she'd soon go broke. Today she set aside a single letter for consideration.

It was all too ironic. Fleeing customers and press pillory notwithstanding, the city's salesmen and charities continued to woo her.

Lea sighed and stared into space. Something had been nagging at her all morning. Suddenly the image of Joy Nugent on the phone with the management consultant came to mind.

That was it, she realized. She tried to remember what Joy had said about Anderson Pruett. It was odd. Why had Keith consulted him?

On impulse she dialed directory assistance and got the number for Kincaid Jenkins & Moore International on the Peninsula. After being transferred twice, she reached a woman named Sharon Dare, who identified herself as Pruett's secretary. As Lea was explaining the reason for her call, Sharon cut her off. "Dr. Pruett is out of the country," she said in a syrupy voice. "But he does call in every day. If you give me your number, I'm sure he'll get right back to you."

Lea's heart sank, and she bit back a retort. Anyone who uttered that phrase usually meant the exact opposite. She gave Sharon her numbers at home and at the restaurant and hung up irritably.

Now what? She toyed with the idea of calling Brooke Evans, a friend who hosted a radio talk show at studios two blocks away. Brooke had been in for lunch yesterday and had offered to help. If nothing else, she could canvass the station's reporters for the latest news—or rumors. As much as Lea hated to ask for a favor, she picked up the phone.

Brooke was just going into a meeting with her station manager, but she promised to check out the scuttlebutt. With any luck, she said, she'd stop by Panache with news at closing time that night.

Lea must have looked discouraged when she returned to the kitchen.

"Don't worry," Gerard teased. A perennial optimist, his mood had brightened since the salmon incident. "If we get desperate, we can advertise a special ostrich-meat dinner, followed by port and cigars in the bar."

"Oh, how trendy." Lea smirked

Gerard grinned, and he clicked on a portable radio he kept tuned to WFAR, the all-news station. A fledgling investor, he liked to check the mid-morning and closing stock market reports from the Pacific Exchange. Gerard clapped his hands as the announcer gushed about a hot new stock issue for an Internet firm. "What a country!" he enthused. "Everyone here can play the market. It's your capitalist sport!"

Brian, one of the line cooks, beckoned to Lea, and she went to the stove to taste a Breton lobster sauce he'd made for the Petrale sole *quenelles*.

Her lips curled as soon as a drop hit her tongue. *Yechh!* Lea groaned inwardly.

"So how is it?" Brian asked. His brown eyes grew anxious as he awaited her verdict.

Lea paused, careful not to vent her annoyance. She had long ago accepted her self-critical nature and knew she was her own worst critic—berating herself about errors and goading herself to improve. That was the price you paid to produce a quality product.

But she knew that others were not as self-critical, and that a harsh word from her could wound or embitter. She also preferred, on principle, to let her staff learn from their own mistakes. Yet she had a restaurant to run, and customers who noticed every lapse.

By now the other cooks were also watching her apprehensively, and the kitchen had grown silent. Lea tasted the sauce again and chose her words carefully. "The sweetness of the lobster comes through." *It ought to, at the price I paid to have it flown in.* "But I'm afraid you've added a bit too much salt, and way too much tarragon. They overwhelm the delicate flavors." She glanced at her watch. "Do we have any lobster stock left?"

Brian, who was subdued, nodded slowly.

"Then let's make up a new batch before lunch. You'll just have time—if you hurry."

Brian nodded again, and Lea watched, her heart heavy, as he poured out $90 worth of sauce. Few inexpensive mistakes occurred in a kitchen like hers.

At 11:15, the servers gathered in the dining room for their lunch and daily meeting—men and women alike attired in white shirts, black slacks, and black shoes. As everyone helped themselves from a buffet with chicken and vegetable wraps, Gerard emerged from the kitchen with three plates bearing the day's lunch specials. He placed the dishes in the center of the servers' table and proceeded to describe them: risotto with fresh chervil, marjoram, and *Ricotta Pecorino* cheese; ragout of escargots with sweet corn and fresh sage; and organic, baby garden greens with house-smoked sweetbreads and hazelnut oil. Forks flew as everyone speared bites.

"Fabulous!" pronounced Heather, a petite brunette, as she licked a drop of ragout from her lower lip. "Where were the corn and the sage grown?"

Gerard briefed everyone on the provenance of the dishes, and Lea distributed copies of the day's menu, run off on the laser printer in her office. Finally, Stuart the sommelier, an enthusiastic evangelist for California wines, described the six Napa and Sonoma vintages being offered by the glass.

At 11:30, Lea went to the locker room to change from her turtleneck and slacks to a camel sheath dress. She combed out her hair—from the ponytail she often wore while in the kitchen—and slipped into a pair of low heels. After hastily applying lipstick, she got to the dining room just in time to seat her first arrivals, a party of expensively suited trial attorneys who had to catch a flight to New York. She agreed to expedite their orders.

Next came five almost identically dressed Japanese executives from Moritoba; Wyatt Worthington, the crusty state senator; Ted Cushing, the septuagenarian author from the Gold Country; Buffy Stone and Cynthia Llewellyn, whom some insisted were the most soignée of all the San Francisco "ladies who lunch;" and a trio of garrulous fashion designers from Milan. Lea brought the latter their requested Campari.

She was short a server again that day, so Lea helped the staff deliver and clear plates. When a customer complimented her on the coriander-scented *gelato* with pistachios and asked how she managed to stay so slim, Lea laughed. It helped to be on your feet 12 hours a day.

"Next course for Table 27," she said to Gerard as she deposited a tray of dishes in the kitchen.

Gerard stood at attention at the line, directing the flow of orders. The cooks, in a blur of white jackets, were in constant motion in the aisle between the gas range, grill, and ovens—which lined the wall—and the stainless steel counters and shelves opposite, which held raw ingredients. Gerard in turn stood across from the cooks—in front of the stainless steel counters.

Acting as expediter, Gerard plucked a ticket from the row of orders hanging at eye level and called out the next dishes for Table 27. The cooks repeated the orders back. Satisfied, he executed a diagonal slash, from right to left, through the appetizer order on the ticket. It formed an X with the left-to-right slash he'd made as appetizers were taken to the table. Gerard then moved the ticket from the row on his left, where he monitored the progress of appetizers, to the center row, where he kept track of main courses.

"Where's that swordfish for 14?" Heather called to Gerard as she bounded in from the dining room.

Gerard in turn addressed Todd and Nicholas, two cooks who had their hands full at the fish station. "Where's that sword?"

"Coming up," said Nicholas, the senior of the two. Without breaking stride, Todd expertly coated a swordfish filet with olive oil, salt, and herbs and handed it to Nicholas, who slapped it on the grill.

Gerard scrutinized a plate of veal scallops that had just come up. "A little more sauce," he commanded, sliding the dish over the counter. CeCe, the meat cook, complied, and Gerard handed the dish to Lea, who was waiting. "Five," he said.

Lea glanced at the ticket for Table 5 and placed the veal in the right corner, or the second position, of a large rectangular tray. When two plates of pasta were ready a moment later, she placed them in the number one and three positions, to correspond with the seating at the table. That way any server could see at a glance who had ordered a dish.

Lea turned to Heather, who was on her way out. "Table 5," she said, thrusting the tray at her.

Heather grabbed it, pivoted smartly, and rushed out the door.

Lea followed Heather back to the dining room and spent the next half hour seating guests. Gradually, however, she began to feel self-conscious. People were too polite to gawk, but she was aware of surreptitious, curious stares. What were they thinking? Each day brought fresh media scrutiny into Keith's death and her own acquaintance with the man. Were her customers wondering if she'd been involved in a murder? Or was she simply an object of gossip—or worse—pity?

By 1:20, it was apparent to Lea that Panache would lose money on lunch yet again. The 110-seat dining room was now only half full.

"How are you holding up?" a masculine voice inquired. Lea turned to see Carter Weberling, the man who had funded Paul's start-up, and whom Paul had once regarded as his mentor. Carter's venture capital firm was nearby, and he occasionally came in for lunch. Today his silver hair was freshly trimmed, and his gray eyes probed hers. "I know the last week has been brutal," he said.

Lea felt a surge of gratitude for his sympathy. Then chagrin that she should so welcome the kindness of a relative stranger. Me and Blanche DuBois, she thought.

She smiled, more bravely than she felt. "What worries me is that the press seems to be out for fresh blood. Mine!"

Carter nodded. "I know. The Whitten board is doing all it can to contain the damage, but the media seem to have a morbid curiosity about Keith's death."

Lea suddenly flashed back to Keith's collapse—his painful breathing, his contorted torso. It was a recurring image, and she willed herself to suppress it.

She took a deep breath and changed the subject. "Paul's told me about the special auditors he had to bring in, and how worried he is about financial discrepancies."

"So am I," Carter said. "I have a distinctly negative feeling about it." He paused, weighing his words. "It's beginning to look like we'll have no choice but to restate earnings. Maybe even report a loss for the last quarter." Carter's expression was grim. "What I can't understand is why Keith didn't catch this. Francine Reese grotesquely inflated the value of our receivables. She assumed we'd collect 98 cents on every dollar, which is virtually impossible.

"Francine also overvalued our inventory. She assumed we'd get top dollar at a time when everyone else was cutting prices." Carter shook his head in amazement. "The thing is Keith knew he'd have to meet the discounted prices. He and I had a long talk about it. I simply don't see how he could have let the first quarter report go out as it did."

"Has anyone been able to locate Francine?" Lea asked.

Carter's face darkened. "No, not yet."

"What do you think is going on?"

Carter's troubled eyes met hers. Lea sensed he knew more than he wanted to reveal.

"At this point, I just don't know."

After she seated Carter, Lea became aware of another man who apparently was waiting to talk to her. He had finished lunch and was standing by the host station.

He spoke up as Lea approached. "Miss Sherwood? I'm Adam Pfeiffer. I suppose the name doesn't ring a bell?"

She admitted that it didn't and studied him for a clue. He was of medium height, with thinning dark hair, and was neatly dressed in a business suit. She couldn't remember meeting him before.

"I've known Paul for several years," he explained. "I just thought he might have mentioned me. I've been reading about Keith's death, and the mess it's been for both of you." Adam flushed slightly. "I used to know Keith too. In fact I once had business dealings with him, and I can't pretend to be sorry he's dead. For a while, I wanted to kill him myself."

Lea raised her eyebrows and waited for him to elaborate.

Adam laughed ruefully. "I hate to admit it, but I was a chump. I thought doing business with Keith would make me rich. I actually trusted him, which was my biggest mistake. You see, I developed a specialized cost-control program for hospitals, and I believed it had enormous potential. It took me a year to write, in my spare time. Then I shopped it around. It generated a lot of interest, but Keith was the highest bidder. You probably know that Whitten Systems has been trying to diversify and develop new types of applications software. Anyway, Keith's offer seemed too good to be true. He offered to pay me a minimal upfront fee, with the bulk of the payoff coming from royalties. That way my income seemed unlimited."

"Then what happened?" Lea hoped Adam would get to the point.

Adam grimaced. "Keith started marketing the program seven months ago, and it took off all right. But I've only seen a trickle of income. There's no question—Keith was screwing me out of my share. So I hired an attorney, and we've been fighting to get access to his books. Now with Keith dead, maybe I actually have a chance of getting my money. He can't stonewall me from the grave."

Lea felt an odd sensation—part sympathy and part awe. Keith had been more brazen than she'd known. What else could he have been involved in? And where would he have drawn the line?

"Why are you telling me all this?" she asked.

"Because I've always thought Paul was a decent guy. I just hope he knows what kind of company he's keeping over at Whitten Systems. The others aren't much better than Keith was. Please tell Paul to watch his back."

"I'll tell him," Lea said, subdued. As if Paul needed more bad news.

"Oh, by the way, I was surprised to hear that Paul brought in Harry Coulter to manage his software development."

"Why are you surprised? Harry worked with Paul at his old company."

"I know. It's just that after I heard Harry discussing a job with Keith, I assumed that he and Paul had parted ways."

Lea was stunned. "There must be some mistake. Are you sure it was Harry?"

Adam nodded, surprised at her reaction. "Absolutely. They were having lunch at Cooper's in San Mateo. I walked by their table and heard them talking about salary and bonuses. They were so caught up in negotiations, they didn't even notice me."

Lea was more confused than ever when Adam Pfeiffer left the restaurant. She watched him wend his way down Jackson toward Battery Street and mentally replayed her last conversation with Harry. She was sure he had denied ever knowing Keith.

But if what Adam said was true, it would certainly account for why Harry might have lied.

Sydney Toth was changing into her chef's whites when Lea entered the locker room after lunch. Sydney frowned as Lea picked up a discarded copy of the morning's *Herald*.

"It's all right," Lea said. "I might as well know what they're saying about me." She braced herself as she held up the front page. Nothing, however, could have prepared her for this latest volley.

Chef a Suspect in Silicon Valley Murder, the boldfaced headline screamed. In breathless prose, the *Herald* announced that it was now official: the SFPD was investigating Keith Whitten's death as a homicide.

The story went on to recap Lea's acquaintance with Keith and then delved into her friendship with Paul, the alleged rivalry between the two men, and Keith's "hostile takeover" of Paul's firm. The reporter then salaciously noted that Lea herself had served Keith's last dinner.

"Braying yahoos!" Sydney exclaimed. She grabbed the paper from Lea and tossed it in the trash contemptuously.

At 3:05, Lea, Gerard, and Sydney met in the dining room to discuss menu revisions. Several dishes they all liked hadn't been selling well.

Sydney, who was in charge of the dinner service, was from Bath in England and had also worked with Lea in Brussels. At 32, she was slender and lithe, with short chestnut hair that tended to mat and form spikes over a steamy stove. Her piercing violet eyes dominated her narrow face. Sydney had studied drama while in her early 20s and had acted for a year in London's equivalent of off-Broadway plays. Concluding that she had neither the talent nor the disposition for the Thespian life, she'd enrolled in culinary school and had gone on to work at several of the top restaurants in France. Sydney brought to her cooking the same intensity she'd exhibited on stage, and it was often said that she didn't suffer fools gladly. Off-duty, her mode of dress was a cross between the beatnik and the mod; her favorite shoes were pointy-toed, black leather lace-up boots that reminded Lea of the Wicked Witch of the West. Today, in a black pullover and snug black jeans under her chef's whites, Sydney resembled an edgy black cat.

Evidently Sydney was still smarting from a squabble with their linen supplier, who had failed to deliver clean linen that morning. "Mendacious blighter!" she complained. "He had the nerve to tell me his employees went out on strike. But I checked, and we're the only ones within five blocks that he stiffed."

Lea gulped. Their problems with suppliers would only get worse, she knew, so long as Panache was under a cloud. She tried to put that out of her mind for the moment, however. The menu now demanded their attention.

"Okay. What should we do about the steak *marchand du vin*?" Lea asked. "I know it's the vogue to eat less red meat, but we ought to keep at least one beef dish on the menu."

"Let's change the name," Gerard proposed brightly. "Update the image. How about describing it as a dry-aged loin of beef with Merlot sauce, served with potato-celery root *galette*?"

"Perfect," Lea pronounced. She looked inquiringly at Sydney, who nodded crisply and for once, withheld comment. Lea annotated her copy of the menu.

Gerard grinned. "Remember M. Beaulieu?" he asked, referring to their former boss in Brussels. "Whenever a dish didn't sell, he rewrote the menu. I remember when he got diners to order the duck breast by referring to it as smoky, rare medallions of duck with mango *jus.*"

"I know," Sydney said in a rare burst of enthusiasm. "In London we had people scarfing up 'roasted root vegetables' who'd never before gone near a turnip, much less a rutabaga. But M. Beaulieu elevated the practice to an art!"

Lea clapped her hands in delight as she recalled their assorted tenures under the imperious chef. M. Beaulieu was a notorious perfectionist, and a benevolent despot. "Remember the night he kept yelling at Pascal Pelletier, who quit in a huff?" she asked gleefully. "Pascal left six dinners on the stove." M. Beaulieu fit the classic French stereotype of a screamer—acting on the conviction that emotional turmoil kept his staff in line. Lea, like many young American chefs, shunned this approach on the grounds that a calm disposition begat stable cooks and consistent cuisine—not to mention peace of mind for chef-owners such as herself.

Sydney shuddered. "Bloody tyrant! M. Beaulieu may be a brilliant chef, but he and I never got along. His kitchen was like a locker room—all those strutting men trying to prove how macho they were. The testosterone level was way too high for me."

Lea chuckled and flashed back to a particularly trying night, when a 40-minute power outage had backed up the dinner orders. It reminded her that men and women had vastly different styles in the kitchen, and that they reacted differently to pressure. The men that night had yelled and cursed—but they'd quickly regained their composure after the crisis had passed. The women had kept their focus under pressure but had fallen apart afterwards. Lea now preferred to work in kitchens where both sexes were present, keeping extreme behavior in check.

"I am, perhaps, not the right person to be objective about M. Beaulieu," Gerard said. "I was far too young and much too terrified when I served my apprenticeship under him."

He grinned. "But I do remember being thrilled when he finally let me start trimming the filet mignon. I said to myself, this is progress!"

They all laughed and exchanged warm glances.

"I remember M. Beaulieu had a soft spot for you, Lea," Gerard said.

"Really?" she asked with exaggerated disbelief. "Was that why he insisted women didn't have the stamina or the creativity to be great chefs? Or why he claimed they wilted under pressure?"

Gerard tittered. "That was just his way of pushing you. But he liked you, *certainement*. He even gave you that going-away present, the pretty gold wine-bottle opener. What was engraved on it? "A meal is a celebration of life," Gerard quoted.

Lea nodded slowly, recalling both the gift and the bear hug that had accompanied it. Somehow it all seemed part of another lifetime. "So, tell me," she demanded, "how would M. Beaulieu reinvent this dish?" With a bold stroke, she underlined the next spurned item on their list.

By 3:45, they had arrived at five menu revisions, but Lea fretted privately that it might be too little, too late. At this point, Panache needed far more than a cosmetic polish.

A s her last guests lingered over coffee that night, Lea took a moment to reapply her lipstick and to smooth her camel sheath, which she'd been wearing since lunch. Her thoughts kept returning to her earlier conversation with Carter Weberling. How did he truly feel about Keith? Carter, after all, had sanctioned the merger, only to discover that Keith had misrepresented vital facts. At the very least, Keith had tarnished Carter's pride and reputation. And no man likes to be played for a fool.

Lea was still lost in thought when Brooke Evans bustled in shortly before 11:00. "Bet you never thought I'd get back to you," Brooke said, shrugging off her jacket. "I'd have gotten here earlier, but it's been crazy at the station!" Brooke waited impatiently as Lea said goodnight to a party of six.

When Lea was free, Brooke tapped her on the arm and hummed a menacing tune. "Guess what I found out about Francine Reese! It's a lulu," she hinted.

"What?" Lea demanded.

Brooke squared her shoulders and drew herself up. "Only that she's suspected of attempted murder back home in Baltimore!"

7

Lea led Brooke to a table in a quiet corner, away from the servers who were cleaning up.

"Do you mean there's a warrant out for her arrest?" Lea asked excitedly.

"No, no," Brooke said. "Let me start at the beginning."

Brooke, the host of her own talk show, *Brooking No Nonsense*, had copper-colored hair and sea-green eyes. She didn't look her 43 years, and she brimmed with an exuberance that Lea envied. She was an eclectic reader, and a formidable debater on the air—more than a match for any caller. Invariably she received as much hate mail as fan mail, which she proclaimed to be a desirable ratio. Brooke's show currently swept the local ratings, and she was being wooed by at least two rival stations. She and Lea had met the week Panache opened.

"You know that Francine came here from Baltimore after she got divorced a year ago," Brooke said, an undercurrent of intrigue in her voice. She pushed the sleeves of her emerald sweater dress up to her elbows.

"I heard someone mention it." Lea's pulse quickened.

"What you probably don't know is what a bitter custody battle she faced. Both she and her husband wanted Tommy, their 8-year-old son. Anyway, one night hubby went over to Francine's—she supposedly was expecting him—and when she didn't answer his ring, he let himself in with his old key. It was dusk, and the lights were off in the house. When he walked into the living room and reached for a light switch, Francine shot him ... twice. In the stomach. He had a real bad time of it. He was in and out of hospitals for months."

"Francine admits shooting him?" Lea pulled a face.

Brooke fluttered manicured hands. "She claims it was in self-defense. She'd forgotten he was coming over and thought he was a prowler."

"Oh," Lea said, somewhat deflated. "And the police believed her?"

"Well, they investigated for a while. The husband is a prominent banker in Baltimore. But there wasn't any solid evidence, so the cops couldn't make it stick. Francine then convinced a judge to let her keep the boy, and she moved out here when Keith offered her a job."

"What's the word on the grapevine? Did she really intend to shoot him?"

"Among the people who knew them both, the answer is an unqualified yes."

Lea frowned. "People sometimes do things in the heat of a custody battle that they'd never do otherwise. Especially a mother trying to keep a child."

"Maybe," Brooke said doubtfully. "But that's not all. Keith had Francine investigated before he ever made her the job offer."

"That seems a little extreme, even for a sensitive spot in Silicon Valley."

"What's peculiar is that Keith hired her after he got the report." Brooke rested her arms on the table and leaned forward conspiratorially. "Keith's private investigator learned that Francine was on the verge of being fired by her Baltimore firm. There were complaints about her work, and some kind of unpleasantness was being hushed up. Plus she rubbed people the wrong way. Nobody wanted to go to bat for her."

"Keith *knew* that?"

Brooke laughed. "It's odd, isn't it? It's almost as though he intended to hire someone with a murky past."

"So he'd have leverage over her?" Lea asked uncertainly.

"You tell me." Brooke waggled her eyebrows.

Brooke extracted a manila envelope from the leather portfolio that doubled as her purse and briefcase and slid it across the table. "Courtesy of our affiliate in Baltimore. They faxed me these today."

Lea opened the envelope and pulled out a stack of press clippings. She riffled through them, pausing at a photograph of Francine in a dress-for-success suit. The accompanying news story announced that Francine Reese, 41, had been named vice president and chief financial officer of Whitten Systems Corp. Ms. Reese was quoted as looking forward to the challenge of working with the outstanding management team of such a dynamic Silicon Valley company.

"Look at this!" Lea said. She held the clipping aloft, pointing to a paragraph. "Francine left her Baltimore job after only ten months. She sure has a talent for getting into trouble quickly." Lea scanned the remaining articles, which traced Francine's professional history as a financial analyst and manager. She leaned toward Brooke expectantly. "What else were you able to find out about her?"

"Nothing about her lifestyle, except that she just bought a million dollar house in the Valley. Pricey, but then so is everything down there. You probably couldn't buy an outhouse for under 50 grand. And whether Francine is living above her means, I couldn't say. I wasn't able to find out how much her divorce settlement came to. My Baltimore source said Francine complained about getting a raw deal. But who knows what that means?"

"Maybe she felt she needed money," Lea speculated. "But why would she get mixed up in financial fraud? That would hardly guarantee long-term security."

"Maybe she was planning to take the money and run. In fact it's looking like she may have done just that. Paul still hasn't been able to reach her, right?"

Lea shook her head. "Maybe she's a risk taker. Some people are. Normal life is too tame for them." Lea stared at Francine's photograph, as though she could divine her character.

"From what I hear, financial fraud cases are dicey to prove," Brooke said. "They're expensive for the state to prosecute, and so complicated that it's hard to get a jury to return a guilty verdict."

"Which only encourages white-collar crime," Lea suggested. She sighed deeply and set aside the picture. "This is all quite provocative, but the only thing we've confirmed so far is that a woman can be just as incompetent or venal as a man."

Her friend was silent, and Lea felt a stab of guilt. She hoped Brooke hadn't mistaken her frustration for ingratitude. "But I can't thank you enough for digging this up! You're a terrific reporter," Lea said.

Brooke gave her a reproving look. "Puleeze. I can't pretend to be that. We both know I went into journalism as a way of trying to see and do everything. This way I can poke my nose into everybody's business." Brooke tossed her head and smiled wickedly. "But I do hope you appreciate what I went through to get you the information."

"Oh? And what was that?" Lea asked in mock horror.

"I had to bribe our Baltimore station manager. Dinner with me here next time he comes to town."

"Anytime," Lea promised gaily. "It's on the house."

"It'll be soon," Brooke warned. "The man's been asking me out for months."

"In that case, I'll be sure to give you a romantic table." Lea cocked her head suggestively.

Brooke giggled. "No, please don't. He's a success-at-any-cost kind of guy. Not exactly my type."

Lea's jaw dropped. "Wait a minute! Just what is your type, anyway? Since I've known you, your men friends have had nothing in common. First there was the sculptor who brewed his own ale. Then the divinity student who played the bass in a jazz combo. Not to mention the vegetarian who ran marathons and spent eight years getting a doctorate in Chinese studies."

Brooke vamped and batted her eyelashes. The emerald hue of her dress made her eyes look like jade. "They all shared a transcendent Zen quality that I find irresistible."

Lea laughed again and looked up to see Sydney emerging from the kitchen. She bore down on them with a filigreed silver tray.

"It's not the traditional Port and Stilton," Sydney said, "but I thought a foray into the unknown would do no harm." She set the tray down and uncorked a bottle of Rex Hill Pinot Noir, which had been a hit at a recent Panache tasting of Oregon wines. "I thought you could use some nourishment, if not inspiration."

Lea, who had not eaten dinner, murmured her thanks as Sydney poured. She helped herself to Humboldt Fog, a specialty cheese produced on the northern California coast, and to slices of fresh Bosc pear and shelled black walnuts.

"Ummm. Smell this *Brie de Meaux*. It's heaven." Brooke shaved off a sliver and chewed it delicately. She moaned. "It practically melts in your mouth."

Sydney poured a glass of wine for herself, held it up to the light, and swirled the burgundy liquid. Humming, she retired to the kitchen.

Lea and Brooke ate in silence for a while.

"So, what were you able to get on Marshall Schroth?" Lea asked as she munched a walnut.

Brooke took a moment to swallow. "He's well-known in the industry, according to Karen Dixon, our Silicon Valley bureau chief. She's interviewed him twice. But Karen says he's considered baldly aggressive by Valley standards. For one thing, Marshall doesn't pay lip service to the prevailing ethos. You know, the miracle of technology. He's in it strictly for the cash and the glory." Brooke took a sip of Pinot Noir.

"He's got the MBA, and an impressive résumé with progressively responsible jobs at Valley firms. He joined Whitten Systems last year after a stint as marketing chief for TYBER Semiconductor."

"He sounds like a lot of ambitious men in other fields," Lea observed dryly. "The Bay Area is loaded with them."

"Maybe. Karen did find his Achilles heel, though," Brooke added. "When she asked him where he got his MBA, he hemmed and hawed. Wouldn't tell her. It turns out he got it at night school—not at some fancy Ivy League institution. He's quite touchy about it."

Lea smiled. "Tom Wolfe had it right in the '70s. Sex is no longer the great taboo. Now it's class and status. And Marshall certainly struck me as a man who would consider himself a failure if he didn't make CEO by the time he's 40." Briefly she told Brooke about her encounter with Marshall in his office.

Brooke speared a slice of pear. "There's one more thing. Word has it that he's livid about Paul beating him out for the top spot at Whitten Systems. In fact Karen says Marshall's doing everything he can to sabotage Paul."

Lea groaned and poured them each more wine. "I just don't understand men like him. He was obviously trying to intimidate me in his office. But why? It was almost instinctual. The funny thing is, I've read that arrogance often masks insecurity. But when someone acts like an SOB, the last thing they arouse is my sympathy."

"Really," said Brooke. "Marshall sounds like a corporate climber with an inflated ego. I've met my share. Frankly, I'm surprised they all manage to keep from killing one another."

"You mean that most of them do," Lea said darkly. "Look at Keith."

Brooke shrugged.

"I wonder," Lea mused. "Marshall must have hated playing second fiddle to Keith. And Keith loved to make people squirm."

"It sounds like they deserved each other."

Suddenly Lea remembered Keith's alleged rendezvous with Harry Coulter. "I heard something strange today. Tell me what you think." She recapped the high spots of Adam Pfeiffer's story.

Brooke frowned. "You're wondering if Harry was a mole for Keith during the time he was trying to take over Paul's company."

Lea sighed. Her fear wasn't so farfetched after all.

"What are you going to do? Tell Paul?"

"I don't know yet," Lea said slowly. "Paul has enough problems right now. And he badly needs Harry's expertise. I don't want to create a rift between them for nothing. There may be a perfectly reasonable explanation for what happened. That is, assuming Adam Pfeiffer really did see Harry and Keith together."

Brooke shot her a look. "Don't kid yourself."

"Did you find out anything else?" Lea asked, eager now to change the subject. Even though she was keeping Adam's story from Paul for the right reasons, she still felt guilty about it.

Brooke reflected. "There was one curious thing. Gossip is circulating about Keith's former girlfriend. You know, the Web designer who looks like a character out of a Tolkein fable?"

"Former girlfriend? What do you mean? I had a long talk with Georgeanne the other day, and she said the relationship had been cooling off, not that they'd broken up. *Au contraire*, they'd gone out to dinner the night before."

Brooke cocked an eyebrow. "I heard they'd split up several weeks before the murder. But I suppose if Keith had been desperate for his super-duper pills, he might have persuaded Georgeanne to meet him that night."

Their eyes locked.

"Noooo," Lea said.

"Why not? Somebody did it. And she had the perfect opportunity."

Lea pictured the delicate, otherworldly Georgeanne. She seemed incapable of swatting a fly. "But why would she do it that way? Why deliberately cast suspicion on herself?"

"Precisely. It's fantastic, and therefore a logical person would not suspect her. She's smart, remember."

Lea considered. "We still don't know what poisoned Keith. That might tell us something about the person who did it."

Brooke smiled wryly. "They say poison is a woman's weapon."

"But what could Georgeanne's motive be?"

"Maybe Keith told her to get lost and she took umbrage. Or maybe she doesn't want to be a cyber-groupie all her life. She might have planned to marry Keith and spend her days meditating and doing Tai Chi on their estate in the Santa Cruz mountains."

Lea groaned and pushed her chair away from the table. "Damn!" she said. "None of this makes any sense."

8

The naughty neon signs on Broadway glowed brightly as Lea drove home through North Beach. It was past midnight, but the tourist Mecca still hummed with prurient thrill seekers. Waiting at a red light, Lea spied a balding man eyeing an X-rated movie marquee.

When the light shone green, Lea headed west through the Broadway Tunnel and turned right onto Larkin Street, up Russian Hill. Here the traffic thinned, and she became aware of a light-colored Ford sedan behind her. She couldn't be sure, but she thought she'd seen the car pull out of a space on Jackson as she and Brooke had said goodnight. Chiding herself for her overactive imagination, Lea made another right turn and watched her rearview mirror. In seconds the Ford slid around the corner.

A vise gripped Lea's stomach. She lowered her car window and inhaled the cold night air. *"You're imagining things,"* she scolded herself. Still, she didn't dare drive home.

She made a right at Filbert and headed east, then hooked a left on Hyde. As she sped down the hill toward the bay, the illuminated towers of Ghirardelli Square blazed against a moonless sky, momentarily distracting her. She checked her mirror again. The sedan was still there. Lea could make out a lone figure in the car but couldn't tell whether it was male or female. At Fisherman's Wharf, she made a dizzying series of turns in a maze of one-way streets. Finally, she appeared to have lost her pursuer.

Lea stopped the car at a curb and took deep breaths. The bayside air carried a whiff of the sea. Then she nosed the Renault west again and drove home, periodically glancing in the mirror.

She found a parking space two doors down from her apartment at the corner of Larkin and Chestnut. Nervously she scanned the shadows. Both streets appeared deserted. A streetlight was out, however, and a dark patch lay ahead of her. Lea eased the car door open and got out cautiously. She took several steps, heard a rustling in the bushes, and froze. A marmalade cat soared out of a hedgerow and streaked across her path.

Lea heaved a sigh of relief when she finally unlocked the front door to her building and let herself in. She latched the door behind her and climbed the stairs to her apartment.

The message light was blinking on the answering machine when Lea entered the living room. She collapsed onto the sofa and hit the replay button. A woman's unfamiliar, reedy voice announced that she was Lea's second cousin from Boston. Lea had met her once years ago. The cousin asked if she and a friend might visit Lea for a week—they would *so* love to have her show them San Francisco. Lea buried her face in a sofa pillow and groaned.

A second message was from Lea's high school French teacher. Mrs. Livesy's clear lilting voice filled the room. "Lea, my dear, I got the strangest phone call this afternoon. It was from a police detective who asked a great many questions about you. Rather intrusive and impertinent. Along the lines of whether you had any trouble getting along with others, or if we had records of any psychological tests. I just thought you should know."

Mrs. Livesy paused. "Naturally I don't believe half of what I read in the newspapers, but I've seen enough to know that you're going through a difficult time. I trust everything will work out well for you. You always showed initiative in solving problems, and I'm sure you'll land on your feet. Take care, my dear. Call me sometime when you get a chance."

For the first time since Keith's death, Lea eyes welled with tears. The police were digging into her life, no doubt contacting a variety of her acquaintances. And innocent or no, their questioning carried a taint.

Lea thought of her parents, who had been out of the country for almost a year. Her father, an archaeologist, divided his time between digs in the Middle East and the Balkan Peninsula; occasionally he lectured at European universities. Her mother, a painter of note whose work hung in museums around the world, accompanied her husband on his jaunts. Her last e-mail had been from Turkey.

Lea felt a familiar pang of loneliness. Her parents had been away for months out of the year when she was growing up. In their stead, she was raised by her father's sister, Vivian, a reserved maiden lady not partial to displays of affection. Lea had spent long, solitary hours in her bedroom, reading and daydreaming. She would wander from room to room in the big house by the Presidio, mindful of her aunt's constant vigilance, lest she break anything. When her parents finally did sweep in from exotic points, she reveled in their conversations about foreign cultures and art, music, and books. Steeped in the lore of Gertrude Stein's salons by her mother, she would eavesdrop on their dinner parties, intrigued by an adult world that seemed to promise both wit and adventure, order and sensibility. Later, restaurants became an extension of that world for her. Her aunt had died five years ago, and the Presidio house was now empty, awaiting her parents' return.

Lea got up, walked to the window, and gazed out over San Francisco Bay. The beacon on Alcatraz Island blinked. A foghorn moaned.

The view was at once familiar yet mesmerizing. Lea had never lost a sense of awe about the bay, or forgotten its potential for danger as well as romance. With its treacherous currents and dense fog, it was one of the world's most precarious passages—its rockbound shoals a graveyard for countless ships and seafarers.

A sense of gloom enveloped Lea. It was now almost 1:30, and she doubted that she'd be able to sleep. She still felt jumpy and unsettled. Clearly, she would have to be on her guard. But on guard against what? And whom?

She sank back onto the sofa and kicked off her pumps. At least here, for the moment, she was safe. She drew comfort from the familiar surroundings. Her one-bedroom apartment was one of four in a rambling, three-story English Tudor built after the 1906 earthquake. She had lived here for over a year, since her return from Belgium. In a corner of the high-ceilinged living room, beside the marble fireplace, stood a *shoji* screen from Japan, a gift from her parents. Shelves of novels and books on art and European history lined the walls, framing a favorite painting by her mother—an abstract canvas of forest and sea. The ivory upholstered sofa and chairs were from the Presidio house; the Oriental rug she'd purchased at auction.

She sat in the dim lamplight, nerves alert to the foghorn's plaint. This was the time of day she felt most vulnerable, most alone. The fears she'd been repressing all day now engulfed her, and the memory of the car that had followed her returned. Her stomach churned, and she fought against a rising panic.

Clearly, she stood to lose everything she had worked for all these years. She winced at the thought of her anxious investors. Not a day went by that several didn't call. These were the people who had believed in her. Who had come through for her. The possibility of failing them made her ache.

Business, however, showed no signs of picking up. On the contrary, it continued to dwindle. After paying this month's overhead, she would be awash in red ink. Nostalgically she recalled her struggle to start her own restaurant. She'd had to acquire skills to deal with bankers, suppliers, accountants, lawyers, and her employees—and she'd undergone a trial-by-fire in running a service-oriented business. She'd trained her staff, developed the menu and wine list, transcribed the recipes, and tasted *everything*. And every day now she wore 15 hats; it was not unusual for her to go home without having so much as peeled an onion.

Despite the relentless pace, Lea was hooked. The work was addictive, the pressure kept her sharp, and in the end the rewards surpassed the anxiety and fatigue. She loved giving people the pleasure of good food and considered herself lucky to get immediate feedback, unlike Paul and Harry, who had to wait months or years to see a finished product. Also, she basked in the glow of her customers' praise; to be told that Panache was their favorite restaurant never failed to make her day.

Lea's thoughts drifted to her staff. They were top-notch, she thought with pride and sadness—and they had become her extended family. Yet unless she could conjure up a miracle, she would have no choice but to let some of them go.

Her eyes strayed to a framed photograph of Paul on her bookshelf. He was standing on a trail on Mount Tamalpais, the wind in his hair, looking carefree and happy. She was reminded of his resiliency—of how he'd picked up the pieces after losing his company and started all over again. As devastating as his loss had been, his innate enthusiasm for life had seen him through. Paul's steady gaze seemed to reach across the room to calm her.

Before she had met him, Lea had wondered if she would ever fall in love. It had seemed a heady, elusive dream. Oh, she had been fond of a few men. But she had tended to value them for their individual traits—warmth, a keen sense of humor, imagination. Paul had changed all that.

She thought of their first evening together. They'd gone to dinner and then taken a long walk through the Marina and Fisherman's Wharf. He'd admired her pluck and resourcefulness in opening Panache, and she'd been smitten by his vitality, and his determination to make the most of his life. They'd agreed that you had to follow your passion—wherever it led you.

She'd been fascinated by his endless curiosity about things. Was there anything he *wasn't* interested in? History, religion, art, sports, philosophy—he spoke more intelligently and more compellingly about each than anyone she'd known. It was obvious he thought for himself and intended to live life on his own terms. At the same time, he didn't take himself too seriously.

Unlike other men she'd known, Paul had also been interested in who *she* was. He wanted to know what she thought and felt. And he was the first man who saw her as she saw herself—and to whom she felt truly visible. It was as if she'd met a missing part of herself.

They'd laughed beside the barking seals by the pier, eaten cotton candy, and sat arm in arm on the shore as the stars glittered above the bay. The next day he'd sent her a bouquet of bird of paradise flowers, and a card that thanked her for the best night of his life. She'd nearly swooned as she read it and had blushed furiously when the kitchen crew had winked and nodded knowingly.

But a rogue voice inside her fretted that it was all too good to last. True, her parents' romance had endured for 40 years. Lea knew it was possible. It was just that for so many lonely years, love had been unattainable.

She gazed out at the bay, hugging her chest. What did the future hold for her and Paul?

9

L ea pulled open the heavy wooden door of the old Potrero Hill coffee warehouse that had been converted to residential lofts—and that Harry Coulter now called home. She took the industrial-size elevator to the second floor and rang Harry's bell, praying he was home this Sunday morning. After an almost sleepless night, she'd decided to confront him about whether he'd been spying for Keith.

On the third ring, Harry opened the door a crack and peered out. His graying hair was tousled, and his Visit Planet Mars T-shirt was half tucked into his jeans. His eyes widened when he saw her. "Lea? What on earth are you doing here?" He stood aside, puzzled, and let her in.

Lea stepped into the vast room and stopped abruptly. She hardly knew where to turn. The scuffed floor was littered with circuit boards and other computer innards. The patches of flooring not obscured by computer parts were stacked with manuals. Tucked into various nooks were early-model Apple computers—the techie's equivalent of the Model-T Ford. Presiding in the center of the room was Harry's old magician's guillotine, a legacy from his days as a semi-professional entertainer.

"I'd be happy to give you a demonstration," Harry said, following her gaze. He sidled over to the instrument and hoisted its blade. "Here, just lean forward and put your head down."

Lea shuddered and instead navigated a path to a stained velvet sofa. "May I?" she asked.

Harry laughed and nodded, taking a seat at the other end. Lea sat down gingerly. Her foot brushed a plate smeared with what she hoped was dried green *salsa*. As she shifted, attempting to secure clearer ground, she inadvertently kicked a wadded-up pair of striped pajamas. They landed nearby, draping a vintage lava lamp. Lea stared as blobs of sickly yellow lava coalesced, then collapsed, in the primeval, murky ether. She turned to Harry in dismay.

"I know, I know, it's a relic of the '70s. But hey, so am I." Harry grinned. "Can I get you anything to eat or drink?"

Lea swallowed and shook her head. For a moment, she'd almost forgotten why she was here.

Harry, however, had recovered from his initial surprise at seeing her. He now seemed delighted to have the company. He waved a hand grandly, taking in the expanse of his loft. "I know it may seem cluttered, but the beauty of my system is that I know where everything is. I always have a backup if a part fails, and I can lay my hands on it in seconds." He wagged his head. "When I'm defending virtual Planet Earth from extraterrestrial invaders at 2:00 A.M., the last thing I need is a system failure."

Lea smiled weakly and pulled up the neck of her pullover sweater. It was chilly in the loft.

"Here, look at this." Harry reached down to the floor and picked up the instruction booklet for an elaborate computer war game. His eyes lit up like a 10-year-old's. "This game is positively addictive. I was up all night playing it." He bounced to his feet and walked over to the nearest computer. "Come here. I'll show you."

Lea felt her courage ebbing. Harry, she knew, could go on like this for hours. She cleared her throat. "I came here to ask you something. It could be important."

He stared at the computer screen, oblivious to distractions.

"You're not responding," Lea said.

"Huh? Oh," he said guiltily and laughed. "That's what my ex-wife always said." He still had one eye on the screen. "What was it you wanted?"

"I need to talk to you about Keith."

Harry's face darkened. "That guy. I spent all week trying to straighten out a mess he created. Did you know that Paul had to add more staff to our help line? Customers were either getting busy signals or they were stuck on hold for 35 minutes. All to resolve problems that Keith should have prevented." Harry shook his head in disgust. "I don't know what he was thinking when he released our latest accounting package. It's slow and cumbersome, and users have been flooding our lines asking how to fix glitches. Not only did Keith alienate buyers with a shoddy product, we're now paying through the nose for it. Each call costs us from $20 to $100."

"That's not what I…."

"Now I'm not totally naive," Harry interjected. "Any software company that tries to release a product with no bugs will never ship a product. But some firms act like all their problems are due to user error. That's just crazy. So the question really becomes: what level of dysfunction will you and your customers tolerate?"

"Keith insisted he was scrupulous about debugging," Lea said. "He used to claim that any problems with his products usually cropped up in specialized applications."

"Keith was a sanctimonious jerk," Harry said. "I can tell you he put a lot of people off with his holier-than-thou attitude, and his high-pressure sales tactics. Not to mention the way he touted vaporware."

"Speaking of Keith…."

"I know people at Whitten Systems are grumbling about Paul," Harry interrupted again. "Those who want to coast," he added, catching Lea's astonished look. "Oh, they may not have respected Keith, but it was easier to play his game.

You could toady up to him. But Paul expects the best from everybody. That can make you downright uncomfortable if you're used to getting by with style over substance."

Lea gaped at Harry. He obviously detested Keith. So why had he spoken to him about a job? Harry didn't strike her as someone who'd put money over principle. Or was he feeling guilty because he'd been tempted to do so? Was he trying to redeem himself by denigrating Keith?

"I have to ask you something *now*," Lea declared.

"Uh-oh!" His eyes widened in mock alarm. "That's the tone of voice my ex-wife used. What have I done this time?"

Lea sighed in exasperation. "Let's be serious. When I was at your office, you told me you'd never met Keith. But the other day at my restaurant, someone mentioned he'd seen you together. Talking about a job."

Harry froze, and anger flared in his eyes. Then he looked away, his face a mask.

Lea studied him. Was he stalling? Concocting an impromptu story?

"Are you asking me or accusing me?" Harry said finally.

"I'm asking you," she said miserably. "That's why I came here. I didn't want to say anything to Paul until I knew what had happened."

Harry clenched his jaw and turned to stare at Lea. Slowly, his expression softened until he appeared sheepish. "It's, uh, kind of embarrassing, actually." He walked back to the couch and sat down.

"Here's the thing," Harry said. "Keith called me one day when I was working for Paul. Yes, he was interested in buying Paul's company, although I didn't know it at the time." Harry paused.

"And you met for lunch," Lea prompted.

"Yeah," he said. "At Cooper's in San Mateo, which apparently isn't as out of the way as I'd thought. Anyhow, Keith told me he'd heard about my work and wanted to offer me a job. He flattered me. He mentioned big money. Mind you, this was when I knew Paul's company was in trouble. I figured the odds were that I'd be out on the street before long. Under the circumstances, I thought it wouldn't hurt Paul if I started protecting my own interests.

"But halfway through lunch, I started to get a funny feeling. I got wise to Keith. It became obvious he was just pumping me for information. Well, I felt like a fool. A really disloyal fool. The kicker was that when I called him on it, he threatened me. He said if I told Paul, he'd insist it had happened the other way around. That I'd gone to him for a job, offering to trade inside information." Harry shrugged helplessly. "I wanted to tell Paul, to warn him. But I just couldn't. I knew how he felt about Keith. He would have been furious with me just for meeting him. So I felt guilty, but I kept my mouth shut."

Harry looked so forlorn that Lea concluded he must be telling the truth.

Then the implications dawned on Harry. "Wait a minute," he said. "Did you believe I might have acted as a mole for Keith? Helped him take over Paul's company? Or that I killed Keith when he threatened to expose me?"

It was Lea's turn to be sheepish. She turned up her palms apologetically. "I don't know what to think about anything anymore."

They were silent for a moment. Harry seemed lost in thought.

"You're not going to tell Paul, are you?"

Lea hesitated. At best, it would create a strain between the two men; at worst, it would foster a distrust that might continue to grow. Still, she had never kept anything from Paul before. Reluctantly she shook her head. "I don't plan to tell him, no."

10

A brisk wind ruffled Lea's hair as she and Paul walked across the courtyard to the stone pagoda at the Japan Center.

They entered a wing housing a vast replica of a Japanese village. Storefronts bore traditional carved-wood facades. Gaily colored paper lanterns bobbed beside signs in Japanese characters. Plastic replicas of *donburi* and other Japanese dishes beckoned from restaurant windows, and the aroma of ginger filled the air. Lea peered into a restaurant with a U-shaped wooden bar. A chef in the center was busy shaping morsels of *sushi*; once launched on miniature boats, they floated, glistening, past patrons on a moving counter.

"This was a good idea," Paul said. He took Lea's hand and squeezed it. "I can't remember the last time we spent an afternoon together."

Lea felt a surge of hope—and joy. She had all but forgotten the morning at Harry's and now wanted only to renew her intimacy with Paul. Since Keith's death, they had hardly seen one another, and their few conversations had centered on the murder investigation.

They wandered past shop windows, admiring black pearl necklaces and embroidered *obis*. The lilting sounds of a flute echoed as they skirted a small rock garden, artfully framed by stalks of bamboo.

At the far end of the building a crowd had gathered around a wizened old man in a red *kimino*. Seated at an easel, he appeared almost in a trance as he wielded an artist's brush. A sign on the wall above him read "*Shodo.*"

"Look!" Paul said, his eyes lighting up. "I love Japanese calligraphy. When I was in Japan with Carter we went to a *shodo* exhibition, and I was blown away."

Lea studied the intricate Japanese characters that appeared to flow effortlessly from the man's quick brush. "What is it you especially like?"

Paul replied without taking his eyes off the artist. "The abstract beauty—and the individuality. Calligraphy is supposed to be writing from the heart, and to create it, the artist taps into his own true self." He was whispering now. "The artist's feelings and reason merge, and his soul is reflected in the brush strokes. It reminds me of a good system design, or an elegantly crafted program."

Lea was struck by both the lushness and the austerity of the art.

Paul gestured at the canvas. "See, he's telling a story with the characters, and while it may not look like it to us westerners, he's painting them in his own individual style. That's one of the reasons calligraphy is sometimes called 'moving meditation.' " Paul's voice held a note of wonder. "The Japanese also prize it for its spontaneity. You can never retouch any of the strokes, so you have just one shot at getting it right."

Lea was about to ask Paul another question when the artist ceremonially laid down his brush, stood, and bowed. Apparently the demonstration was over.

Paul grabbed her hand. "Come on," he said.

Smiling, he pulled her away from the crowd—past the video store showing Kabuki theatre, the spa advertising *shiatsu* massage, and the *ikebana* society with its artful floral displays. In a nearby studio, one *sumo* wrestler flipped another, who landed on his back with a grunt and a thud.

"Come here," Paul said after he'd led the way out of the building to a mushroom-shaped fountain on the plaza. He stepped behind her and wrapped his arms around her waist. "Tell me what you're thinking."

Lea's eyes danced as she leaned her head back on Paul's shoulder and looked up at him. The spray from the fountain tickled her face. "I'm thinking what a fascinating man you are, and how I want to discover everything about you."

Paul gave her a James Bond look. "Hmmm," he said. "What is it you'd like to know?"

Lea smiled playfully. "If you could choose to be anywhere else on earth right now, where would you would be, and what would you be doing?"

Paul laughed. "That's easy. I'd be with you, and we'd be on the ocean, somewhere in Hawaii."

"*On* the ocean?" Lea asked in mock horror. "Pray—doing what?"

"Windsurfing." Paul chuckled. "I've always wanted to try it."

Lea turned in his arms to face him and wound her arms around his waist. The intense blue of his eyes in the sunlight startled her. "Is this a recent enthusiasm, or have you always had a secret yen to frolic like a dolphin?"

Paul tossed his head back and laughed again. "I think it would be exhilarating. But what about you? If you could be anywhere right now, where would you be?"

Lea pursed her lips and pretended to be deep in thought. "You and I would be in Portugal," she pronounced. "In Lisbon's Alfama—the old African quarter. It's got narrow dirt streets that twist and turn like in a maze, and if you're not careful, you can get seriously lost. When Sydney and I were in Lisbon once, I couldn't stay away from it. It's dirty and a bit dangerous, but thrilling. I told myself I'd go back with the man I loved."

Paul became serious, and his look was caressing. "As far as I'm concerned, we have a whole world of thrilling things to discover together."

Lea smiled dreamily, enveloped in a warm glow.

They went back inside and found a tiny restaurant filled with the aroma of hot *miso* soup. The waitress who seated them poured green tea, and they settled on *tatami* mats and cushions to face each other over a low tabletop.

Lea sipped her tea, observing Paul, who had a faraway look.

He caught her eye and smiled apologetically. "Sorry. I was thinking about my father."

"What about him?" she asked softly.

"I was thinking of something he told me right before he died. He said the most important thing in life is to pursue an ideal, no matter the sacrifice. I've never forgotten it."

She waited for Paul to go on. She loved feeling so close to him.

"He taught me that life is full of intriguing challenges— that in fact you should seek them out. Otherwise your own life will be colorless and dull. My father died young, but he did live intensely."

"You take after him," Lea suggested.

"I guess I do. Our minds work the same way. Once I took an aptitude test, and my profile came back as a system builder. If I have to do the same thing twice, I devise a system for doing it. My profile also said I live to do everything optimally, and to create or discover things. My father was just the same."

Lea cupped her tea in her hands. She suspected that, like Paul, his father had also insisted on thinking for himself. Paul was not impressed by titles or credentials but evaluated a person according to individual merit.

"I may sound naive," Paul said, "but for a long time I assumed that most men were like my dad. I assumed they lived according to their convictions."

"That's not unusual when you're young. I think most of us are born as idealists. It's just that we're forced by life to become skeptical."

"I know, but when I think back now, I marvel at how deluded I was. I remember thinking how exciting it would be as an adult to work with smart people. How our ideas would feed off one another's. I actually looked forward to learning from guys who were smarter than me." Paul smiled wryly. "Instead, look at me. Do you know how I spend my days? Playing politics and stroking egos."

"You're doing what the situation demands."

"Maybe. But when I ran my own company, I had a strong reason to get up in the morning. I knew that in order to survive, my decisions had to be right most of the time. And that I had to keep coming up with creative ideas." Paul shook his head. "There's something about playing bet-the-company with each decision that at least makes you feel alive."

Lea smiled ruefully. "I know what you mean."

"I just don't get it," he said. "No one at Whitten Systems really seems to care about the products we're making. What drives them is their careers—their own petty ranking in the universe. And how they can feel good about themselves when all they do is spend their time playing corporate politics...." Paul broke off, at a loss for words. "I have to tell you, I'm sick of the conniving, the shading of truth." Anger flashed in his eyes.

"I'd hoped things were getting better."

"Hardly. Marshall Schroth is spinning tales to his cronies on the board, and they're starting to question every move I make. And Randy Derrough wants to have his hand held. He seems to require daily positive feedback." Paul sighed. "Then we've got this financial Pandora's Box hanging over us. Who knows what's going to crawl out?"

"I don't suppose this would be a good time to bring in your own people."

Paul frowned. "If this were any kind of normal situation, I would clean house. But under the circumstances, it would do more harm than good. Our shareholders are anxious enough as it is."

They fell silent as a *kimono*-clad waitress approached and took their order. Sinuously, she dipped to table level, poured fresh tea, then rose in a single motion before padding away.

"I don't understand why the directors pay attention to Marshall," Lea said. "After all, they chose you to be president.

Why won't they give you a chance to turn the company around?"

Paul slumped back against the cushions. "Who knows? Maybe it's because our problems originated on their watch. Maybe they're trying to find a scapegoat to divert attention from their own negligence."

"But that's crazy," Lea protested.

"Sure. Unfortunately, it's also human nature. When you get right down to it, most people don't think clearly. They let self-interest cloud their judgment. Then they rationalize their actions."

"What about Carter Weberling? Isn't he a voice of reason on the board?"

"Yes, but even he's getting worn down. Frankly, I think he's sorry he got himself into this."

The waitress arrived with black lacquer soup bowls. "*Suimono*," she said as she set them down. Tiny cubes of tofu and green scallions floated on steaming clear liquid.

They ate the soup in silence.

When it had been cleared, the waitress placed a copper *mizutaki* pot in the center of the table. As beef stock bubbled, she dipped raw sliced steak and vegetables into the broth and swirled them with chopsticks. "*Shabu-Shabu*," she said. Lea remembered that the name of the dish was derived from the splashing sound the beef made in the liquid.

Lea spoke first when they were alone again. "How have you been getting along with Bennett Alston?"

Paul worked his chopsticks. "Bennett? He's been avoiding me. And I've been too busy to press him about our legal affairs."

"Have you resolved the suit against CadSure yet?" Lea recalled her conversation with Georgeanne Hughes.

"No. But I've instructed Bennett to drop the whole case, not even to try for a settlement, like Keith did. But he's dragging his feet."

Lea smiled. "You're cramping his style."

"I suppose so. But this case bothers me. Keith was trying

to use patent law as a weapon to eliminate CadSure as competition."

Lea thought of Adam Pfeiffer and the way Keith had taken advantage of him. She finally told Paul about Adam's visit to the restaurant, and she passed on his warning.

Paul shook his head. "Keith was a bully. Rather than create something new himself, he'd rather prey on others. Take this thing with software patents. Who needs them? The software industry's been booming for 20 years without any patent protection. It's like trying to copyright piano keys. The whole idea in programming is to build on work that's come before you." Paul dipped spinach into a dense sauce sprinkled with sesame seeds.

"For years legal experts have agreed that programmers should be allowed to copy certain software features. Otherwise, programming would be incredibly restrictive. The problem is that modern operating systems are so complex. You might have a program with over a million lines of code that's made up of a series of ideas, maybe even thousands of ideas. What programmers do is find creative ways to combine common ideas and techniques. But almost all the ideas that go into a program are derivative. We're building on decades of invention. And if every programmer had to stop and consider whether any one idea or subroutine infringes on a patent, development would come to a standstill. You wouldn't be able to write a line of code without consulting an attorney." Paul swirled a leaf of cabbage in hot broth. "And once a patent suit gets before a judge or a jury—well, you never know which way a ruling will go. You should hear Harry on the subject. He and a lot of older hackers are up in arms."

"A suit like Keith's could have ruined you when you were starting out," Lea said.

"Absolutely."

Over green tea ice cream, Lea broached the subject of Keith's safe. To her surprise, Paul looked pained.

"That was another fiasco," he mumbled.

"But what was in the safe?" Lea scanned his face anxiously for a clue.

"Nothing important."

"You mean there were just routine items like company contracts—nothing else?"

"That and...." Paul appeared to be weighing his words. "Really, Lea, it's not worth discussing." He raised his hand abruptly and signaled for the check. "Ready to go?"

Lea wanted to press Paul further, but he was already rising from his seat. His expression clearly indicated that the subject was closed.

They left the Japan Center and returned to her apartment, where Lea was determined to restore their earlier, lighthearted mood. She led Paul to her living room sofa facing the bay, and they talked for more than an hour about their families, friends, and happier times.

When Paul kissed her, Lea felt a rare sense of reprieve. She took him to her bedroom, and they made love slowly as the foghorns echoed across the bay. She felt herself melting into him, losing herself completely to his touch. Afterwards, as she lay in his arms, she felt a new yet uneasy peace. More than ever, Lea realized, Paul was essential to her happiness.

11

S hortly before dawn, Lea had her recurring chef's nightmare.

"We're out of the sturgeon!" Gerard yelled.

"Damn, I just took three orders for it," Robert said, exasperated. "And where are my appetizers for Table 7? People are sick of waiting." He glowered at Lea and Gerard, who, improbably, were alone in the kitchen attempting to feed a full house.

"I ordered lamb *noisettes* a half hour ago!" cried Heather, rushing in from the dining room. "Where on earth are they?"

Gerard, wringing his hands, informed Lea that they were out of half the menu items. He flung off his chef's coat and announced that he could no longer work under such conditions. Pouting, he retired to the back of the kitchen, where he pulled out a deck of cards and began to play Solitaire.

Lea begged him to return to the stove as she shuffled a growing stack of unfilled orders. She coaxed and she wheedled, but Gerard refused to budge.

In desperation, Lea began cooking maniacally. But where was the clarified butter? Where was the fish stock? She was missing basic ingredients.

Gerard tuned his radio to KJAZ and cranked up the volume. The strains of Duke Ellington's "Take the 'A' Train" filled the kitchen as Lea searched for fresh basil.

Gradually, Lea became aware of an ominous, rhythmic thudding emanating from the dining room. She left the stove and went to investigate. Scowling diners sat bolt upright, with knives and forks protruding from their clenched fists. In unison, they pounded their silverware on the tabletops. A low growl spread like a wave throughout the room.

Lea's heart pounded, and her breath came in gasps. She ran back to the kitchen, but her customers rose and pursued her. Lea turned and saw their anguished faces, ghoulishly pale from hunger thwarted. She glimpsed bulging eyes, and lips curled back to reveal fangs.

Forks raised high, the diners advanced in slow motion. "Lea Sherwood, Lea Sherwood!" they chanted.

Lea scrabbled backwards, searching for a means of escape.

Gerard, still enthralled by the music, hummed along to Ellington and played an imaginary xylophone.

Lea fell to her knees and crept through the kitchen to the walk-in refrigerator, where she spied crates of mangos and limes. She grabbed one crate and then another— attempting to barricade herself from the mob. But the din grew louder, and Lea heard a voice cry out. "She's getting away! Stop her!"

Lea awoke with a start, drenched in sweat. She sat bolt upright and fumbled with the covers, trying to fathom what had just happened. The dream had gone further this time. Usually she woke up when she got to the dining room.

A glance at her alarm clock told her it was 4:42 A.M. on Monday. Paul was sleeping soundly as moonlight cast dappled patterns across the bed. Lea staggered into the bathroom, splashed cold water on her burning face, and then crawled back under the blankets. She shivered several times and eventually fell into a shallow slumber until 5:30, when her eyes popped open again.

She lay awake thinking until Paul stirred about an hour later.

Paul reached for Lea and kissed her neck gently. "Last night was wonderful," he murmured.

"Ummm. I'll say." Lea snuggled up against him.

"Did you sleep well?"

"Yes," she fibbed.

"So did I." Paul put both arms around her and buried his face in her hair.

"Are you hungry?" he asked after a few moments.

"Famished."

"Me, too."

Lea smiled. While she always liked to wake up slowly, Paul was usually ready to get up as soon as he opened his eyes. "Not so fast," she said, moving against him again and tilting her head to give him a long kiss.

"Keep that up, and we'll never get anything done today," he teased when they finally broke apart.

Lea yawned and stretched like a cat as Paul got out of bed. He was wearing blue pajama bottoms, and his dark hair fell over one eye. The notion of not getting anything done today definitely had its appeal.

"You stay put," he said. "You look so comfortable." He headed for the bathroom and called back, "I'll make us breakfast."

Lea burrowed happily under the covers, her nightmare forgotten.

The aroma of French roast coffee roused her fifteen minutes later, and she got up, showered, and dressed. When she entered the kitchen, Paul was at the stove, shirt sleeves rolled up.

Lea peered over his shoulder. "That smells wonderful. What is it?"

"Scottish highland eggs. My father used to make them on Sunday mornings. They're basically scrambled eggs, but with a splash of vinegar and a touch of cream."

She sat down at the kitchen table and sipped the glass of orange juice Paul had poured. She sniffed appreciatively as he gave the eggs a final stir, served them, and took a seat facing her.

Paul watched with anticipation as she ate her first bite.

"This is wonderful," she said, marveling at the unexpected yet appealing flavors. Then she noticed a pink baker's box with two croissants on the kitchen counter. He'd gone around the corner to DeCharme's to get them.

"You're spoiling me, and I love it!" Lea crowed.

Paul grinned. "You deserve to be spoiled."

They finished breakfast and lingered over second cups of coffee, watching the fog curl over the Golden Gate. Neither of us wants to leave, Lea thought.

"So, what's on your agenda today?" she asked finally, setting aside her mug. "Something enjoyable, I hope."

Paul's smile was wistful. "Don't I wish. I'm still trying to locate the elusive Francine Reese. Talk about your suspicious disappearances."

Lea nodded slowly and reached across the table for his hand. "Remember to be careful," she said.

L ea spent the early morning in Panache's kitchen and at 9:15 went to her office. Impatiently she dialed the number for Anderson Pruett. It had been days since her initial call to him, and she still hadn't heard from the management consultant.

Sharon Dare, the secretary with the syrupy voice, answered on the sixth ring. Yes, she had relayed Lea's message, she replied in a wounded tone. No, she would not give Lea a number where Dr. Pruett might be reached. And no, she couldn't say when he might be returning to the states. Dr. Pruett was an extremely busy man.

Lea muttered under her breath and hung up.

She sifted through the mail and took calls from salesmen and two of her investors. Absentmindedly she picked up the phone when it rang again.

It was Brooke, and she sounded excited. "I just got word on the poison that killed Keith," she said. "A police source leaked it to one of our reporters."

Lea was suddenly alert. "What was it?"

"A substance called clonidine. It's a white crystalline powder used in high blood pressure medicine. The police actually found a prescription bottle with legitimate medication in Keith's bathroom. Apparently it was planted, because when they checked with the pharmacy, there was no record of Keith ever ordering it."

"You mean whoever killed Keith hoped it would look like an accidental overdose?"

"Right. He—or she—didn't figure on Keith having the doctored smart drugs in his pocket when he died."

Lea remembered Keith's body, racked by seizures.

"The funny thing is how little it takes to kill you," Brooke said. "The normal dose is about 0.1 milligram, but a lethal dose can be under 5 milligrams. You'd get that much if you dipped the end of a toothpick in the stuff. And whoever killed Keith wasn't taking any chances. According to the coroner, there were 30 milligrams in the doctored pills."

"But where would you buy it? I assume you can't extract it from a blood pressure pill."

"No, but clonidine isn't a controlled substance. You could get it by ripping off a pharmacy or a medical lab. I imagine that wouldn't prove too great an obstacle if you're intent on committing murder. Oh, and it kicks in fast. If you take a lethal dose, you'll start to feel the effects in a half hour."

Lea shuddered. "Then Keith must have taken one of his pills after he got here. Right after I seated him."

"It sure looks that way." Brooke sighed. "There's something else." Her voice had dropped two octaves.

"What is it?" Lea steeled herself.

"The police want to know if either you or Paul had access to the drug. In fact, they're starting to make inquiries."

"What!" Lea yelled.

"I know, I know," Brooke said. "But you can't entirely blame the cops. Paul admitted he had access to Keith's desk."

"But what about the others in the office?" Lea asked. "Why haven't the police linked any of them to the murder?"

"From what our reporter said, they're still investigating. But they seem to have run into dead ends. Excuse the pun."

Lea groaned. "That's just great."

"Listen, I hate to say this, but I'm late for a meeting. Can I call you later?"

"All right." Lea hung up irritably.

She spent the next hour trying to stretch funds to pay her bills, but Brooke's news played havoc with her concentration. Shortly after 11:00, she went back to the kitchen. Sydney had just arrived and was goading Gerard.

"Look at this man, Lea!" Sydney cried. "He's gone irrevocably American!"

Lea stared at Gerard, as did everyone else in the kitchen. Then she laughed for the first time that morning. He was wearing what passed for natty chef's attire—baggy pants in a loud print of red chili peppers, accessorized by red wool socks inside his black clogs.

"America is just one big carnival to you, isn't it?" Sydney demanded.

"C'est bien." Gerard had a wicked twinkle in his eye. "But this is nothing. You should have seen me yesterday, roller-blading past Rhododendron Dell in Golden Gate Park. Afterwards I went home and listened to my Scott Joplin collection and read Tom Wolfe. Did you know I'm halfway through *The Kandy-Kolored Tangerine-Flake Streamline Baby?* By the time I finish, I'll have a whole new vocabulary! *Mau-mauing. Flak catchers.*" Gerard pronounced the words with relish, his French accent making them sound even more absurd. He winked at Lea. "Really, it's so refreshing the way you Americans poke fun at yourselves. You have a sense of humor about your culture that Europeans lack."

Sydney snorted. "American culture! That's an oxymoron."

Lea stopped laughing long enough to say, "I don't think all of Tom Wolfe's subjects appreciate his work as much as you and I do, Gerard." In college Lea had often stayed up late reading Wolfe's hilarious essays on American mores, to the detriment of at least one term paper.

Gerard smiled knowingly. "Do not let Sydney mislead you, Lea. She too is full of surprises. She once confessed to me that she even watches court TV!"

"Ah, but that simply reinforces my native British cynicism!" Sydney retorted. "Courts are all about the human spectacle. Five people testify that their neighbor's beastly dog barks all night, keeping them awake, while the owner whines to the judge, 'It's not *my* dog. My dog would never do that!' "

Sydney went on. "Frankly, I fail to see how you can claim that any civilization that coined the verb 'to party' is not on the decline. And if I hear the phrase 'Yo, dude' one more time, I'm going to spit."

"Amen!" Lea agreed. She was going to say more when Minette walked by with a bowl of tiny, crimson field strawberries.

"Oh, what fun!" Lea exclaimed.

"They were picked two hours ago," the pastry chef said.

"I can tell," Lea replied. Lured by the aroma of the ripe fruit, she followed Minette to her station, plucked a berry from the dish, and popped it into her mouth. "Ummm," she moaned. "This is luscious! I could survive on these alone."

Minette grinned. "Not *too* sweet, do you think?"

Lea made a show of selecting another berry, taking a whiff of it, and chewing it slowly. "*Never!*"

Gerard clicked on the radio, and Lea caught a snippet of a news announcement. "Wait a minute," she called to him. "Did he say there'd been a kidnapping?"

"I think so." Gerard turned the volume up.

The announcer's deep voice could be heard throughout the kitchen. "This morning's abduction marks the latest in a string of Silicon Valley kidnappings. The Fremont computer executive, ambushed as he left his home, was forced at gunpoint to admit his abductors to one of his company's warehouses. He and four employees were bound, and the thieves fled with $11 million in computer equipment. The identities of the Fremont man and his firm are being withheld."

"What bloody cheek!" Sydney cried.

The announcer continued. "Police suspect that today's heist is linked to three other incidents in which kidnapped executives have been forced to let thieves onto Silicon Valley sites. Ironically, police say that strict new on-site security measures adopted by many Valley firms may have encouraged these attacks against individuals."

Gerard paused on his way to the pantry and emitted a long, low whistle. *"Hélas! C'est dangereux là-bas!"*

L ate that afternoon, Lea was checking the evening's reservations list at the host station when Francine Reese walked in. Lea, startled, turned to stare at her. The last she had heard, Francine was still incommunicado, and Paul had little hope that she would reappear.

"Oh, good, I caught you!" Francine said. "I hoped you might be free about now."

Lea managed a taut smile. She couldn't imagine why Francine would come to see her. "So you're back in town," Lea said bluntly. She felt cold just looking at the woman.

Francine, however, didn't catch her drift. "Could I talk to you?" she said. "It's incredibly important. I need your help."

Lea stiffened.

Francine stepped closer. "I don't know where else to turn," she said. "You seemed like a sympathetic person when I saw you at the funeral. Someone who'd listen with an open mind." She glanced around the dining room as the servers, laughing and chatting, began to set up for dinner. "Isn't there somewhere we can talk? Please!" Francine's tone bordered on the shrill.

Unsure if she was doing the right thing, Lea led Francine to the small bar off the foyer. The bartender, Raoul, rakishly flashed his dark eyes at Francine. He gave Lea a questioning look.

"Would you like something to drink?" Lea asked at Raoul's cue, having almost forgotten her manners. Francine asked for sparkling mineral water with lime, and Lea seconded the request.

Lea led the way to a table and took a seat opposite her unexpected guest. Francine smoothed the skirt of her slim, pistachio-hued suit and tucked wisps of short blond hair behind her ears, revealing diamond-stud earrings. She was lean and attractive in a rather mannish way, with a prominent nose and a strong jaw. Fine lines above her upper lip suggested she had been or was a smoker.

Lea thought she detected in her a skittish quality, perhaps even recklessness. It was a quality she disliked.

"I suppose you wouldn't remember it," Francine said, "but Keith brought a few of us from the office to dinner here one night." She laughed airily. "I must say, it was the best expense account meal I've ever had." Without waiting for a response, Francine surveyed the room as if she'd been called in for an appraisal. "You've done a nice job with this restaurant, but I've read that you don't become wealthy running just the one. You have to operate a chain." She ran her hand across the marble tabletop. "How much will you net in your first year?"

Lea nearly choked. "It's a labor of love," she replied frostily.

Francine murmured her thanks as Raoul served their drinks with dishes of tiny, sweet Spanish peanuts and green olives from Provence. She nibbled at an olive speculatively. "These are fine, but I've had even better from an importer on the Peninsula. I'll get you his name," she offered. "You should serve his instead."

Lea groaned inwardly, her patience ebbing. Whatever was the woman here for?

"I just got back in town last night," Francine began. "It's true my mother was sick, but I also needed to get away. I needed time to think."

"And you went back to work this morning?" Lea prompted.

Francine's face crumpled. "I met with Paul for over an hour. He told me he'd called in the auditing team. I just can't believe it!" she blurted. "Paul actually suspects I've been cooking the books!"

"I don't think the auditors have drawn any conclusions yet," Lea said carefully.

"But I told them this morning what happened! It was all Keith's idea. We were having a temporary sales slump, and he was afraid that if we announced it, we'd lose more ground and never recover market share. The competition is brutal, you know. Keith insisted it wouldn't do any harm to fudge a quarterly report. He was sure we'd recoup the sales by year-end. Then the annual figures would be accurate, and the stockholders would be happy. He even argued that this way, we'd be preserving shareholder equity." Francine's eyes were bright with the outrage of one unjustly accused.

Lea's jaw dropped, and she made no attempt to hide her shock. "And if sales didn't bounce back?"

"Keith was sure they would, but he said we could retroactively adjust the quarterly figures if necessary. We could announce we'd unintentionally recorded some shipments as final sales and placed too high a value on inventory. He didn't think it was a big risk, or that we'd hurt anyone."

Neither had all the white-collar-criminals serving time in California prisons, Lea thought. And fudging the figures once made it easier to do so a second time, and a third. "You didn't have to go along with it," she said.

"Oh no?" Francine's tone was bitter. "What choice did I have? Even though it wasn't my fault, I left my last company under a cloud, and Keith knew it. He made it clear that if I didn't comply with his wishes, he'd find someone who would. Two black marks against me would have crippled my career."

"Not if you explained the circumstances," Lea insisted.

"Hah! Don't be naive." Francine shot her a withering look. "Keith was extremely influential. If he'd wanted to smear me, he would have."

Lea swore under her breath. Was Francine telling the truth? Or had she juggled the books for her own profit— and killed Keith when he found out? Still, one thing did lend support to Francine's story: Keith had hired her after investigating her past. Lea also suspected that Keith wouldn't have been above a few dirty tricks if he'd felt his back was to the wall. Since he'd considered himself intellectually superior to others, he probably would have assumed he'd get away with it. He also might have felt this was how the game was played. After all, look at what he'd done to Adam Pfeiffer. Again Lea wondered what Keith had been capable of.

"You don't believe me!" Francine yelled when Lea didn't answer. "I'm telling you, *I'm* the one who got used!"

Lea, astonished, stared at Francine. The woman seemed to have a perpetual chip on her shoulder—Sydney said the British called it "chippiness."

Then it occurred to her that Francine might be telling the partial truth. What if she'd gone along with Keith and later learned he was angling to make her the scapegoat?

"I can understand why a couple of those jokers at the company don't believe me," Francine said heatedly. "When you stretch the rules yourself, you're apt to believe the worst about someone else. But there's a difference between padding your expenses and committing outright fraud. I would think Randy Derrough would realize that." Francine mumbled something Lea could not hear and appeared to be talking to herself. Then she sat bolt upright, crossed a leg, and jiggled her foot. Splotches of red appeared high on her cheeks.

"Why on earth did you come here?" Lea shot back. "What do you expect me to do?

Francine leaned across the table and grabbed Lea by the wrist. "You can talk to Paul! He'll listen to you. I just know he wants to fire me! But all I need is a second chance. If you ask him to, he'll give it to me."

"A second chance?" Lea echoed in disbelief. Francine's nails were cutting into her.

"Don't you see? It's all so unfair! I was only following orders. Besides, I'm good at my job, and I haven't gotten half the credit I'm due."

Lea wrested her arm free.

"I'm made major contributions to Whitten Systems," Francine argued. She tapped her chest with her index finger. *I'm* the one who put together the financial package that allowed Keith to acquire Paul's company. Believe me, it wasn't easy. We were short on cash, and I had to come up with creative financial instruments to pull it off. But I made the deal happen."

Lea grimaced and shook her head resolutely. This would hardly commend her to Paul.

Watching her, Francine laughed shrilly. "A technical person like Paul may not realize how crucial it is these days to cultivate good financial management. But more than ever, it can be key. Don't you see? I've got that expertise. I can help him turn the company around."

Flabbergasted, Lea stood up. She'd heard enough.

Francine rose too and held out her arms. "You've got to speak up for me! You're my only hope. I don't know what I'll do otherwise."

Lea gave her a long, pitying look. "I'm sorry, but I can't tell Paul how to run his company. In any case, he'll only do what he thinks is right."

"You won't help me?" Francine gaped at Lea. Tears sprang to her eyes. "You won't even put in a word for me?"

Lea remained mute.

"I thought I could appeal to you as a woman," Francine almost shrieked. "You've got to understand, I'm a single mother. If I get fired, my ex-husband will jump at the chance to brand me an unfit parent. He's just waiting for an opportunity to take Tommy away from me." Francine picked up her glass, and Lea thought she would hurl it at her.

"Here you sit—so smug—in your own restaurant! You think you've got it made. And you don't care what happens to me." Francine spat out the words and let the glass, half-full, tumble to the carpet. "But you're no better than anyone else. Why do you think you deserve to be happy and I don't? What gives you that right?" She opened her purse and yanked out a tissue, swiping ineffectually at the rivulets of black mascara cascading down her cheeks.

Lea, aghast, shrank back as Francine advanced toward her, face contorted with spite.

She halted within inches of Lea and all but hissed. "You may think you've fooled everyone else, but believe me, I can see right through you! It's obvious to me now that you know far more about Keith's death than you pretend."

Lea stared, slack-jawed, as Francine flounced out of the bar.

12

Two days later Gerard handed Lea a certified letter. "This just came for you."

Lea tore it open, read the brief message, and gasped. "I can't believe it. I'm being sued for breach of contract. Three of our investors want their money back. Now!"

Gerard gulped. "How can they do that?"

"In this country you can sue anybody for anything. A judge and jury may or may not go along."

"But how are our investors claiming that you broke your contract?" Gerard was wringing his hands. "It makes no sense."

Lea forced herself to reread the letter. "They cite reports in the press suggesting that I engaged in criminal activity. And that by so doing, I broke the implicit terms of our agreement to act responsibly, thus endangering their investments."

"In other words, they've got cold feet and are trumping up charges to try to get their money back. *Comme c'est fou!*"

"Yes, it is. But when people panic, they do strange things."

Gerard was agitated. "How much cash are we talking about?"

"It's the money from the Millers, Piersons, and Jabots," Lea said, referring to regular customers. She calculated. "About $45,000 total."

Gerard winced. "That could push us over the edge."

"True. Not to mention the chaos it will cause if other investors join in the suit." She shivered as the full implications of the threat began to dawn on her.

"Ma foi, Lea! What are you going to do?"

"What else can I do?" she said testily. "Hire a lawyer and fight them."

S ydney was tasting a *perigueux* sauce when Gerard clicked on the radio after lunch. As the Pacific Exchange reporter began his spiel, Sydney banged the saucepan down on the stove.

"Sydney is a little tart today," Gerard informed Lea.

"Who's calling me a tart?" Sydney retorted.

Lea gave her a weak smile. Even Sydney appeared to be on edge after hearing about the lawsuit.

Absorbed in her thoughts, Lea didn't realize the reporter was discussing Whitten Systems until she heard Paul's name. She moved closer to the radio.

"The already-hammered stock took another dive today on rumors of financial irregularities. Whitten shares fell 8 points at the opening bell, then recovered slightly to close down 7. But the fire sale may not be over. According to an inside source, Whitten Systems has been overstating earnings for the last quarter and is soon expected to announce a big loss for that period. A special audit team is also trying to ascertain whether funds are missing. Oops, I see the stock is down another 2 points in after-hours trading. Talk about volatility!"

Lea held her breath as the reporter continued. "Our source, who asked not to be identified, charges that Whitten Systems President Paul Boyd has tried to conceal the irregularities from stockholders. Mr. Boyd, as you may recall, was questioned extensively by the police in regard to the murder of company founder Keith Whitten."

"That's outrageous!" Lea cried. "Marshall Schroth must have leaked this lie to smear Paul!"

"Whitten Systems had no comment on the allegations but did announce that as of today Vice President and Chief Financial Officer Francine Reese is no longer with the company. The firm declined to say whether she resigned voluntarily, or whether any criminal charges might be pending."

Gerard turned off the radio. They exchanged uneasy glances.

"What a bloodbath!" Lea moaned. "The stock is dying, and they make it sound as though Paul is responsible."

Gerard, the old market pro, attempted to reassure her. *"Attendez!* The market, it always overreacts. It hates uncertainty and assumes the worst. And you know how volatile tech stocks can be. Once the facts are known, Whitten shares will recover."

"Once the facts are known," Lea repeated darkly. "That's the problem. What are the facts?"

"Do you really think Marshall Schroth planted this to give Paul a black eye?" Sydney asked.

"Who else?" Lea said. "He's the only one who stands to gain if Paul fails." The notion filled her with dread.

"But the board passed him over for president in favor of Paul. What makes Schroth think they'd appoint him next time?" Sydney persisted.

"Ego," said Lea. "The man has an enormous ego."

Sydney shot a suspicious look at Gerard. "I've read that in men's dreams, there are actually winners and losers. And that men have more unpleasant dreams, because they involve aggression. What is it with you male creatures? Why are you always competing?"

"Don't look daggers at me," Gerard warned. "I only compete with myself!"

"That reminds me," Lea said. "Do you know what Keith once told me? I thought it was odd. He said that in any business transaction, there's always a winner and a loser. And that men know exactly who they are."

"Poor Keith," Gerard said, drawing down the corners of his mouth. "He died so quickly. He never had time to realize that he himself was the loser."

Lea frowned. "What I want to know is: who came out the winner?"

At 4:00 P.M. the servers for dinner arrived and began to set up their tables. They worked quietly, polishing wine glasses with linen napkins before placing them on the starched white tablecloths.

"Everything is laid out in squares," Lea heard Robert instruct Jayne, who had just joined the staff. "The glasses should form a perfect square. Then you align the silverware with the center of the wine glasses." He bent to minutely adjust a fork. "Next set the butter knife across the butter plate with the knife point in line with the tip of the fork." Robert stepped back to survey the effect. "See? If you look at the table from any direction, everything is in squares."

At 5:00, Lea surveyed the dining room with satisfaction. The chair backs along the banquette formed a straight line. Cutlery gleamed. The standing silver ice buckets, in a niche along the wall, were perfectly aligned, as were the linen napkins laid diagonally across the top of each. All was ready.

Promptly at 5:15, the servers gathered for their evening meal and meeting. Lea ran through the list of dinner specials. "For the appetizer, we have soft-shelled crabs on a bed of watercress and herbs, sauced with a coriander *vinaigrette*. The day's fresh oysters are *belons* from Tomales Bay."

"Those are cultivated from seed oysters, right?" Robert asked. His pencil was poised over his pocket-sized notepad.

Lea nodded. "And for the main course—roasted veal medallions with star anise and a Zinfandel sauce." The servers dove forks into plates of each special that Sydney had prepared.

"And for dessert...."

"Don't tell me!" Jayne interjected. "I saw Minette preparing it—plum fritters with a clover honey and pine nut sauce." Jayne pretended to swoon. "It is to die for," she informed the others.

Someone coughed reproachfully, and an awkward silence ensued.

"Okay," Lea said. "Special occasions and guests. We have a 10th anniversary at Table 16. Tables 8 and 23 are birthdays. A bouquet was just delivered for 8. Table 31 is Bill Endicott, a VIP from Security Bank. He's allergic to shellfish, frowns on veggies, but loves the cheese course and port."

Lea turned to a waiter on her right. "Josh, that's your table. Let's give him a complimentary glass of the vintage Warre."

Josh nodded and scribbled a note to remind himself.

"At Table 15, we'll seat the Schiavos, of the Mendocino winery. They'll be pleased to see we've added their Syrah to our list. And last is Table 28, which is celebrating Mazie Johnson's big promotion. Her husband Stan dropped off a surprise gift, which he asked us to present." Lea looked around the table. "Any other business?"

Robert cleared his throat. "Speaking of dying, or at least Jayne was...." he said archly.

Jayne glared at him.

"I just thought I should mention that I got a call at home from a reporter named Kenny Mariner," Robert said. "He asked me about the night Keith Whitten died. I told him I didn't know anything, but he kept insinuating that I might remember something I saw. Nasty fellow. What I'd like to know is how he got my name and number."

"That's nothing," Dominique piped up. "He accosted me on the sidewalk when I left here last night. At first I thought he was your ordinary dipsomaniac. I mean he reeked. But then he showed me his press card and pestered me for four blocks until I caught my bus."

"Is there anything in particular we should say?" Jayne asked. "I mean if customers ask us about it."

Lea's heart sank. Now even her servers were in the line of fire. She scanned their faces. They were waiting for her answer. "Just use your best judgment," she finally said. "It should all blow over before long." She sounded far more sanguine than she felt.

L ea was subdued as she seated guests that night. Paul was the topic of conversation at more than one table. One critic suggested, within her earshot, that Paul lacked the savvy to rescue Whitten Systems. Another said the board was losing faith in him.

She circulated through the dining room, trying to put Paul out of her mind. Snippets of conversation came her way.

— "What time tonight does your plane leave for Seoul?"

— "No matter how good you are at your job, you still have to deal with people."

— "You want to know my definition of success? Your work is your play, and your play is your work."

— "Honestly, you won't believe this, but we ended up spending the night in Sweden!"

Lea gently extracted a cork from a bottle of fine Barolo and decanted the wine for a party of five foodies who came in once a month. Typically, they ordered myriad pairings of food and wine, and frequently were the last guests to leave. Tonight they appeared to be in high spirits, as usual. Lea envied their gaiety.

When she returned to the host stand, a man was waiting. Lea studied him—somehow, he looked familiar. She realized with a start that it was Bennett Alston.

"Have you come for dinner?" she asked. She'd never seen the lawyer here before.

"Yes. I'm meeting friends from out of town." Bennett appeared ill at ease. "They particularly asked to come here after reading a review in a travel magazine," he added sourly.

Bennett had a lean, angular frame and stood over six feet tall. His face was chiseled, almost gaunt, and was dominated by his eyes, which were dark and luminous. They were framed by bushy black brows threaded with silver. His lips were thin and his nose long, with a slight crook in the middle. The attorney's still vigorous black hair was brushed with gray, and two deep horizontal lines creased his forehead. Dressed in an impeccably tailored, dark pinstriped suit, he had an imperious air.

Lea consulted her seating chart as Bennett waited. Then she had another surprise. As she looked past Bennett's shoulder, Paul walked in.

"What are you doing here?" she asked, giving him a hug.

"I spent the afternoon at Carter's office to get his advice on a few things. Since I was so close, I thought I'd stop and see you." Paul looked curiously at Bennett. Neither man appeared pleased to encounter the other.

"I'd ask you to join me and my friends for dinner, Paul, but I'm sure you have more pressing matters to attend to," Bennett said.

"Actually, Bennett, I can't believe I've caught up with you. Whenever I've tried to see you in the last two weeks, you've claimed you couldn't spare a minute."

"I have been extremely busy."

"Well, I'm glad to see your schedule has cleared a bit. How about meeting in my office tomorrow morning? Say at 11:00?"

Bennett hesitated. "Unfortunately, that will not be feasible."

"Tomorrow afternoon?"

"I'm afraid I have prior commitments then too."

"Tomorrow evening, then. You name the time." Paul was growing exasperated. "I don't care what else you have to cancel."

Bennett's eyes glowed in reproach. "Really, Paul. I see no reason to be peremptory."

"And I see no reason to keep dragging out our lawsuit against CadSure. I sent you a memo about it three days ago, asking for an immediate response. So far I've heard nothing."

"Paul, you know as well as I do that we can't back down on that complaint. We initiated it with great fanfare. We'll look like fools if we withdraw it."

"I know that you personally might lose face. But I'm more concerned about doing the right thing."

Bennett Alston had grown pale as Paul had spoken. Now he regarded Paul with undisguised dislike. "We have a court hearing on a key motion next week. I am sure we will prevail."

"No, we will not prevail, Bennett, because we are dropping the suit. I order you to file the proper papers with the court by the end of this week."

"We'll see," Bennett said evenly. "I'm sure that when you and I meet alone, I can persuade you that the facts are on our side." He glanced at Lea in annoyance, as though she had intruded on a confidential tête-à-tête.

Paul squared his shoulders. "Bennett, there is no way you are going to convince me to exploit the patent process. You and Keith were abusing the system, and I'm putting an end to it. There are times when it's legitimate to protect your intellectual property, but this isn't one of them."

"We'd best discuss this in private," Bennett reiterated.

"No, Bennett. There is nothing to discuss. I'll expect the papers on my desk tomorrow, ready for my signature."

Bennett opened his mouth to speak but was interrupted by the arrival of a well-dressed middle-aged couple, who apologized to him for being late.

As Lea led the threesome to their table, she couldn't help but look back at Paul. His eyes were narrowed, and pinned on Bennett.

13

Gerard crossed the ballroom and handed Lea a flute of bubbling Champagne. "Compliments of the house," he said grandly, gesturing to a booth opposite them. Lea took a sip. It was yeasty, her favorite style. She waved her thanks to Nat Timmons, whose Hawk Ridge Vineyards in Calistoga was known for its sparkling wines.

Lea smoothed her white silk cocktail dress and surveyed the three-story, Edwardian-era salon of the Pacific Park Hotel. It was Thursday night, and patrons in evening attire swarmed across the gleaming parquet floor, nibbling hors d'oeuvres and quaffing California wine. At $145 a head, the proceeds from the event were earmarked for local literacy projects. Lea admired the room, with its ornate, wedding-cake molding and tear-drop, Czechoslovakian crystal chandeliers. Throughout the years, it had been the site of countless glittering soirées, and no doubt intrigues.

She scanned the booths arranged around the periphery of the floor, recognizing most of the restaurants and wineries who were donating their wares for the evening. Her own contribution was a *ballottine* of wild Pacific Coast salmon with golden caviar and crayfish. Gerard, not to be outdone, had prepared a pear *dacquoise* with warm raspberries, macadamia nuts, and Chambord sauce.

Gerard nudged her, inclining his head toward the booth to their right. Lea turned and caught a whiff of grilled squab. A discreet, engraved card on the serving table indicated that the squab not only hailed from Sonoma but that it was being served with *pancetta* and dried fruit. The bird was improbably perched on a pinnacle of wild rice peppered with Bing cherries. Gerard sniffed disdainfully. "Tall food," he said. "I thought that fad was over. The poor bird looks like it's preparing to ski downhill."

Lea laughed and directed Gerard's attention to the booths cattycorner to their left. "Look," she said, pointing to the signs of restaurants serving regional Italian cuisines. "Umbria, Liguria, Piedmont, Tuscany, Emilia, Lombardy," she enumerated. "Soon every Italian region will be represented in the city."

"You know what I want to try," Gerard said. "Dishes from that new Hakka restaurant. And the Tibetan one, too."

The decibel level in the room was rising. A happy hum was punctuated by the clinking of glasses and sudden trills of laughter. Aging yuppies prowled the floor, seeking new taste sensations. Blond women of indeterminate age in little black dresses air-kissed one another and tilted their heads rapturously as they accepted the conversational gambits of silver-haired men in black tie. The revelers seemed to swoop down upon the booths in waves, pressing first against one and then another, pausing intermittently to gain strength for their next culinary assault.

"Look." Gerard tapped Lea's arm. A young woman with flowing red hair in a snug, cherry-red strapless dress approached them. Her floral designer perfume wafted toward Lea as she leaned over their table, displaying a creamy décolletage. Gerard beamed and sliced her a choice piece of the salmon.

He sighed volubly a minute later as the woman sauntered away to join her escort. "I must confess," he said. "*La jeune fille me donne de l'inquiétude.* One false move *et* ... phhhht!" His arms flew up protectively across his chest.

Gerard left to greet friends and sample dishes, and Lea soon lost track of time. She chatted with dozens of patrons, but the insistent gaiety of the evening eventually wore on her. She felt increasingly alone.

Ordinarily she would have made the rounds herself, but tonight she hung back, unsure of her reception. Several restaurateurs she had counted as friends had inexplicably snubbed her as they'd all set up for the night. Then Daphne Davis, a buxom brunette who laughingly referred to herself as "big and beautiful" and who owned a catering service in Mill Valley, had stopped by to get in her own dig. Lea replayed the scene in her mind. "Frankly, Lea, I'm surprised to see you here," Daphne had drawled, a knowing gleam in her eye. "If it were me ... well, I guess some people just don't care what others say about them."

"*Schadenfreude,*" Gerard pronounced when Lea told him of the incident. "Do not be saddened by those whose lives are brightened by the misfortune of others," he admonished her.

Lea knew Gerard was right, yet Daphne's words still stung. She wondered how many others in the room shared her opinion.

With only a half hour left until closing, Lea was startled to see Francine Reese suddenly appear at the Bent Mountain Winery booth to their immediate left, just steps away. Lea murmured to Gerard, reminding him of who she was.

Francine wore a sleeveless, midnight-blue velvet sheath that revealed her sleek, firm arms. A single diamond, suspended from a delicate gold chain, sparkled in the well of her neck. Her blond hair was pulled back in a stylish chignon; she would have looked soignée but for her smeared mauve lipstick and an unnatural glint in her eye.

As Lea watched, Francine surrendered her empty glass to a passing waiter and accepted a fresh one from her winery host. Then she turned and walked over to Lea.

Gerard coughed discreetly and offered Francine a taste of the pear *dacquoise*, which she declined.

Lea took a step back from the table. The animosity of their last encounter was still fresh in her mind.

"Ms. Sherwood." Francine's words were slurred. "You can now gloat."

"I beg your pardon?" Lea asked.

"You know." Francine waved her right hand, which held her wine glass. Beads of Burgundy splashed onto her velvet bodice. She appeared not to notice. "I've been booted out of the company," she declared. "Paul fired me, and most unceremoniously. So now I have no prospects in sight. In fact I may be facing criminal charges." She giggled, then pursed her mouth in distaste.

"Why do think that makes me happy?" Lea inquired. Francine repelled her anew.

"Oh, I know your type! There are two kinds of women, those who help other women, and those who'll do anything to compete against them. You've proven which type you are."

Lea cast a stricken look at Gerard. His return glance confirmed he was thinking the same thing. Was Francine crazy or merely soused?

"Thanks to you and Paul, I am now persona non grata in the tech industry," Francine said. "I can't even get a crummy job interview." She thrust her face close to Lea's. "How do you think that makes me feel? I've got house payments to make, and a son to support. Who, no thanks to you, has been having nightmares because of all this!"

Lea had heard of blaming others for your own problems, but this took the proverbial *gâteau*. She moved another step back from the table.

Francine's voice rose to a wail as she grew increasingly sorry for herself. "How can I promise an 8-year-old-boy that we'll be all right when I don't even believe it myself?"

Lea shifted uncomfortably. People were beginning to stare.

"But you don't care about my problems!" Francine cried. "Oh, no. You're too self-centered for that. But just wait until you have to disappoint your own children. On second thought, the way you're going, I don't suppose you'll ever have any!"

Lea gaped. Was Francine truly this irrational?

Before Lea could respond, Gerard stepped out of their booth and put a cautionary arm around Francine. She squirmed, resisting as he tried to escort her off the floor. Strands of blond hair had pulled free of her chignon, and a run was visible in her stocking. Everyone around them had stopped to watch, and Lea caught a glimpse of Daphne Davis, smirking.

Francine yelped as Gerard attempted to steer her toward the door. She shoved him with her free hand, simultaneously flinging a ruby-colored wine into his eyes. Sputtering, Gerard released her. Francine brushed a few glistening drops of the liquid from her velvet waistband and drew herself up.

Slowly she turned in a semi-circle until she faced Lea again. Perversely, she seemed to enjoy the audience. "This is hardly the way I'd expected things to turn out," Francine said. "I'm fed up with all the insinuations about me, and I'm sick of all my so-called colleagues at Whitten Systems, who've abandoned me. Not even Marshall Schroth, who can't even cover his own tracks, will support me now. Then of course there's the fact that I don't enjoy taking the fall for others. Do you have any idea how that feels?"

Francine's eyes swept the crowd. "But there is one thing that gives me a modicum of pleasure. And you can probably guess what that is."

Lea stared at her blankly.

"Please! Such assumed innocence." Francine sneered. "You know what I'm talking about. I want to hear you explain yourself to the police after all the things I told them about you!"

Two women in the crowd gasped. Lea struggled to maintain her composure.

Francine flashed Lea a nasty smile. "Oh, don't think I haven't told them what I know about Keith's murder. Or about you and Paul. I was at police headquarters all afternoon, and my, weren't those two detectives interested in what I had to say."

Gerard gestured to two security guards, who began to thread their way through the crowd.

Francine tittered. "I imagine it will keep you busy for quite a while. Huh. I can't wait."

14

The fog had squatted above the city all morning, finally giving way to a radiant noon sun. It was in the mid-70s—virtually a heat wave for San Francisco—as Lea strolled down Market Street. She shrugged off her blazer, brushed her hair back, and lifted her face to the sun's warming rays. San Francisco's weather, cool and breezy most of the year, never ceased to confound tourists and natives alike. When Lea was considering names for her restaurant, a wag had suggested she call it The One Season.

Lea checked her watch: 12:41—plenty of time before Paul's speech at 1:30. Paul had called last night after the benefit to remind her that he'd be speaking at Quest West, the much-ballyhooed computer conference. Lea felt a flutter of excitement—and relief—that Paul wanted her to be there. Increasingly, she was aware of a growing distance between them. And it wasn't just that crises at Whitten Systems were consuming all of Paul's time. Unaccountably, Paul seemed to be pulling away from her.

At Mission Street, Lea took the path through the park by the Yerba Buena Arts Center. Workers on their lunch break sprawled on the lawn. In a clearing, a reggae band played a lilting, carefree tune. A small crowd swayed to the beat, and Lea allowed herself a quick hip wiggle. To Lea's left loomed the striated black-and-white tower of the Museum of Modern Art, its inscrutable eye staring unblinkingly at the sky.

Dodging taxis and shuttle buses, she crossed Howard Street and approached Moscone Center. Futuristic in design, it resembled an albino space station marooned in the heart of San Francisco. Lea entered through the massive glass doors, obtained the pass Paul had arranged for her, and took the escalator down to the subterranean exhibition rooms. There she stepped into a crush of voluble conventioneers.

The *couture du jour* varied from shabby T-shirts and stained jeans to silk designer suits and Italian leather shoes. The median age appeared to be 35. Men outnumbered women by three to one. Hundreds of booths touting a dizzying array of computer products lined the vast main hall. Lea inched down a crowded aisle, trying not to make eye contact with the hungry sales reps poised to pounce. She knew that many of them were entrepreneurs who had staked everything on their start-ups; if they failed here now, they might not survive to try again next year.

She found herself blocked by a cluster of fans swarming around a demo, and she took a minute to consult her floor map. Whitten Systems' booth was two aisles over. She edged her way back the way she'd come and turned a corner. Suddenly she came face to face with Randy Derrough.

Randy scowled and attempted to walk around her. The sales manager was natty as always, sporting a double-breasted charcoal suit with thin cobalt-blue stripes and a red silk pocket handkerchief.

"Wait," Lea said eagerly, laying a restraining hand on Randy's arm. "Could we talk for a minute?"

Randy stopped and glared at her. "I can't imagine we have anything to discuss."

"It's just that you were with Keith on the night he died," Lea said. She tried not to sound accusatory. "And Joy Nugent said you were in his office earlier that day, when someone must have tampered with his pills. I've been wondering if you saw anything suspicious—maybe someone else hanging around." She withdrew her hand.

Randy flushed. "Why won't anyone believe me? I was nowhere near Keith's office that morning. I had a client visiting, and I was with him until we left for lunch."

"But you could have excused yourself for a few minutes," Lea blurted out.

"Listen," Randy said. "I don't have time to worry about Killjoy and what she thinks she saw. I'm sick of her games. She plays favorites, and I'm not lucky enough to be one of them, okay? She controlled access to Keith, and now she's doing it with Paul. I've been trying to get past her for days to see him."

Lea stared at him in astonishment. "That doesn't sound like Joy."

"Oh, she's pleasant to you. You're close to the boss."

"Maybe she's trying to protect him."

"Hardly." Randy shook his head. "Joy Nugent is a barracuda. I don't know about Paul, but Keith was incredibly naive when it came to women. Especially ones like Joy. He couldn't see past her ornamental qualities. Believe me, she's ambitious. And she has her own agenda. With Keith she played the loyal secretary, but ... what's that quaint expression? Secretly she set her cap for him."

"There's nothing wrong with that," Lea observed.

"Not if it's above-board," Randy agreed. "It was the way she went about it. Using feminine wiles. First she had no ride home when they both worked late. What could Keith do but drive her home himself? Then she got him to take her out to dinner. Poor thing. She'd been so busy working she hadn't eaten all day. Then she bought tickets to a Giants game and claimed her date canceled at the last minute. Keith went along with that too."

Lea thought back to the way Joy had lingered over Keith's picture. Maybe she *had* been in love with him. Poor Joy.

"What about Georgeanne Hughes?" Lea asked. "Joy knew all about her."

Randy smirked. "Not for a long time, she didn't. And you should have seen her when she found out. She pouted for days. For some bizarre reason, she even whined to me about it."

"Isn't it possible that they were ... ah ... intimate, and that Joy felt Keith betrayed her?"

Randy considered this. "I doubt it. I can't say I understood Keith, but it was clear that he felt intellectually superior to the peons on his staff. He was so cocky that I honestly think it would have bothered him to sleep with a woman he considered his mental inferior. I watched Joy work on him a few times. She'd subtly rub up against up him, lean over his shoulder when he was at his desk. But Keith just had no reaction. The only conquest he cared about was taking over Paul's business."

"But what...."

"Enough." Randy cut her off. "I have to go, Ms. Sherwood, but I will give you some advice." He laughed disagreeably. "If I were you, I'd concentrate on keeping Joy Nugent away from your friend Paul. She's already in his office more than she needs to be."

Lea was so startled that she let Randy pass.

She was still brooding about Randy—and chastising herself for suspecting the worst about Joy—when she spotted another familiar face. Harry Coulter was ambling down the aisle toward her but stopped to talk to a young marketing rep in a three-piece suit.

Harry looked up as she approached. "Lea, what on earth are you doing in this zoo?"

She reminded him of Paul's speech, surprised that he evidently wasn't planning to hear it.

"Oh, that's right. I forgot. Maybe I'll drop in. I sure could use some inspiration."

Lea laughed and gestured with a hand, taking in the hall. "Isn't this enough for you?"

Harry looked skeptical. "I suppose it depends on your point of view."

"What do you mean?"

"I mean just look at these people," he said. "The start-up guys all want to hit it big. You can almost see the stars in their eyes. But for every one who makes it, 10 others will crash and burn. The guys who aren't completely devastated will pick up the pieces and try again. If they're lucky, their wives and kids won't have walked out on them. Of course no one ever wants to talk about burnout and divorce, but the rates in this industry are astronomical."

Lea shifted uneasily. She'd never seen Harry in this mood. "Haven't you ever wanted to start your own business?"

Harry grunted. "Me? All I want is to be left alone so I can write code. And play computer games." He scratched his beard. "For one thing, I couldn't hack dealing with the *vulture* capitalists. Talk about your Hobson's choice. Either you have no capital to get your company off the ground, or you cede majority ownership to a bunch of scavengers. Come on. Those guys portray themselves as white knights, but they don't care about nurturing your dream. Why should they? They take their cut when your company goes public. Or when *they* decide to sell it. Look at what they did to Paul. The guy put three gut-breaking years of his life into his firm, and they tossed him out and served his company on a silver platter to a charlatan like Keith. And talk about *chutzpah*! When the vultures needed Paul again, they asked him to come back and run the merged company like nothing ever happened. I tell you, I'm surprised Paul did it."

Lea stared at Harry, trying to fathom his meaning. Had he lost respect for Paul because he'd agreed to run Whitten Systems? But if so, why had Harry accepted Paul's job offer?

Harry shrugged elaborately, as if to dispel negative thoughts. "We averted a crisis this morning, anyway. Or rather Paul did. Joe Clooney over at Entimax, one of our biggest clients, has been complaining about the bugs in the software Keith sold him. Last week he even announced he was pulling his business. But today Paul talked him out of it. Paul personally guaranteed our new release."

"That ought to improve morale," Lea suggested. She felt a surge of hope that Paul was already beginning to turn Whitten Systems around.

Harry's face clouded, and Lea looked over her shoulder to see why. Marshall Schroth walked past and barely glanced at them. Neither he nor Harry attempted to say hello.

"Not your favorite person?" Lea asked.

"You got that right. I do everything to steer clear of that guy. He's all style over substance." Harry grimaced. "When I try to explain our design problems to him, he doesn't even listen. He thinks he already has the answers. But mainly he isn't capable of hearing another person's point of view without regarding him as an adversary." Harry glanced at Marshall's retreating back. "It's like he went to this 'Image' school of management, where they teach secret tactics to achieve corporate power. In Schroth's case, he seems to have been taught that if he intimidates enough people, they'll assume he knows what he's doing and won't challenge him."

"That's odd for someone in his position," said Lea. "And in this industry. I mean if you're smart, you recognize how much there is you'll never know. The more you learn about any subject, the more you realize that."

Harry laughed shortly. "I don't know how smart Marshall is. Cunning is more like it. He only sees things in terms of power and status."

Lea peered at her watch, suddenly aware of the passing time. She would have to hurry to get to Paul's speech. She promised to save a seat for Harry and headed for the exit. After two false turns in the labyrinthian corridors of Moscone, she found the indicated meeting room and slid into a seat just as the moderator was concluding his introduction. She looked up expectantly.

Paul, who appeared tired, stepped to the podium. He hesitated at the applause, apparently surprised by the warm welcome.

"I've been asked to speak to you today about the need for vision in our industry," Paul began as the applause waned. "We may move at breakneck speed to get new products on the shelf, but rarely do we stop to assess the implications of our actions.

"I suppose most people in this country are surprised at how many changes computers have brought about in a fraction of their lifetime." Paul paused and scanned the room. "But personally, I'm amazed that there's been so little change, when you consider the vast potential.

"We're lucky enough to live in one of the most exciting times in history, and we're on the threshold of amazing new discoveries that will alter human destiny. But the computer industry is still in its infancy. Ten years from now, we'll be four or five generations along in hardware, and new software will bootstrap our brainpower. We'll develop new tools that actually augment our intellects. We'll see this across the board—in medicine, genetic engineering, all levels of science and industry. And on a personal level, computers will continue to automate more functions and give us more time for personal development. Interactive networks will let people of all ages approach problems collectively in new ways. We're talking about breakthroughs that will unleash vast reserves of creative energy.

"It's hard to imagine limits to what we can do. Look at history. At the end of every century, people thought they were reaching the limits of what there was to know. This was especially true at the dawn of the 20th century. But look how far we've come since. Who in 1900 expected astronauts to walk in space, or to see us land a probe on Mars? Who expected to see heart transplants? Artificial insemination? Cloning?

"And just look at our economy. At the turn of the century, raw materials companies were kings. Today a large percentage of the profits in this country are made by firms that didn't even exist 25 years ago."

Out of the corner of her eye, Lea saw Harry slide into the seat next to her. He nodded and winked as Paul launched into a discussion of new products now on the drawing boards.

Paul paused again as he took in the audience. His tiredness had evaporated, and a wistfulness crept into his voice. "There's just one thing I don't understand. With all the potential for innovation, there are still thousands of companies in our industry who—let's face it—are only working out the variations of a theme. Think about this. In a few short years, the prevailing standards have been set by a handful of companies. We all know who they are. Yet there are countless ways to design computers and applications. So why are we sitting on our hands? Why are we satisfied? Our greatest threat is not the technological challenge. It's our prevailing complacency."

Paul met the eyes of various members of the audience.

"Who among you is going to defy the status quo? Which of you dares explore the unpopular—or the untried? I'm sure you remember, like I do, when the challenge of solving problems was more important than the money. Yet today I see too many of us hiding behind stock options and bonuses, when we all know it's the quest for unconventional solutions that will keep our society—and our own minds and spirits— alive.

"I think most of us still believe in our hearts that true satisfaction in life comes from making intellectual leaps. From creating something out of nothing. What could be better than using our intelligence and imagination to create products that change lives? What could be better than using our faculties to the fullest extent?

"I believe everyone here still lives for these ideals. I also think everyone in this room would like to leave a legacy for future generations. And yes, we need vision to do that.

"But it seems to me that what we more urgently need is character. To fight the status quo. To stand up to marketing whizzes who argue that a design isn't *commercial*. To persuade management to hang in there when development gets tough. And to keep fighting the complacency within ourselves.

"Let me leave you all with this thought: vision is essential. But, it isn't nearly enough. What we all need—from the most junior programmer to senior CEOs—is the strength of character to realize our vision."

The audience was silent for a moment. Then it erupted in applause. Lea felt a burst of pride as the crowd surged forward to congratulate Paul. He stood for more than 10 minutes, shaking hands and talking.

Lea joined Harry in the back of the room, where she noticed Marshall Schroth conversing with a florid-faced man. The two spoke warmly, and at one point Marshall tossed back his head and laughed. Lea marveled. She had never seen Marshall so agreeable. Evidently he could turn the charm on and off.

She nudged Harry. "Who is Marshall talking to?"

Harry followed her glance. "Oh, that's Ross Merriweather. He's a securities analyst here in the city. I'm glad he made it today. A good word from him could really boost our stock."

When Paul finally broke away from his well-wishers and joined them, he looked happier and more relaxed than he had in weeks.

Harry immediately began to rib him. "Hey, you missed your true vocation in life, fella. Lea, don't you agree? Can't you just see Paul on the missionary circuit? Why waste all that zeal?"

But Lea was barely listening. Marshall Schroth and Ross Merriweather had moved closer, and Paul's rival was making no attempt to lower his voice.

"Confidentially," Marshall said, "I don't think the board will keep Paul Boyd on much longer. He's lost their confidence. He hasn't made any headway on our design problems, and he's been ineffectual in stemming our bad publicity."

Lea gasped. She didn't dare look at Paul.

"Frankly, I've had to step in to save us from losing one of our biggest clients. Joe Clooney of Entimax has been quite unhappy at the poor treatment he's gotten from Boyd. It wasn't easy, but I convinced him to stay on for our new release. The board was quite gratified too. I informed our directors just before I drove up here."

Lea choked audibly. Marshall was simultaneously dissing Paul *and* taking credit for his accomplishment!

When her gaze met Paul's, she knew he had heard every word. His eyes narrowed, and a muscle twitched in his jaw.

Ross Merriweather, realizing that Paul had overheard, bid Marshall a hasty good-bye.

Paul walked up to Marshall and clapped a hand on his arm. Marshall squared his shoulders and regarded Paul condescendingly.

"How dare you?" Paul demanded. "Have you no scruples whatsoever? I don't care what you think of me personally, but how can you fuel more rumors about the company? How can you cashier the welfare of everyone you work with?"

Lea stepped back nervously. For a moment she thought Paul might actually haul off and slug Marshall.

Marshall said nothing, but a glimmer of satisfaction flashed in his eyes.

Lea stared at him in dismay. Had he deliberately been goading Paul?

"I know you resent me because you wanted my job," Paul said.

"Correction," Marshall said. "Want had nothing to do with it. I fully deserved the position. And I was amazed that the board awarded it to a neophyte whose only previous experience was bailing out of a failed start-up."

Paul blanched. "You've been trying to sabotage me since the very beginning. But do you really think the board would name you president now when they've already passed you over?"

Marshall flinched ever so slightly. The one chink in his armor, Lea thought.

"I ought to fire you this second," Paul stated. "The only reason I don't is that it would give our critics more ammunition. But I'm putting you on notice. Consider your days numbered."

Marshall responded with a bland look. "You're overreacting, Boyd. As usual. Ross is merely an old friend, and I was giving him my opinion in confidence. He'll respect it."

"Ross Merriweather has a pipeline to everyone in this industry, and you know it. I'd suggest you stop playing politics and start doing your job for a change."

Marshall shifted his gaze from Paul to Lea. Unaccountably, he smiled at her. Then he returned his attention to Paul. "In this world there are winners and losers, Boyd. A few winners, and many losers, to be precise. And let me assure you both, I have no doubt which side I'm on."

15

Lea had just arrived at Panache on Sunday morning when she heard an insistent knock on the front door. Expecting to see Zoe—she and the bookkeeper were going to review her finances—Lea peered out the window. On the sidewalk stood three Chinese men in boxy suits, smiling and waving to her.

As she opened the door to explain that Panache was closed, they each reached out enthusiastically to pump her hand. They then introduced themselves as independent investors from Hong Kong and asked if they could look around. Perplexed but unwilling to appear impolite, Lea let them in.

Immediately the men separated and began to scrutinize the walls, ceiling, floor, and fixtures. They murmured excitedly.

After several minutes, Lea approached the eldest man, who appeared to be in charge. "Excuse me, but I think there is some misunderstanding," she said in confusion. "Could you tell me what you're doing?"

"No misunderstanding, miss," he said. "We're examining the property. We're in town to scout locations for a new

Hong Kong-style night club. This neighborhood seems ideal, so close to Chinatown and Broadway."

"A Hong Kong-style night club?" Lea echoed. She almost laughed at the unexpected response.

"You know, one with separate areas for disco dancing, *karaoke* singing, video games—even billiards."

"That sounds very interesting," Lea managed to say. She thought she knew how Alice must have felt in *Through the Looking-Glass*. "But as you can see," she gestured about her, "this is already a restaurant."

"Oh, we know. We'll do all the remodeling." He smiled coyly. "I do hope you won't be too difficult about the price."

A second man joined them, rubbing his hands with pleasure. "It's just how Sandy described it," he said.

"Sandy Warner?" she asked. Light began to dawn, and a knot formed in her stomach.

He nodded. "We met with him this morning. He may come in as a partner with us."

Sandy Warner ran one of San Francisco's largest real estate development firms. He had brought a party to dinner last night. Lea couldn't believe it. Evidently the word around town was that she wouldn't last long.

With barely concealed disgust, Lea ushered the protesting men to the door, reiterating that Panache was *not* for sale. As her temples throbbed and her heart raced, Lea faced the indisputable fact that the vultures were out. And circling.

L ea's mood continued to darken as she and Zoe went over the books. Red ink was everywhere.

"I wish you'd at least *consider* charging a fee to split plates," Zoe admonished her. The bookkeeper peered over her bifocals at Lea and wagged her head. Strands of Zoe's gray hair broke free of a bun on the top of her head. "Why not? Other restaurants are doing it."

Lea stiffened. "I don't like it," she said. "It makes people feel like you're trying to nickel and dime them to death."

"Okay. How about raising your wine prices? People who can afford a good bottle of wine would pay a few dollars more, and the going rate is at least double the retail price. You're not even charging that!"

Lea crossed her arms. "No. Wine is supposed to be a part of the meal. Not a license to charge the moon. A lot of my customers would be put off if I raised prices. I might *lose* business."

Zoe clucked. "I don't suppose it would do any good to suggest that you push bottled water as a substitute for tap?"

Lea exploded. "*That* is the worst! It's a blatant grab for money. Not to mention being pretentious, and setting your customers up to feel either inferior or superior. I'm sorry, but that I can't do."

"Very well. It's your funer ... ah, restaurant," Zoe said, gathering up the outstanding bills. "I was only trying to help."

Georgeanne Hughes called after lunch.

"I just remembered something about Keith," she said. "I'd forgotten it when we met at the café, and I thought it might be important."

"And what is that?" Lea asked, surprised to hear from Georgeanne.

"Something happened when we were at my parent's house last month. I'd gone upstairs to talk to my mother, and Keith was in the library with my father. When I was ready to go, I went downstairs and overheard them arguing. My father told Keith he was pursuing a course—I think these were his words—that would get Whitten Systems in trouble. Well, I didn't like eavesdropping, so I went into the library, and you could just feel the tension between them. On the way back to the city, I asked Keith what my father had meant, but Keith laughed and said he was being overly scrupulous. Keith didn't want to talk about it." Georgeanne sighed. "Knowing how they felt about each other, I put it down to some kind of personality difference. At the time, I didn't see how Keith could do anything to jeopardize the company. It was his life."

"But Keith always believed that whatever he did was right," Lea pointed out.

"That's true," Georgeanne agreed. "And until a few days ago, I would have told you that Keith could walk on water. I mean, he was such a success. But now his murder has me wondering. I've been going over the last few times we saw each other. He was definitely preoccupied, even worried, I can see that now. Unfortunately I had my own problems at work, and I didn't pay Keith as much attention as I might have. But ever since I remembered that night in the library, I've been asking myself if it could be related to Keith's death. I don't know, maybe Keith got in over his head."

"Have you asked your father what he was referring to?"

Georgeanne did not reply. Was she afraid to ask him?

"Have you told the police? They ought to know."

"No," Georgeanne said vehemently. "I despise the police. Besides, if Keith was living on the edge, I'd hardly be doing his memory a favor by exposing him. And Keith's paid dearly enough for it. I mean if this did have anything to do with his death."

"Why are you telling me all this?" Lea asked.

Georgeanne hesitated. "I thought it was only fair to warn you and Paul. I know Paul's on the hot seat. My father's been talking about how everyone is waiting for him to stumble. So in case Keith left any land mines behind...." Her voice trailed off.

"Hmmm," Lea murmured. Her thoughts went back to Brooke's comments about Georgeanne. "I heard something odd the other day," Lea said. "Someone told me you had broken up with Keith right before he died."

She was met by silence on the other end of the line.

"Georgeanne?"

The young woman's delicate breathing came over the phone. "Oh, you caught me by surprise," she said. "I was just trying to think why anyone would have said that. It doesn't make any sense." Georgeanne paused. "There was something else I wanted to mention."

"What?" Lea's patience was wearing thin.

"It's just that I was pretty hard on my father the day we talked. I probably made him out to be some kind of monster. I wanted you to know that although we've had our differences, I've never thought he was capable of murder. I still don't."

Now it was Lea's turn to be silent. She didn't know how to respond. Was Georgeanne guilt-ridden because she'd criticized her stepfather? Biting the hand that had fed her all these years? Or was she trying to convince herself that Bennett Alston wasn't involved in Keith's death?

Rain pelted the windshield of Brooke's Volvo as she maneuvered the car over Noe Valley's slick streets later that night. "You're awfully quiet," she said to Lea.

"I guess going to the movies wasn't such a good idea after all," Lea replied. She had been on edge all evening.

Brooke groaned. "It was supposed to cheer you up. I thought *Vertigo* was one of your favorite films."

"It is, but I'd forgotten how disturbing it can be. After all, Jimmy Stewart is used as a pawn in a murder. Then he gets betrayed by the woman he loves."

Brooke gave her a sidelong glance. "There was one light moment. Remember when Stewart and Kim Novak drove past that Nob Hill intersection under construction? I drove by myself the other day and a hard-hat crew was still working on it. No wonder the audience howled."

Lea smiled weakly.

Brooke squinted at the fogging windshield as the storm gained strength. Streetlights cast an eerie glow on Victorian houses and stucco storefronts, and car taillights throbbed red through sheets of rain. Suddenly the minivan ahead of them hit a pothole, dousing three women waiting for a Muni bus. Brooke sighed in relief when they reached her Liberty Street condominium.

"Can you believe this weather?" Brooke yelled as they sprinted for her door. "I didn't know it could rain like this in June in San Francisco."

Inside, they dried off and Brooke went to the kitchen to make coffee. Lea wandered through the living room, studying a modern watercolor and a 1939 painting by a Portuguese artist that Brooke had recently bought. She pulled up the collar of her wool turtleneck against the evening's chill. Rummaging through Brooke's compact discs, she selected an album of Erik Satie's piano pieces. She inserted it into the CD player and curled up on the chintz-covered sofa as Satie's haunting strains filled the room.

Lea was lost in reverie when Brooke returned and handed her a cup. Lea lifted it to her face and let the steam warm her.

"Why so preoccupied?" Brooke said.

Lea sighed. She was thinking of Paul, and the fact that she had hardly spoken to him in days. She knew how busy he was, yet she wondered if he was using that as an excuse to put distance between them. Was it her imagination, or was he really avoiding her?

"It's Paul," Lea said. "I just don't know if we're going to make it through all of this." As she said the words, she felt a stab of pain. Stating aloud the fear she had only voiced privately now made it all the more concrete. She looked sadly at Brooke. "He seems so far away lately. It's like he's lost a part of himself, and now he doesn't care if he loses me."

Brooke reached over and pressed her hand. "Lea, I'm sure it's only temporary. I can't imagine the two of you not being together. You seem so right for each other."

Lea winced. "I thought we were too."

"You are," Brooke insisted, "in so many ways. You're both idealists—a dying breed. You both believe one person can make a difference. You both have a passion for what you do, and each of you has created something to be proud of."

"And which we each stand to lose," Lea observed. A dull ache enveloped her. The thought of losing both Paul and the restaurant was almost more than she could bear.

"But he has another chance. And so do you. Keith's death is on everyone's mind now, but it will all blow over soon. You'll see. A new scandal...." Brooke paused, biting her lip. "A new crisis will capture the public's imagination."

Lea shook her head. "There are times, like tonight, when everything seems so futile. As if it doesn't matter what I've achieved in the past, or what I do in the future." She cupped her chin in her hand. "I'm scared, Brooke. You know the wonderful, exhilarating feeling you have when you're young? That life is an adventure and you can shape it? Well, maybe you can't after all. Maybe I can't."

"Lea, I've never heard you talk this way before!" Brooke said in alarm. "You've always risen to every challenge."

Brooke's words, though meant to soothe, had the opposite effect. Lea hung her head. She feared she'd lost the ability to take decisive action.

"Listen to you." Brooke leaned over and shook Lea by the shoulder when she didn't respond. "I can't believe what I'm hearing. You're one of the most resilient people I know. Look at what you've done. You've taken an enormous risk to make a dream come true. And—no easy feat— you've created your own world. You surround everyone with beauty and taste. I've seen people walk into Panache looking tired and discouraged. But they leave feeling on top of the world. Really, Lea. You perform a kind of magic. Personally, I don't know what I'd do without it."

Lea smiled in gratitude. "You're a good friend."

"It's true," Brooke said firmly. "In a world where so few people seem to care, where so much is screwed up—you're an alchemist. I go to Panache just because you make things work. And believe me, I know how hard it is to do."

Lea sighed again. "Sometimes I feel like I'm living in a surreal universe. It's no disgrace today to cut corners or lie. People inflate their résumés, take credit for what others have done. Not so long ago, people prided themselves on earning

a good reputation. Now people like that are called suckers."
She pulled at the fringe of a throw pillow. "We've created a
civilization where decent people feel like failures if they're
not rich or famous. Our role models are movie stars!"

Brooke nodded. "I know. Celebrity has replaced
accomplishment. And achievement for its own sake hardly
seems to matter."

They lapsed into silence and listened to Satie and the
rain drumming on the roof. A restless wind moaned through
the acacia trees.

"Listen to us," said Lea. "We're both past 30, and still so
earnest. As if we really could change the world."

16

"**I** just can't get through to Harry," Paul said to Lea in his office the next night. "He insists on sticking to his arcane notion of how to design our new system, and he refuses to see it's got disaster written all over it." Paul's voice crackled with frustration. "If I didn't know better, I'd say he was trying to sabotage me."

Lea felt a pang of guilt. She still hadn't told Paul about her talk with Harry at his apartment. "But it's only natural for two designers to come up with different concepts," she said. "The two of you have disagreed before, and you've managed to work things out."

"I know, but we've never been so far apart. And it isn't as if Harry is just standing up for what he believes. That I could respect. But his underlying approach is seriously flawed. I can't understand why he doesn't see the holes in it. He's usually sharp about what will or won't work."

"What are you going to do?"

Paul sighed. "If Harry refuses to work with me, what choice do I have? I'll have to find someone else. But that may not be easy. I called Gary Farrell this morning. He's tied up on an applications job down in Irvine." Farrell was an elite freelance programmer who charged $250 an hour and only took jobs that challenged him. In between projects he went to Los Angeles to surf.

"What about Bat Carey?" Bat had acquired his nickname by pulling all-nighters in dark rooms illuminated only by the light of his computer screen.

"Nope. He's on his honeymoon in Kauai."

"Bat got married?" Lea shook her head in amazement. The programmer was notorious for his red Maserati and his groupies—a coterie of young women who somehow managed to tolerate one another.

"To an emergency room nurse," Paul said. "Not one of his stable. He only met her a few weeks ago."

Paul's phone rang, and he reached for it. From what Lea heard of the ensuing conversation, she guessed he was being grilled by a board member.

Joy appeared at the door after several minutes and beckoned to Lea. She rose and followed Joy to her desk, where a light was blinking on the telephone console.

"It's Francine," Joy said. "She insists on speaking to Paul. I told her he can't be interrupted, but she says she has to talk to him immediately. She's babbling something about knowing more than she let on about Keith's death."

Lea frowned. Was this another of Francine's games? The last thing she wanted was to talk to her. But perhaps she'd better. "I'll take the call," Lea said unhappily.

Joy depressed the console button and handed Lea the phone across her desk.

Immediately Lea was struck by Francine's tone of voice. She had never heard the woman betray actual fear before. Yet now she sounded as if she were skirting panic.

"I have to tell someone," Francine stammered. "It's about Keith. I ... I've known something about his murder, and now I'm afraid to keep quiet. It's gotten too dangerous for me, and my son."

"But I thought you were in touch with the police." With distaste, Lea recalled the scene at the charity benefit. "Why not tell them? They could offer you protection."

"No, it's more complicated than that." Francine was quiet for almost a minute, and Lea thought she might hang up. "Also, I think Paul may be in danger." Lea endured another prolonged silence. When Francine finally spoke again, her voice was tremulous. "I need to talk to somebody. I can't think straight any more. Can you meet me? Now?" she pleaded. "I can't talk about this on the phone."

Reluctantly, Lea agreed to meet her in a half hour. She checked her watch. It was now 7:28.

Francine gave her the address of a steak and ribs joint near her house in the hills. As Lea hung up, she wondered if she was doing the right thing.

She summarized the conversation for Joy and asked her to tell Paul where she was going. Joy responded with a strange look.

"Do you think it's some kind of trap?" Lea asked.

"I'm not sure," Joy said. "All I know is that Francine is peculiar. You never know what she's going to do."

Lea said she'd be back as soon as possible and hurried out to the parking lot. She hoped she still had her dog-eared map of the Peninsula. She had only a vague notion of how to reach the restaurant.

She got into the Renault, found the map at the bottom of the glove compartment, and traced a route that would take her almost to Crestline Boulevard, a snaky hilltop drive beloved by motorcyclists on weekends and couples at sunset. The restaurant was about a half-mile from there.

Lea started the engine and drove out of the lot, only peripherally aware of a dark sedan following her. Distracted by the setting sun in her eyes, she lowered her visor as she headed west toward the heavily wooded Jasper Ridge. Ordinarily she would have enjoyed the drive, but tonight she was apprehensive about what Francine might have to say.

At Quail Court, Lea suspected that she must have missed her turnoff. She checked her watch, then fumbled with the map again until she pinpointed her location. At the next opportunity, she made a U-turn and retraced her route for several blocks, getting caught at a couple of stop lights. It was now dusk, and the sound of crickets echoed through her open window. She gave a sigh of relief when she began the ascent into the shadowed hills.

She reached the Chuck Station at 8:05 and squeezed the Renault into one of the few available parking spaces. The aroma of hickory smoke wafted through the air as she walked to the entrance, reminding her that she was ravenous. Maybe she should go on a cholesterol splurge, even order a cheeseburger. She couldn't remember when she'd last had one.

The restaurant was crowded, particularly for a Monday night. The hostess advised her sternly that her party had not yet arrived and all but commanded Lea to take a seat on a semi-circular, red-leather banquette. The hostess had a bony frame, and her pinched lips suggested to Lea that she derived little pleasure from either people or food. Lea wondered what perverse quirk of fate had brought her here to greet the public.

Lea sat down next to a plump woman with frizzy hair and swiveled her head to take in the decor. Wild West paintings of cattle roundups and moonlit campfires were flanked by worn saddles, branding irons, and other bygone paraphernalia. Lea almost expected to see Roy Rogers enter, twirling a lariat. The booths lining the walls favored comfort over style, and the waitresses wore wench costumes with ruffled, low-cut white blouses and teensy black skirts. Lea could hardly believe she was still in the politically correct Bay Area.

At 8:25, she stood to stretch her legs. Steak sizzled invitingly on the nearby grill. Lea peered out the front window at the parking lot, hoping to see Francine. She watched the lot for a few minutes and then turned around to reclaim her seat. A family of four carrying doggy bags paraded by her, and the teenage son elbowed his younger sister, who burped.

Ten minutes later, Lea was both hungry and annoyed. She walked to the rear of the restaurant, where it was quieter, and pulled out her cell phone near the Cowgirls' room. Its door bore the image of a perky young woman in cowboy boots and a flared skirt. On the off chance that Joy was still at the office, Lea tried her extension. Joy answered immediately but said she hadn't heard from Francine. She was able to give Lea Francine's telephone number and address, however. Lea tried the number and gave up after 15 rings.

Lea walked back to her seat with her stomach growling. She couldn't decide whether to drive to Francine's or stay at the restaurant in case Francine should suddenly appear. Lea couldn't understand it. Francine had said she lived only six miles from here. Surely nothing could have happened to her in the last half hour. Maybe she'd had a flat tire? Or lost track of the time? Some people were routinely late and thought nothing of it.

When the hostess called her name, Lea's growing concern about Francine warred with her hunger pains. The hunger won. Once seated, she felt almost morally justified in ordering a double-thick, blue-cheese burger, and even acquiesced to a side of fries. She ordered a Diet Pepsi out of preference, however, not virtue. At 9:20 she paid her bill and tried Francine's number one more time. Still no answer.

Back in the car, Lea squinted at her frayed map in the faint glow of the overhead light. There were two ways to get to Francine's. The route along Arnold Street seemed preferable to the alternative—a dark and lonely stretch of Crestline. She wrestled with the wisdom of attempting to go to Francine's at all. Who knew what she might find? It could still be a trap.

Suddenly Lea felt queasy. Yet she could hardly call the police. There was no evidence of foul play, or even that Francine was missing. Lea tried to examine the situation from every angle. She only had Francine's word for it that she was in danger. Come to think of it, she couldn't even swear that the voice on the phone had been Francine's.

Lea resolved to at least drive by the house. If anything seemed out of place, she could call for help.

She headed out of the parking lot and cranked down the car window. The June night air was fresh and cool. Lea switched on her bright lights as she approached Arnold. The drive was downhill, through densely wooded terrain. A yellow sign warned of deer crossing, and Lea spotted a skunk scurrying into a stand of pines. For a quarter of a mile, a canopy of fir trees overhung the narrow road. Gradually dense thickets gave way to partially cleared lots, then to a residential neighborhood.

As she turned onto Francine's street, she saw a pulsating red light ahead of her. She checked the number of the house she was passing and experienced a sinking sensation. One way or another, the police had made it to Francine's.

Lea's heart began to race as she pulled into Francine's driveway, where a black and white patrol car was stationed. A lanky man in a police uniform came forward and held up a hand to halt her progress. He walked over to her door and stooped to scrutinize Lea through her open window. "Are you Miss Sherwood?" he asked. She admitted she was, unsure of the implications of his knowing her name.

"Pull over here and remain in the car," he instructed her.

Lea did as she was told while the man walked up the drive to consult with a colleague. In the beam of her headlights, she could see Francine's two-story, nouveau-Victorian on a half acre of partially wooded land. The house itself was dark, but there was no sign that anything was amiss. No gaping doors or windows, no wails in the night.

When the officer returned, he took a moment to appraise her. "Could you tell me where you've been for the last two hours, Miss Sherwood?"

Lea described Francine's phone call and her own movements since then.

"And you're here now because you're concerned about her?" the officer asked in a monotone. His expression, however, was skeptical.

She nodded and inquired in a weak voice if Francine was all right.

He ignored the question and took a step back from the car. "I'd like to ask you to come along with us. You can drive your own vehicle, but we'd appreciate it if you'd follow us down the road a bit."

Lea gulped but agreed to go.

"That's fine, then. Just pull out of the driveway now so we can get by." Lea shifted into reverse, suddenly aware that her knees were shaking.

She followed the patrol car along the quiet street until it turned right on Crestline. Immediately they began climbing. Lea glanced off to her right. The lights of Silicon Valley glowed brightly beyond the steep mountain drop-offs. It was beautiful, albeit spooky.

After a few miles, Lea caught a glimpse of red flares flickering ahead. In the dancing light, she could see orange hazard cones blocking the lane of oncoming traffic. At the side of the road, hugging the steep hillside, were an ambulance, a patrol car with flashing lights, and several unmarked cars. Lea's escorts slowed and signaled her to pull off to the shoulder.

Lea came to a stop behind them and turned off her engine, awaiting further instructions. An agitated policeman stood ahead of her, turning back an approaching car. Two men in rumpled sport coats whom she assumed were plainclothes detectives examined the pavement and shoulder of the road, presumably for skid marks. Her heart sank. Lea no longer had to ask if anything had happened to Francine.

One of the men broke off his examination and turned to speak with her escorts, who had gotten out of their car. The man, who had dirty-blond hair and an athletic build, then turned to stare at Lea before walking over to the Renault. Lea rolled down her window and sat very still, afraid to make any move he might misinterpret.

As he ducked his head to peer at her, Lea got a whiff of his spicy cologne.

"Would you mind stepping out of your car, Miss Sherwood?" he asked after several moments.

Lea nervously opened the door and got out. A brisk breeze was blowing over the crest of the mountain, and the road flares cast an eerie pink glow over the assembled vehicles and crew. Lea shivered in her lightweight blazer and slacks. From the canyon below, she heard shouts. Soon a pair of uniformed men struggled over the shoulder, hoisting a gurney. They were panting from its weight, and their long climb.

Lea's stomach lurched. Had Francine been driven off the mountainside? Lea stared as the men stowed her body bag in the rear of their van and took their seats up front in the cab. The reality of Francine's death began to set in.

Gradually she became aware that the policeman was observing her closely.

He introduced himself as Detective Jake Campbell of the San Ygnacio Police Department and asked her to describe her movements that night.

Lea told her story once more.

"Can anyone at the Chuck Station confirm your presence from 8:05 on?"

Lea remembered the grim hostess and her own harried server, a teenage girl wearing red barrettes and braces. She gave him the particulars.

"That still doesn't account for your whereabouts between 7:30 and 8:05, Miss Sherwood."

Lea explained that Joy Nugent could vouch for the time she'd left Whitten Systems. She also pointed out that she'd had at least a 20-minute drive to the restaurant. That left roughly 10 minutes when she could conceivably have followed Francine. Would he believe that she'd made a wrong turn and retraced part of her route?

Campbell's gaze was impassive. "Who else at Whitten Systems knew about Mrs. Reese's phone call tonight?"

Lea told him about Joy, and presumably Paul.

"Are you sure no one else could have overheard? You said you were standing at the secretary's desk in an open area."

Lea nodded, thinking back. "I suppose someone might have heard us," she conceded. Anyone could have approached Joy's desk from the hall and stood unseen at the corner, listening.

Campbell asked her several more questions. Finally he stood back to appraise the Renault and squatted to shine a light over its tires. "We'd like to keep your car overnight, Miss Sherwood. The lab will go over it in the morning, and you'll probably get it back in the afternoon. We'll give you a ride back to town tonight."

Lea wasn't sure if he was asking her or telling her.

"Wait here," Campbell said as he turned to leave.

The wind had picked up, and the growing chill in the air gave her shivers. Her eyes lingered on the van carrying Francine's body that was just now pulling out onto the road.

The two officers who had led her here returned and solemnly ushered her into the back seat of their car. For some unknown reason, Lea felt guilty. The driver swung the vehicle across the road in a narrow arc, heading back the way they had come. Lea craned her head, looking over her shoulder. Bobbing pinpoints of light revealed men still scouring the hillside and ravine. Spotlights illuminated Francine's white BMW, crushed and twisted in a tangle of brush far below.

Once past the accident scene, the mountain road was quiet and harrowingly dark. Lea leaned forward and cleared her throat. The officer in the passenger seat turned around. "Can't you please tell me what happened?" Lea asked. "You already have my statement, and I'm bound to hear about the accident on the news."

The officer grunted and scrutinized her from head to foot. Finally he looked her in the eye and grudgingly informed her that Francine Reese had been coerced off the road shortly after 8:00 P.M.

Furthermore, an eyewitness approaching from the opposite direction had seen a black Mercedes sedan traveling at high speed behind the BMW. First it had pulled up alongside Francine and tried to crowd her over the edge of the mountain. Francine had swerved violently but managed to regain control. Then the Mercedes surged ahead of the BMW and cut it off. Francine soared over the cliff, and her killer sped up, racing past the approaching car in a blur. The witness, who couldn't catch the Mercedes' license plate, had called police from his cell phone. He'd waited at the scene until they'd arrived.

Lea lapsed into silence for the rest of the ride. A sense of horror vied with fear as she reflected that the killer was not only still at large, but more deadly than ever. Whoever had dared to kill Francine in such a manner would stop at nothing.

Poor Francine, Lea thought. Such a dreadful death. She remembered the day Francine had pranced into Panache, acting as if she knew everything. Perhaps that trait had been her undoing. Out of habit, she may have let on to the wrong person that she knew more than she actually did.

Still ... what was it Francine had said on the phone? That she was afraid to keep quiet about what she knew. Had the murderer inadvertently revealed himself to Francine? Had he made an attempt on her life before this? Or perhaps Francine had been an accomplice in Keith's murder. An accomplice who had since become a liability.

Lea glanced up in surprise when they arrived at Whitten Systems. She had asked to come here but had given little thought as to what might lie ahead. In the glare of harsh lights, a television news crew had set up camp. Lea experienced a sinking feeling. How had they heard about Francine so quickly?

Her companions, who apparently wanted to avoid reporters as much as she did, parked on the far side of the building and bid her a hasty goodnight. Gritting her teeth, Lea got out of the car.

The news team was trotting in her direction before she was even halfway to the door. The cameraman trained his lens on her while a young woman with a microphone ran up and blocked her path. Lea tried to act natural.

As the woman zeroed in, however, Lea recognized her from a news show a few nights earlier. She had delivered an inaccurate and vacuous report on the aftermath of Keith's death. The woman was now inches from her—picture perfect, with expertly styled chestnut hair and bright, raspberry-hued lips. Yet there was a disturbing emptiness in her eyes.

She thrust her microphone in Lea's face. "Ms. Sherwood," she said urgently, "we've just heard a rumor that you've been named a suspect in the murder of Francine Reese. Is this true?"

Lea recoiled, and her heart raced. How could she possibly respond to such a question? Even a "no comment" might imply that the rumor was true. Instead, she grimly stared ahead and attempted to skirt the woman.

The reporter tagged along, peppering Lea with impertinent questions, until they finally reached the front door of Whitten Systems. Lea jammed her finger on the night bell and waved frantically to the security guard, who was seated in the rear of the lobby. The reporter was now doing a little jig, unwilling to let Lea escape without comment.

Lea shut her eyes, held her breath, and ducked her head until the guard let her in.

17

"**I**s Mr. Boyd still here?" Lea gasped. She took a deep breath and tried to recover her composure.

"Yes, miss," the guard said with concern, glancing from Lea back to the reporter, who was shouting and pounding on the door, her face a mask of anger. "Let me call him for you."

When Paul reached the lobby, he rushed to Lea's side and wove his arms around her. "Thank God you're all right! I'd never forgive myself if anything happened to you," he said fervently.

Lea held onto him and buried her face in his chest. She was none too steady on her feet.

"Tell us what happened!" Joy demanded when they got to Paul's office. She leapt up from one of Paul's armchairs. "We've been absolutely sick with worry. Paul drove over to the restaurant, but he just missed you. Then he called the police."

Paul sighed. "When we heard Francine had been killed...."

"We thought whoever did it might go after you!" Joy chimed in.

Lea flopped down onto Paul's sofa. "How did you find out about Francine?"

"Salvador Espiritu, the guard downstairs, heard it on his radio," Joy replied. "He recognized her name and phoned to tell Paul." Joy pushed a strand of hair from her eyes. "What a night. First the stolen car, then Francine's murder."

"Stolen car? What are you talking about?"

"Oh, that happened after you left," Joy said. "It was almost 9:00, and Bennett came storming over to my desk, claiming his Mercedes had been stolen." She rolled her eyes. "Well, I thought he wasn't seeing straight. We've never had a car stolen from our parking lot. But sure enough, it was gone. And so was the car key he kept on a key chain in his jacket pocket."

"What color is his Mercedes?" Lea asked.

"It's dark," Paul said. "Black, maybe." He sat down on the arm of the sofa and began to rub Lea's shoulder.

Lea had a dim recollection of the car that had followed her out of the parking lot earlier. It could well have been Bennett's.

She told them about it. "It meant nothing to me at the time," she said. "I was anxious about meeting Francine. And let's face it, there are tons of Mercedes around here." Lea shuddered. "But if Bennett's key was stolen too, that almost guarantees that someone here took his car."

They exchanged uneasy glances. "Do you think we were overheard talking after Francine called?" Joy asked Lea.

Lea nodded and crossed her arms tightly across her chest. She was still cold, and her throat felt sore.

"But how do we know Bennett is telling the truth?" Paul asked. "He could have taken the car out himself and then reported it stolen."

Lea filled them in on everything she had learned that evening.

Joy's eyes gleamed with excitement. "So unless Bennett has an alibi for 7:30 to 8:30, he could have driven to Francine's, followed her down Crestline, and then come back here and reported the theft."

Paul considered the possibilities. "Maybe he ditched the car and took a cab to the office. The police could check the dispatch records."

"That sounds risky," Lea said. "But he could have taken a cab to one of the hotels on Parkside and walked back here. Bennett's in good shape. He could easily have made it in time."

Paul and Joy nodded.

Lea smiled and reached up to touch Paul's arm. "At least you're out of the loop on this one. The police can't possibly suspect you of being involved in Francine's death."

"Well, I don't know," Paul said uncertainly. He frowned. "I was on the phone most of the time between 7:30 and 8:30. And the police could claim I have no proof that someone else wasn't speaking on my extension. No one actually saw me in my office."

"But Joy was right here," Lea protested.

Joy's face fell. "Actually, right after you left, Lea, I decided to go out for something to eat. It looked like Paul was going to be tied up for a while, so I left him a note. I got back just as you called from the restaurant."

"A little after 8:30," Lea suggested.

"I'm afraid so."

Lea thought for a moment and turned to Paul. "But who were you talking to? The police can call them for verification."

She felt Paul's hand tighten on her shoulder.

"It was ... uh, someone who would rather not have me pass his name along to the cops."

Lea waited for him to elaborate, but Paul said no more.

When the phone rang, they all jumped. Joy took the call at Paul's desk and then beckoned to Paul. She covered the mouthpiece with her hand. "It's Detective Jake Campbell of the San Ygnacio Police Department," she whispered. "He wants to come over and talk to you."

Paul rose, grabbed the phone, and spoke briefly. "He's on his way," he said as he hung up.

The rest of the night flew by in a blur. Campbell and his partner arrived carrying cups of Starbucks coffee and questioned Paul, Joy, Harry, and several other hapless souls who were working late. No one could verify that either Bennett or Paul had been in their offices when Francine was killed.

After midnight, Lea slipped away and went down to the lobby. She wondered who Salvador had seen coming and going that night.

"Can I help you, Miss Sherwood?" Salvador asked, surprised to see Lea approach him. He closed the book he'd been reading and held it in his right hand, which was missing its index finger.

Lea hesitated. Joy had let slip once that Salvador was not one to be taken lightly. In his younger days in the Philippines, he'd fought in the Aquino revolution, and as a POW had been tortured and left for dead. A three-inch scar zigzagged across his cheek.

"Do you remember when I left earlier tonight?" Lea asked.

Salvador nodded without comment.

"Well, did anyone from Whitten Systems go out right after me?"

Salvador smiled craftily. "Miss! You know I cannot tell you that."

"But you don't know how important it is!"

Salvador smiled again, not unsympathetically. "See that?" he asked, pointing to a security camera trained on the door.

Lea nodded.

"The police have confiscated the film, and my night sign-in book. And they have asked *me* to stay mum. So it is mum—not dumb—I intend to stay!" Salvador chuckled at his own joke and raised a finger to his mouth, pretending to zip his lip.

"Could you at least tell me if Bennett Alston left after I did?"

"Now, now." Salvador said. He sat back in his chair and reopened his book.

"Oh, there you are." Joy's voice called out to her.

Lea looked up and saw Joy waving to her from the door leading to the office.

"Paul's been looking for you," Joy said. "The police said we can all go home now."

Lea sighed and turned to go, but one last glance at Salvador drew her up short. He was staring at Joy with a queer look in his eyes.

Was it her imagination, or was he suddenly on guard?

18

After four hours of sleep, Lea awoke seconds before her clock alarm was due to trill. She clapped a hand on the timer, tossed her covers aside, and forced herself up. Once on her feet, she moaned. Not only was her throat worse, but she felt a mounting dread as to what the day would bring.

Gerard and the other cooks greeted her apprehensively when she got to work. Todd and CeCe admitted with some embarrassment that they'd seen her on TV attempting to elude the news crew. She didn't dare look at the *Herald*.

Lea was in her office reading the mail when Brooke called mid-morning. She sounded upset.

"I tried to reach you until all hours last night, Lea. How are you?"

"I'm still pretty shaky," Lea croaked. "You saw me on the news?"

"Yep. I wish you'd hauled off and smacked the woman."

"Oh, that would really have improved my reputation." Lea laughed in spite of herself.

"It's good to hear you laugh," Brooke said warmly. "Listen, I've been talking to Karen Dixon, our Silicon Valley bureau chief. She just heard that they found Bennett Alston's

Mercedes, abandoned, on a side street about a mile from Paul's office."

Lea felt a surge of hope. "Do the police think it was the car that shoved Francine Reese off Crestline?"

"Bingo. It's the one, all right. They matched the paint from Francine's BMW where the Mercedes swiped it. The only thing they don't have are fingerprints. The door and steering wheel were wiped clean."

"Bennett could have killed Francine and then wiped the steering wheel himself. To support his claim that someone else used the car and removed the evidence."

"Right. But maybe Bennett's telling the truth. It makes me wonder. What about that daughter of his? The exotic one who gave Keith the death pills. Didn't she sometimes go to the office?"

"Yes, but I don't think she's been there since Keith died."

"My point is that she *might* have showed up."

"But why would Georgeanne choose such a risky way of killing Francine?"

Brooke clucked. "It's obvious that someone overheard you telling Joy about Francine's phone call. Whoever it was knew Francine was desperate, and that she was on her way to spill the beans to you."

Lea had a funny feeling. "How did you know about the phone call, and my conversation with Joy?"

"Karen heard it early this morning. By now, I'm sure it's all over the Valley."

Lea's heart sank. The more she tried to clear her name, the more notoriety she attracted.

"Listen, my dear. I have to run. I have a meeting with my producer, but I'll call you later. In the meantime, as my mother would say, 'Keep your chins up.'"

A after lunch Lea hitched a ride to the Peninsula with Heather, who was driving to Santa Clara and had offered to drop her off in San Ygnacio. The police had phoned earlier to say Lea could pick up her Renault at any time.

Sydney, who was in British Columbia attending a cousin's wedding, had also called to confirm that she was flying back late that afternoon. Lea had agreed to pick her up at the airport.

After Lea retrieved the Renault, she took stock of the time. It was almost 4:00, and Sydney was due in at about 5:30. More than an hour to kill. She pulled out her cell phone and called Paul. As usual, Joy answered and said he was in a meeting, so Lea brought Joy up to date on the discovery of Bennett Alston's Mercedes. Then, on impulse, she asked if Bennett was in the office.

Joy laughed. "He's just gone home to change for the evening. Apparently he has to escort his wife to a charity gala in the city."

Unwilling to waste the next hour, Lea asked Joy for Bennett's address. She didn't flatter herself that she could unmask a skillful liar, but she was curious to see how Bennett was reacting to Francine's death.

Joy put her on hold for a minute and then came back with the particulars. "Just remember," she warned, "you didn't get this from me."

Lea consulted her map of the Peninsula. Bennett lived in Altamira, an exclusive enclave nestled in the foothills of the Santa Cruz Mountains, about 10 minutes away. She started the car and headed southwest. After a few miles, she started climbing; the Renault hugged the narrow roadway as it snaked high into the hillside. Lea inhaled the camphor aroma of eucalyptus and craned her neck to gaze at the towering old trees, peeling bark. Far below, strips of pale blue marked the southern tip of San Francisco Bay. As Lea navigated a hairpin curve, a roan horse in a corral switched its tail lazily.

Perched at the top of the hill, with a panoramic view, was Bennett's estate. An imposing stone wall surrounded the property, but Lea found the gate open, and she drove unimpeded down the drive lined with massive live oaks. Presently she came to the house, a sprawling, Mediterranean-style mini-palazzo of pink stucco, with roses in vibrant hues of red running the length of the terrace. She parked in the semicircular drive, crossed a stone portico, and rang the doorbell.

Almost immediately a plump, middle-aged woman in a peach shirtwaist dress opened the door. Her fading brown hair was held back by a tortoiseshell headband and tucked under in a neat pageboy. She smiled tentatively when she saw Lea.

"Mrs. Alston?" Lea asked.

"Oh my goodness, no," the woman replied, startled. "I'm Mrs. McGredy, the housekeeper." She spoke with a slight Scottish brogue. "Mrs. Alston is dressing for the evening. She's chairing a benefit dinner for Bay Area drug prevention centers." A note of pride sounded in her voice. "May I tell her who's calling?"

"Actually, it's Mr. Alston I was hoping to see. My name is Lea Sherwood. I wanted to talk to him about Francine Reese."

A cloud passed over the woman's face, and she raised a hand to her heart. "Oh, the poor lady who died last night! So young, and so bright and vivacious."

Lea stifled a retort. She would hardly choose those terms to describe Francine. More like high-strung, insecure, and bossy. Mrs. McGredy, however, seemed genuinely affected.

"Did you know her?" Lea inquired.

"She was here in the spring for a dinner party, and very high-spirited she was. I remember she and Miss Georgeanne raved about my *charlotte Russe*."

Lea followed Mrs. McGredy into the tiled foyer and waited as she went to tell Bennett that Lea was here. So Georgeanne and Francine had known each other.

Soon the housekeeper returned and led Lea to the library. "Mr. Alston will be with you soon," she said pleasantly.

Lea smiled her thanks, relieved that Bennett had chosen to observe the proprieties rather than expel her from the grounds. She stood in the center of the room and surveyed it with interest. The walls were entirely paneled in walnut, and the built-in shelves held fine collections of leather-bound books. Lea crisscrossed the richly hued Kirman carpet to

study them. Bennett's taste was grounded in the classics—
he appeared to have the complete works of Victor Hugo,
Jane Austen, and Henry James—but extended to such
modern authors as Eliot, Fitzgerald, Rattigan, and O'Neill.
The room was a refuge of gentility. If Bennett were
threatened with the loss of all this, Lea wondered, how would
he react?

She sank into a tufted red leather chair as late afternoon
sunlight streamed through the French doors. Idly, Lea
contrasted the ideal modern home with that of a century
ago. Gone entirely was the library. In its place was a sterile
"media room" with a wide-screened television. The dining
room had likewise been usurped by the "family room," in
actuality an extension of the kitchen but stocked with
couches and often another TV. Sofas in the kitchen were
bad enough, but Lea could not bear the thought of hearing
prating commercials as she cooked. Worst of all, the
banishment of the dining room threatened to abolish the
art of conversation. Lea had once advanced the opinion to
Brooke, only partially tongue-in-cheek, that the "family
room" was in fact a pernicious contributor to the decline of
western civilization.

Bennett entered the room brusquely, interrupting her
reverie. He was dressed in black tie.

"Miss Sherwood, I have very little time, as you can see,"
he said, gesturing to his attire. "My housekeeper said you
had additional news about Francine Reese?"

Lea was taken aback. Had Bennett only agreed to see
her because Mrs. McGredy had misinterpreted her message?

"Actually, I came to ask you a few questions about
Francine," Lea replied.

Bennett scowled and remained silent. Only the entrance
of Mrs. McGredy served to remind him of his manners. He
took a seat opposite Lea in an upholstered wing chair as the
housekeeper advanced with an ornate silver tray bearing a
decanter of amber-hued liquid and two crystal glasses.
"Sherry?" Mrs. McGredy inquired.

Lea nodded, deeming it impolitic not to accept. She suppressed a smile as Mrs. McGredy poured. Bennett was obviously struggling to maintain the facade of genial host.

Once the housekeeper had left the room, however, Bennett eyed Lea stonily. "I regard it as incredibly impudent of you to disturb me at home, Miss Sherwood. Let's make this as brief as possible." Bennett's bushy eyebrows formed a "V" as he frowned.

Lea took a sip of sherry and put down her glass. Perhaps she could establish some common ground. Surely she wouldn't get anywhere by being confrontational. "I was just admiring your collection of Henry James," she said. She glanced around the room. "His characters would feel right at home here."

Bennett thawed slightly. "Yes, I suppose they would. Do you enjoy James, Miss Sherwood?"

"Very much. I think *The Golden Bowl* is my favorite of his novels. I just reread it last year."

Bennett almost smiled. "Indeed, four exceptional people; four unfulfilled lives. A literary tour de force. How sad that of all of James' extraordinary work, the average person has read only *The Turn of the Screw*."

Lea leaned back in her chair and nodded. Mindful of the time, however, she pressed on. "I know this must be a sad day for you, Mr. Alston. I understand Francine Reese was a friend of yours."

"A friend?" Bennett said, his suspicions rearoused.

"Your housekeeper said you had her to dinner not long ago."

Bennett stiffened. "Miss Sherwood, surely you are sophisticated enough to know that one does not always work or dine with people for whom one feels unalloyed affection. We frequently have dinner parties to which we invite business colleagues."

"What was your personal opinion of Francine, then? I must confess that I found her rather trying."

A corner of Bennett's mouth twitched. "Ah, there lies the problem. I found her on the whole impetuous. Not a disciplined thinker. If you must know, I was extremely distressed at her suggestion that Keith persuaded her to doctor our books. It's preposterous. I hold her fully accountable for any damage we've sustained."

"Do you think Francine might have been siphoning off company funds?"

"I do, yes. I also had thought it likely that she killed Keith when he found out about it." Bennett turned up a hand. "Now, however, I don't know what to think."

"Do you have any idea who might have taken your car last night?"

"Beyond the obvious, that it was someone who knew me, no."

Lea's eyes strayed to a framed photograph of Georgeanne and Bennett on his writing table. "I've met your daughter, Mr. Alston. She's quite intelligent."

"Yes, she is," he said, obviously surprised that they had met.

"I don't suppose she stops by the office much anymore."

"Not since Keith Whitten died," he replied coldly.

"If you don't mind my asking, why were you so opposed to Georgeanne seeing Keith?"

Bennett lifted his sherry to his lips with a cultivated air. "I fail to see what concern it is of yours, Miss Sherwood. It is entirely a personal matter."

"Georgeanne said that you and Keith had your differences."

"Naturally. That is to be expected."

Lea decided to play devil's advocate. "But everyone says Keith was brilliant, and he was successful. Why would you object to him as a potential son-in-law?"

Bennett rested his elbows on his chair arms and wove his fingers together. With deliberation, he crossed a long leg, pointing his toes toward the floor. He could have been auditioning as host of *Masterpiece Theatre*. "Unfortunately, like many entrepreneurs"—Bennett gave the word a pejorative twist—"Keith combined a technical aptitude with an intellectual immaturity. In all but the technical sphere, his was a narrowness of vision. I had to act as his advisor in a number of corporate affairs."

Lea raised her eyebrows. Yet Bennett appeared to be perfectly serious. As she searched for the proper response, Lea recalled a joke Harry had told her—the one about the techie who considered a well-timed belch the epitome of social repartee. Unbidden, images of Keith came to mind. Yes, he'd had his rough edges, but he hadn't been a yokel. And had Bennett really fancied himself as the power behind the throne? If he was that deluded, where else might his faulty judgment have led him?

"One thing has been bothering me," Lea said. "What did you mean when you told Keith that he would get the company in trouble?"

Bennett's eyes darkened. "Where did you hear this?"

Lea hesitated. She didn't want to implicate Georgeanne. "I don't remember, precisely. There's been so much speculation as to why Keith might have been killed."

"Well, I would advise you to spread this rumor no further. No such conversation ever took place. It is wholly unfounded. Moreover, on behalf of the company, I could sue you for slander. Such speculation could impair our stock price and erode our market position."

Lea gawked at Bennett, wondering if he was aware of his own *non sequitur*. Surely Paul, as chief executive officer, would not allow Bennett to sue her, which in itself would generate negative publicity. But she supposed Bennett was used to having his bluster rewarded with acquiescence. Still, why was he so sensitive on this point? What was he trying to conceal? Something that would reflect unfavorably on his own actions as legal caretaker?

As if to forestall more questions, Bennett stood up abruptly and glanced at his watch. "I must say good-bye now, Miss Sherwood. My wife will be frantic if we are late to her cherished affair. She has been working on the preparations for months." Bennett's tone of voice was impartial, but his eyes were like ice. "Mrs. McGredy will see you out."

Without waiting for her response, Bennett Alston turned his back on Lea and strode stiffly from the room.

19

Lea arrived at SFO with 12 minutes to spare. She followed the signs to the international terminal, parked the Renault, and took the elevator up to the gate area. Dodging an Irish tour group and giggling Italian girls hugging skateboards, she made her way to the overhead monitors and scanned the list of arrivals—theoretically, Sydney's flight from Vancouver was on time.

The duty free court was thronged with Asian passengers clutching shopping bags from tony San Francisco shops. They crowded into the *udon* bar, ordering noodle dishes, as an apparently urgent message in Japanese was broadcast over the loudspeaker.

Lea glanced at the cocktail lounge, dimly lit even in daytime, and did a double take. A man who could be Paul's twin was seated in a far corner, absorbed in conversation. His companion was a slight Asian man, his torso wreathed in curls of cigarette smoke. Lea watched for several moments. The man who resembled Paul shook his head vehemently, and the other man leaned forward, jabbing a finger into the air to make a point. They appeared to be arguing.

Moving on, Lea paused before a glass display case filled with geodes and imposing slabs of raw jade. The airport was known for its eclectic exhibits; this month it was marine life and geological specimens. Lea studied a coconut crab six times the size of her hand, and a giant clam at least two feet high.

Her curiosity was piqued again when she glimpsed the Asian man and his companion leaving the cocktail lounge. They walked a short distance to the security check-in area, where the tall, familiar fellow turned in her direction. Now there was no question: it was Paul.

Lea watched as he stooped and shook hands, almost reluctantly, with the Asian, who then went through security. The man quickly reclaimed his briefcase and some keys, strode down the concourse, and melted into the crowd. Lea turned back to intercept Paul only to see him enter an elevator, apparently headed for the garage.

Rather than yell to him across the crowded terminal, she checked her watch and darted over to the security check-in line. Maybe she could follow the Asian man to his gate.

A portly security agent quickly stopped her, however. "Your ticket and ID, miss?" he asked. She attempted to explain, but he took her by the elbow and pointed to a sign forbidding unticketed passengers from proceeding to the gates.

Frustrated, Lea backtracked to the monitors and scanned the list of departing flights. Within the hour, planes would leave for Osaka, Guam, Taipei, Stockholm, and Bangkok.

Lea was still puzzling over Paul's apparently clandestine meeting when Sydney waved at her and called her name.

"You'll never guess who I saw while I was waiting for you," Lea said after they'd collected Sydney's luggage and were driving back to the city.

Sydney gave her a sidelong glance and raised an eyebrow.

"Paul was in one of the airport cocktail lounges talking to an Asian guy."

"So?"

"So why is he taking precious time out of his day to drive to SFO to meet someone? Why didn't the guy go to Paul's office instead?"

"He had a short layover?" Sydney frowned. "I hate to say this, Lea, but I've been worried about you lately. I don't like seeing you so consumed by what's happening at Whitten Systems. Maybe you're reading too much into things. Like this business with the Asian bloke."

Something snapped in her. "Damn it!" Lea cried. "What on earth do you expect me to do?" As she spoke, she felt a stab of pain. Now even Sydney doubted her.

Sydney didn't reply for several moments. "I was only trying to help," she said at last.

Lea bit her lip. "I'm sorry."

Sydney was quiet again.

"It's not just the restaurant, you know," Lea said when Sydney didn't respond. "I'm worried about Paul."

"You really do love him, don't you?" Sydney said wonderingly, turning in her seat to stare at Lea.

"Does that surprise you?"

"A little."

Lea started and was on the verge of another sharp retort when Sydney said hastily, "Oh, I don't mean it surprises me about you in particular. I just mean that I'm always a little amazed when people fall in love and believe it can last. I guess because I've never had much luck in that department."

"You had Tom," Lea said, referring to the man Sydney had seen for a year when they were living in Brussels. "He was a good man."

"Exactly. And we couldn't make it work. Tom wanted to, but he was so *private*. It was such a struggle trying to get him to open up." Sydney sighed. "Typical Englishman. And I guess I was too independent. I resented his wanting to know where I was whenever I wasn't working."

"Are you saying you don't expect to ever get married?"

"I'm saying I'm ambivalent about it. And that love can lead you astray. You have to be very careful you don't compromise yourself in order to maintain a relationship. Or get so invested in it that you lose track of your own priorities."

"Is that what you think I'm doing?"

"I don't know, Lea." Sydney shifted uncomfortably in her seat. "I do know your life would be far simpler if you weren't so wrapped up in Paul."

"Thanks for the advice," Lea said, taking her eyes off the road to give Sydney an enigmatic smile. "I'll definitely consider the source."

W hen they arrived at Panache, Sydney went to the locker room to don her chef's whites, and Lea, who was to fill in that night for an ailing meat cook, followed. After changing, she tied her hair back into a ponytail and slipped her feet into a pair of well-worn clogs.

In the kitchen, all was ready. The pantry, fish, meat, hot vegetable, and pastry stations were fully stocked. Arrayed before the cooks on one side of the line, in clear plastic containers, were the products of hours of prep work: peeled asparagus; morels braised with virgin olive oil, garlic, and shallots; saffron potatoes; roasted red peppers; coral butter; squash blossoms; garnishes of chives and other herbs; lobster oil; basil oil; and the other myriad ingredients required to execute the dishes on the menu.

The six line cooks stood poised expectantly, waiting for the first wave of orders. They appeared intent, like runners at the starting line. All in their 20s or early 30s, they were graduates of culinary academies and veterans of two or more restaurant kitchens. Sydney stood opposite the cooks, ready to direct the flow of orders. Lea took her place at the meat station at the end of the line.

At 7:00, Sydney began to pace. "We've got five parties seated, four more due any minute, and still no orders. Everything's going to come in at once!" she snapped. Sydney wagged her head and swiveled to confront Robert, who had just entered the kitchen. "Tell your cohorts to get their orders in!" Sydney lowered her chin, hunched her shoulders, and resumed pacing.

Several minutes later, the first orders of the night whirred out of the tiny terminal on the counter beside Sydney. A ripple of electricity ran through the kitchen. Sydney snatched the order tickets and separated them. She posted the white copies on the line at eye level and handed the yellow copies to the appropriate stations. "Fire a halibut and a crab," Sydney yelled. The cooks sprang into action.

By 7:25, the kitchen had reached fever pitch. The intensity was almost palpable. As the heat rose from the stoves, concentration and tension were etched in the cooks' faces. Together they danced a crazy jig, suggesting a pantomime. Arms and hands flew as six bodies pivoted and spun, from counter to stove and back again. Under pressure, no cooks spoke except Sydney.

A dozen aromas mingled into one heady rush of gastronomic scent. One might as well post signs: "Caution. Olfactory Swoon Area."

Servers virtually exploded into the kitchen to snatch up plates. "Behind you, behind you!" they cried urgently, dashing within inches of one another while hoisting loaded trays.

"Five abalone left. Tell all your friends," Sydney barked to Robert on his way out. Sydney's eyes darted up and down the line. Her every sense was alert; no detail escaped her. Her brow furrowed as she checked each finished plate to wipe a dribble of sauce or correct a garnish.

At the rear of the kitchen, pots and pans clattered as the dishwashers raced to keep up with the cooks.

To the uninitiated onlooker, Lea realized it must all resemble barely controlled frenzy. Yet, like a theatre presentation, the production of more than 100 dinners a night was the result of an elaborate orchestration involving cooks, waiters, and even dishwashers. Every member of the ensemble was attuned to the nuances of the other players, and each reacted nimbly to the unexpected. Each night, they gave a virtuoso performance.

For the next two hours, time flew as Lea lost herself in her work. One of her specials that night was rack of lamb, and orders for it proved steady. When demand finally slowed to a trickle, Lea stepped away from the hot stove, grabbed a glass of ice water, and sighed. She just might break even tonight. For Panache to be viable over the long-term, however, the rush would have to continue for another hour, at least.

As she placed one more rack of marinated lamb in the oven, Lea's thoughts strayed back to the airport and to Paul. Something about his companion had been strange. Not only had he seemed, well, seedy, but he had exuded an arrogance that she wouldn't expect of a business colleague or a client. It was almost as though he'd had some hold over Paul.

Lea was still brooding over the incident when Dominique pulled Jayne, the new server, aside. The two huddled nearby.

"Maybe no one has mentioned this to you," Lea overheard Dominique say, "but we never remove an appetizer or dinner plate from a table until everyone there has finished eating. I noticed you just took a single plate from Table 14."

Jayne's eyes widened in surprise. "That's what we did at my last restaurant. What's wrong with it?"

"It's a little rude," Dominique answered.

"Not only that, it's barbaric!" Sydney, who had sharp ears, interjected. "You might as well throw the bones over your shoulder." She waved an order ticket at Jayne. "Dining is a social occasion. If you take one or two plates away, it makes those who are still eating uncomfortable. Or worse, they'll think you're trying to get rid of them so you can seat another table. Either way, the mood is broken." Sydney frowned. "M. Beaulieu in Brussels once fired a waiter for removing plates before everyone had finished. But if you're lucky, perhaps Lea will give you another chance."

Lea, who'd been annoyed a moment before—she'd made a point of telling Jayne herself about the plates—now smiled at the young woman. Jayne had grown pale, and Lea reminded herself that excess criticism can backfire. "You'll do just fine," she said.

After the last diners had left, Lea clicked on the light in the wine cellar and stooped to replace a bottle of old Bordeaux a customer had decided against.

As she rose, the lights suddenly went out. Strong hands shoved her against the wall and then thrust her to the floor. She tried to stand, but the hands forced her down again. Wobbling on one knee, Lea was unprepared for what came next.

Smack! Lea heard as much felt the blow against the base of her skull. In an instant, she was clubbed again. She screamed as pain exploded, radiating from her neck to the back of her eyes. Shooting stars gyrated against a field of black.

She turned groggily, attempting to confront her attacker. In the dim light, she could barely discern a slight, young Asian man with a thin mustache. In his hands was a wine bottle. Lea cowered as he pitched it to the floor, followed by another and yet another bottle. Jagged splinters pricked her face. She reeled and ducked as wine gushed everywhere, drenching her.

His anger spent, the man grabbed Lea, pinning her to the wall. His breath was hot against her cheek, and his face was contorted with rage. "Let this be a warning to you. In the future, stay out of our way." Then he spun on his heel and fled.

20

Lea, Sydney, and Gerard stood amid the shards of broken glass in the wine cellar the next morning. Along the walls, splinters lodged in virtually every nook and cranny of the custom wine racks. The room reeked of stale Cabernet Sauvignon.

Gerard groaned. "That thug smashed four bottles of the Jacquesson," he said sadly. "That was Napoleon's favorite Champagne."

"Look at this," Sydney said, pointing to stained labels scattered in the rubble. "Three bottles of the Pol Roger. Churchill's favorite."

Lea fingered her throbbing temples. She did not know how she would get through the day. After the attack last night, Sydney had driven her to the emergency room, where she was treated for a mild concussion, and to the police station, where she reported the attack. Now she awaited her insurance adjuster. Capping her misery was the discovery that the invader had smashed a rare Nebuchadnezzar of Chateau Lafite in the restaurant's foyer—a gift from her father on opening night.

Gerard nudged a jagged crescent moon of glass aside with his foot. "I'm so sorry I wasn't here last night. Maybe I could have stopped him somehow."

"I'm the one who should feel wretched," Sydney said. "I was in the kitchen when the beast barged in. By the time I heard the ruckus, it was too late."

Lea attempted a lighter note. "Well, Gerard, if you had been with us, you could have helped Sydney convince the hospital staff that I wasn't a total degenerate. You should have seen the looks I got when they smelled the alcohol fumes. Wino city."

Gerard gave her a melancholy smile. After another look around, he and Sydney left for the kitchen.

Lea leaned against a wall and cocked her head, attempting to estimate the damage. Suddenly she felt dizzy. Her mind flashed back to the first disorienting moment of the attack. A shooting pain erupted at the point of contact, and she gingerly fingered the bump on her head. She forced herself to take a deep breath.

Concentrate on the task at hand, she told herself severely. She consulted her itemized inventory lists. The Jacquesson and Pol Roger had been purchased from the old cellars of Angelina's when the landmark restaurant had closed after 27 years; they were now almost irreplaceable. All told, about 45 bottles had been destroyed. She estimated that the loss, at current retail value, would come to over $3,000.

Lea was startled by an affable voice behind her. "Ms. Sherwood? I'm Herb Picetti, your claims adjuster. Your staff told me to come on back here." They shook hands, and the man's mouth dropped open. "Well, well. It looks like someone threw quite a party, no pun intended."

Lea mustered a small smile.

"You're not going to tell me you had an earthquake, are you?" he teased. "Your policy doesn't cover earthquakes."

As calmly as she could, Lea described what had happened.

"Hmmm, I see," he murmured. He squinted at the damaged wine racks and ran a finger along the wood. "The tricky part is determining the value of your loss. I don't know much about wine, but I imagine that if I went shopping, I'd find varying prices for any given bottle. Normally we'd give you the lowest price. But in a case like this, where it would be next to impossible to determine the cost of so many individual bottles, we'll probably just ballpark it and make you an offer."

Lea's heart skipped a beat. "Actually, I think some of these wines are unavailable commercially. There are probably just a few bottles in private cellars around town."

Herb Picetti nodded with regret. "That makes it even tougher. I know you've got documentation on your original purchase costs, but I also know that wine can depreciate as well as appreciate in value." He pointed to an item on her proffered list. "Take this fancy Jackson Champagne here, or however you pronounce it. Who's to say it hasn't turned to swill? It's your word against ours as to what it would cost." Picetti extracted a surviving bottle of Zinfandel from its niche along the wall and peered at the label. "But hey, what a way to drown your sorrows!"

He left several minutes later, whistling.

Lea went to her office and began compiling a list of the ransacked wines. She would ask Sydney and Gerard to help her call local merchants to document the value of the collection.

She was almost done when Zoe poked her head around the door. "There's a call for you, Lea. On line 2." Zoe scrunched up her nose. "It sounds like someone who thinks he's important."

Lea picked up the phone, pressed the blinking light on her telephone console, and stated her name.

"Ms. Sherwood? This is Anderson Pruett. I just got back from the Far East, and my secretary says you phoned while I was away."

Finally, the management consultant was returning her call! Lea bit her tongue in frustration. So his secretary hadn't told him she'd called earlier.

"Anyway, I thought I'd try to reach you pronto," Anderson said. "Frankly, I don't appreciate your involving me in all this." Anderson's deep voice boomed out at her, and Lea instinctively held the receiver away from her ear.

"I beg your pardon?" she said.

"I've been in touch with the San Francisco police, and I've told them everything I know. I'd rather you not bandy my name about. You're just stirring things up. It could be dangerous."

"Dr. Pruett, what could be dangerous? All I know is that Keith consulted you shortly before he died."

"Yes, and I most emphatically regret that. It's possible that it may have contributed to his death."

"But how?" She was aware that she sounded shrill.

"Ms. Sherwood. I don't know you. I don't owe you anything. But I will offer you a bit of advice. We are dealing with people who can be ruthless if someone interferes with their business. I don't intend to implicate myself any further. And if I were you, I'd stop asking questions about Keith Whitten's death. And that is all, Ms. Sherwood, that I have to say."

Lea started to protest but was met by a click, then a dial tone. She stared at the phone in her hand. Was Anderson Pruett always so testy, or did his brusqueness mask genuine fear?

The throbbing in her skull signaled that it was time to take more aspirin. Gingerly, she brushed the lump at the back of her head. She could hardly dismiss Pruett's warning. She had first-hand evidence that caution was indicated.

As she tried to digest the implications of his message, she was startled by yet another call. It was on an extension she had given only to several people. Hoping it was Paul, she picked up the receiver. Instead she heard her father's gravelly voice.

"Dad, is everything all right?" Lea asked in surprise. Mentally she calculated the time difference between San Francisco and Turkey. She braced herself for bad news.

"That's exactly what we were wondering."

Lea paused, taken aback by his evident concern. "What do you mean?"

"You're mother and I are in London for a few days at a conference. When we were walking to dinner, we saw a story in one of the tabloids. All about what's been happening in San Francisco. Something wild about two unsolved murders and an attack on you in your wine cellar. We didn't know how much to believe."

Written up in a London tabloid! Lea felt a jolt of mortification. The whole story spilled out as she tried to reassure her father, although the more she told him, the more sordid the tale sounded.

Then she repeated it all for her mother's benefit.

"Lea, dear, I'll get on the next plane," Joan Sherwood said, her normally warm voice subdued. "You shouldn't be alone to deal with all this. I'll call the airlines right now."

"No, it's all right. Please don't go to all that trouble," Lea protested bravely. She talked to her mother for several more minutes and continued to insist that she'd be fine, although privately she wasn't so sure. She promised to call if she needed anything and hung up.

Lea buried her face in her hands and fought back a wave of self-pity. Her entire life was in limbo. If only she could discover if the police were making any progress! Brooke, she knew, had mined all her sources on Lea's behalf. Either the SFPD was keeping an extraordinarily tight lid on the case, or the police had little to report. Lea toyed with the notion of calling Carter Weberling, the venture capitalist. Paul had told her he was friendly with Matt Fitzgerald, the police commissioner. It was worth a try, she decided. Ignoring the incessant pounding in her head, Lea picked up the phone.

T he fog was lifting at 11:10 when Lea left for Carter's office. Patches of blue sky were visible through the dissolving haze, and swirls of mist encircled the spires of the city's skyscrapers.

Lea headed west on Pacific through the heart of the old Barbary Coast. "Terrific Pacific," as the sailors and prospectors of the 1850s had called it, was one of her favorite streets. If she closed her eyes, she could almost imagine the saloons, opium dens, and bordellos where sailors had been shanghaied and carried off to sea. Today, in their stead, were genteel antique shops and trendy interior design studios.

At Montgomery, Lea turned south. She recalled reading as a child that the discovery of gold was announced here, triggering the Gold Rush, and that Mark Twain and Bret Harte had lived nearby. Soon she passed the copper plaque commemorating the site of the Pony Express office.

Lea smiled. The old sourdoughs wouldn't recognize Montgomery today. The street had evolved into a narrow, shadowed canyon bordered by soaring office towers. Instead of carousing sailors or prospectors, it was thronged by men and women in business suits, and the old marshalling site for gold prospecting was now the hub of a financial network with instant access to markets in Europe and the Pacific Rim.

The jangle of an approaching cable car reminded Lea that she was nearing California Street, her destination. She turned the corner and encountered a knot of tourists, scantily dressed in shorts and T-shirts. They shivered in the wind, perusing a map. Evidently they had not heard—or heeded—Twain's observation that the coldest winter he ever spent was a summer in San Francisco. Farther on, three Japanese businessmen, bent over by the weight of luggage, hailed a yellow cab that jerked to a stop, narrowly averting a bicycle messenger who raced to beat a changing light.

Lea located Carter's building and took the elevator to the 28th floor. There she found the corner suite that housed his venture capital partnership, entered, and gave the receptionist her name. Moments later she was ushered into his glass-paneled office, where the towers of the financial district loomed against the backdrop of a cerulean bay.

Carter greeted her warmly, and Lea settled into a leather chair in the conversation area of the room. Carter took a seat catty-corner from her. On his bookshelves were tomes on the role of technology in society. A console table held stacks of what looked like business plans by start-ups eager to win his backing.

Carter followed Lea's gaze. "Each plan represents a dream," he said. "But for every hundred I see, I can fund only one. And of the lucky few chosen, only one in seven goes on to become an Apple or a Netscape." Carter leaned back in his chair. "It's tricky picking a winner. Some firms seem to have it all—a great idea, brilliant people—and it still doesn't work out. Maybe because of poor management, bad timing, or even bad luck. But for every start-up that hits it big, there are hundreds of shattered dreams."

"What about Paul?" Lea asked. "He had a great start, and then...."

"A bitter setback when we sold his firm," Carter finished her thought. "I wouldn't count Paul out yet, though. He's still young, and he'll have new opportunities." Carter smiled. "In this business, you develop a sense of what makes a good entrepreneur. Knowing *who* to back is as important—maybe more so—than knowing what to back. A good entrepreneur has to be able to thrive in an environment of tension and chaos, fueled by his doubts as well as his obsessions. After all, he's trying to create out of thin air what amounts to a new reality, based only on his ideas.

"I've also learned that a guy with experience is a better bet than a guy with just the education. But it's important that people have character and, while it may sound archaic, a sense of honor. Paul has both. He's also got the ability to recognize his mistakes. And he can strike a balance between getting excited by the technology and developing useful products. Most of all, he has strong convictions. That's essential."

The receptionist entered the room with a pink and white, flowered china tea service and placed it on the antique English table between them. She poured a fragrant Darjeeling into delicately sculpted cups and inquired as to whether they preferred cream or lemon.

As she poured, Lea studied Carter. At 59, he had an air of distinction. Thick silver hair capped a strong brow, and his clear, intelligent gray eyes conveyed the impression that he could quickly take your measure. Lea knew he had started his own engineering firm in his early 30s and had sold it four years later to an international consortium, thus generating seed money for his first venture capital fund. He had backed a number of the spectacular success stories in Silicon Valley and today held shares in over 30 firms; he sat on the boards of more than 10. Carter was also fit, Lea knew, from 3-mile morning runs between his Pacific Heights home and San Francisco Bay. He kept a 55-foot sailboat at the yacht club, and he and June, his wife of 36 years, often took it out for overnight trips.

Yet for all his wealth and influence, Carter struck Lea as a modest, thoughtful man. His manner was soft-spoken and genial. His passion, she knew, was his work, which he pursued upwards of 80 hours a week.

After the receptionist had gone, Carter was pensive. "You know, I feel extremely fortunate. I can't think of a more exciting field to be in. When you get inventions coming across your desk every day—ideas that can change the world—it's just so rewarding. Having the chance to shape technological change and transform industries is a dream come true for me. You get caught up in the rush, the euphoria of creating companies that are on the cutting edge. And there's nothing like watching people buck overwhelming odds to realize a dream. Getting to know these people—being a mentor to some of the best minds in the world—it's all fascinating to me."

Lea listened with growing appreciation. She could see why Paul thought so highly of Carter. Still, she longed to know if he really believed Paul could weather the current crisis. Just last night she had overheard a customer gossiping that Paul was on his way out as president of Whitten Systems.

Carter smiled sympathetically, as if he could read her thoughts. "I know you're worried about Paul. All I can say is

I hope and trust that reason will prevail among the board. It would be a terrible mistake to let Paul go now."

Lea had a sinking feeling. So it was true. The board was actually debating whether to dump him.

"I also know how frustrated Paul is with the job," Carter said. "And I can appreciate how he feels. I know what it's like to need to make full use of your mind—to immerse yourself in intellectual challenges. Instead, Paul is struggling to solve marketing and personnel problems not of his making in a highly politicized environment."

Carter paused to sip his tea. "It's interesting. The people who start companies usually aren't the ones who end up running them. A lot of entrepreneurs can't make the transition. By nature, they're risk takers. They bring the vision and energy to launch a firm. The qualities that make them good entrepreneurs mitigate against their succeeding as corporate managers. You can imagine, a guy who thinks and moves fast—who's willing to risk it all—can be a threat to a company once it reaches a certain size. He's too used to doing everything himself. Or he may be brilliant technically but lacks a grasp of production techniques, or of markets or finance. And sometimes a company just grows too fast, so you have to bring in someone else to run it.

"I suspect that Paul is one of those people who can fill both roles. That's why I put myself on the line to give him the chance." Carter had a faraway look. "I remember what it's like, you know. You get a high from trying to solve every problem thrown at you, whether it's technological, political, or financial."

"But Paul is bucking his own board. And his staff isn't behind him."

Carter frowned. "I know. He has his work cut out for him. The problems at Whitten Systems are far more extensive than we knew at the outset. And the people Keith Whitten surrounded himself with...." Carter shrugged. "All I can say is, when you're committed to doing your best, it's maddening to work with others who aren't."

Lea smiled ruefully. Talk about an understatement.

Carter's next words surprised her.

"You know, I've heard the vulture capitalist jokes that are making the rounds. And believe me, it isn't amusing being regarded as a scavenger who preys on the hard work of others." Carter sighed. "This business can definitely foster love-hate relationships. I know how disappointed Paul was in me when I made the decision to sell his company. But throwing more money after a problem isn't always the solution."

Lea shifted in her chair, uneasy at the direction of the conversation.

Carter noticed and gave her a reassuring look. "But that isn't why you came to see me. You've been sitting here patiently while I expounded. Now, tell me. What can I do for you?"

She took a deep breath. It wasn't easy to reveal her fears to a man like Carter. "I'm worried about the murder investigation," she said haltingly. "From what I hear, the police aren't getting any closer to finding the killer." Lea could hear the tremor in her voice. "Unless it's cleared up soon, I stand to lose Panache. And Paul and I will both have a cloud over us for the rest of our lives."

"I know," Carter said. "I was thinking about it before you arrived."

"Could I ask what Matt Fitzgerald has told you?"

Carter's eyes were troubled. "At the moment, the chief is furious at the stonewalling he's getting from Keith's inner circle. He's convinced that something's not right."

Lea sensed that Carter was holding something back. "What about Paul and me?"

He hesitated. "Apparently the police have a witness who's made damaging statements— either about you or Paul. The chief wouldn't tell me more than that."

Lea felt a sudden chill. Could they be taking Francine's ranting seriously?

"He did assure me that no one would be arrested without solid evidence, just to appease the public appetite." Carter was silent for a moment. "I know you're in an awkward position, Lea, but we'll just have to give it time. I'm sure it will all get resolved in the end."

Lea thanked Carter for his time and hastily got to her feet.

Carter rose too and walked her to the door, where he gave her a fatherly pat on the shoulder.

She mustered a tremulous smile and had barely managed to close his door behind her when tears began streaming down her cheeks.

L ea fretted all during the lunch service as Carter's discouraging words echoed in her ears. Sydney urged her to take her doctor's advice and go home to rest, but Lea knew she'd only feel sorry for herself cooped up alone.

When the last meals were served, she went to the kitchen to tell Sydney and Gerard about Anderson Pruett's phone call. Maybe together they could make sense out of it.

"What do you think?" Lea asked after she had repeated the conversation.

"Hmmm. I was just reading about all the industrial espionage that goes on in Silicon Valley," Sydney said. "And this Pruett bloke just got back from Asia, where they crave American technology. Maybe Keith hired Pruett to investigate some suspected espionage. Is there any indication that Whitten Systems designs have been stolen?"

"Not so far."

"Maybe Whitten Systems was a takeover target," Gerard suggested eagerly. "Maybe someone was about to stage a hostile takeover and Keith wanted Pruett's help to fight them."

"Oh, you and your Machiavellian corporate schemes!" Sydney snapped. "You listen to too much market commentary."

Gerard, unfazed, sipped a glass of ice water. "No, think about it. Until lately, the company has been highly profitable, has it not? Maybe somebody uncovered the fact that something was wrong with their books. That could amount to a lot of leverage. They could buy the company at a fire-sale price."

"Maybe," Lea said dubiously. "But now that the news is out and the stock has dropped, it's an even better takeover target."

"Could someone have leaked the news for that purpose?" Sydney asked. "Maybe someone inside the company is working with a corporate raider."

"It seems obvious that Marshall leaked it," Lea said. "But I think he did it to discredit Paul. Never mind that all the damage was done before Paul's watch."

"Investors can be fickle," Gerard said. "If they don't get a quick turnaround on their money, they sometimes start pushing for another CEO."

"What about the Pacific Rim angle?" Sydney asked. "That must figure in somehow."

"Maybe someone was selling pirated copies of Whitten Systems' software in the Far East," Gerard said. "Keith could have hired Pruett to check it out."

"I guess," Lea said. "Paul says there are bootleg copies of software all over Asia. But it's a problem every Silicon Valley software firm faces. I don't see why Keith would hire a consultant on his own." Lea remembered the fear in Anderson Pruett's voice. He had stumbled onto something far more serious, she felt sure.

"What did Paul say about Pruett's call?" Gerard asked.

With a start, Lea realized that she hadn't even told Paul about trying to reach the consultant. She also hadn't told him about the attack on her last night.

"Uh, I haven't talked to Paul yet today."

Sydney shot her a penetrating look. "I think Paul would agree with your Dr. Pruett in one important respect."

"What's that?" Lea couldn't imagine what Sydney was talking about.

"I mean," she said with exaggerated patience, "that you should bloody well watch your step."

21

Lea sat in her office at 10:30 A.M. two days later, a cup of coffee untouched beside her. She felt numb. In the past half hour she had hired attorney Donna Eskey to defend her in the lawsuit brought by her investors, and she'd laid off Todd and Heather from her lunch staff. Her employees, knowing how hard it had been for her, had tried to cheer *her* up.

She attempted to rouse herself, but a sadness persisted. Her life was unraveling. How she wished she were smarter—perhaps then she'd see a way out of her predicament. Then she laughed at herself. Paul was smarter, and he was no better off. And of course Keith had been smarter, and it had done him no good.

Lea was still in a bleak mood after lunch as she changed from the fitted black suit she often wore to greet lunch guests into a more comfortable sweater and slacks.

In the kitchen, she found Gerard hunched by the radio, engrossed in the stock market report. Apparently it had been a listless day on Wall Street. Or, as the broadcaster put it: "Indifference is rising to a fever pitch!"

Gerard clucked. He had been nervous about the market ever since he'd bought a biotech stock at 50 and it had plunged to 34. He also seemed pale, and uncharacteristically irritable.

"Is anything wrong?" Lea asked.

"Just that I hardly got any sleep last night," he retorted. "The guy next door played Souza marches until past midnight. Then the woman downstairs blasted Gregorian chants. *Tiens!* As a boy I used to enjoy those chants in chapel, but now I don't know if I'll ever be able to listen to them again!"

Sydney smirked. "If this were anywhere but San Francisco, I'd say you were pulling my leg. However, I offer the perfect solution. I started reading a biography of Violet Makepeace-Cornwall." She glanced at Lea and Gerard for signs of recognition. "You know, the British stage actress? Well, the book is nothing but a hagiography. The author chap is pitifully smitten with her, fawning really. To hear him tell it, the woman was a saint. After three chapters I was so bored I just nodded off. But I can unconditionally recommend it as a soporific."

As Lea started to respond, one of the servers came to the kitchen door. "Lea, someone's out here asking for you."

Lea went to the dining room, where a young woman, her back to Lea, was examining *My Inamorata*, the painting that always generated so much comment. As she turned, Lea recognized Patrice Holbrook from Paul's office—the enigmatic accountant with the gun.

"I hope I haven't come at a bad time," Patrice said. Her blond hair brushed the collar of her tailored maroon business suit; the string of pearls was again in place.

Anytime lately seems to be a bad time, Lea thought. But she said she could spare a few minutes and led Patrice to a table. As they sat down, Lea's curiosity mounted.

Patrice's manner became brisk. "You know I'm heading up the auditing team at Whitten Systems," she stated.

Lea nodded.

"Well, that's only part of the truth. What Paul hasn't told you is that I'm an investigator with a private security firm. Technically, I'm a forensic accountant. I specialize in uncovering white-collar crime."

"You mean you're an industrial *spy*?"

Patrice smiled humorlessly. "We're often called that, yes."

So that might account for the weapon, Lea reasoned. But why hadn't Paul told her? She felt a flicker of annoyance as she waited for Patrice to go on.

"I asked Paul not to tell anyone, including you. Obviously, the fewer people who know, the better. I also couldn't be sure at first that you weren't involved in Keith's death. He did die here, after you served him dinner." Patrice glanced around the room. "But I've done some background checks on you, and I'm satisfied that you're clean."

Lea didn't know whether to be annoyed or relieved. More inquiries into her private life. "Are the other auditors on your team investigators too?" she asked after a moment.

"Yes, we all work for the same firm. And unfortunately, business is booming. Computer technology is so sophisticated today that more companies than ever need our help to track down pilfered assets. I just came from a job where a guy declared bankruptcy, stiffing his creditors. Come to find out, he'd smuggled $24 million into hidden trusts."

Lea blinked. "Do you think Francine Reese could have been diverting money into a secret account?"

"It's too soon to tell. We're still in the middle of verifying corporate assets, sales, inventory, financial transactions. Just following the paper trail."

"You mean to verify things like company checks being made out to legitimate suppliers?"

"Right. Francine could have set up an account in a false vendor name and billed the company monthly. She also might not have been working alone. Francine claimed Keith authorized some accounting sleight of hand to make the company appear more prosperous, but maybe what really happened is that someone else suggested she juggle the books."

"So they could share in the profits."

"Exactly."

Lea thought back to her conversations with Francine. "I don't think she was close to anyone at the company. In fact, she seemed kind of at odds with everyone."

Patrice shrugged. "I would expect her to hide the relationship, particularly if it was with a married man."

Lea considered this. Francine had worked with Marshall, Bennett, and Randy. Presumably all were married. Randy wore a wedding ring, and Lea had seen Marshall at Keith's funeral with a woman she'd assumed to be his wife. "What happens after you've verified assets?" she asked.

"Then we get to look at personal property and bank records to see if anyone's come into any sudden wealth. It can get complicated, though. We check all the electronic databases for ownership of cars, boats, real estate, airplanes, you name it. We also check out court records on liens, bankruptcies, even assumed names." Patrice waved a hand. "But the reason I came here is to ask you about the other night. Paul told me you were assaulted just as you were closing."

Lea winced. Although the attack had occurred two days ago, she had only told Paul about it late last night.

"Can you tell me what happened?"

Lea recounted the story, her voice choking a bit as she relived the horror of being bludgeoned in the dark.

"Did you get a look at the man who did it?"

Lea shook her head ruefully. "All I remember is that he was young, maybe 23 or 24. Asian. I couldn't tell more than that," she said. "After he hit me, I saw stars. And not the kind Dom Perignon saw when he discovered Champagne."

Patrice smiled. "No, I'm sure of that. But what about the voice? Do you recall ever hearing it before?"

"It was full of venom," Lea said. She shuddered. "But did I recognize it? No."

"This may be a long-shot, but what about scents? Did you pick up on any after-shave or cologne?"

Lea shook her head again. "And I'm pretty sensitive to aromas. Most chefs are." She thought back, trying to remember more. "Wait a minute, I did get a whiff of something. There was a menthol smell, almost like a cough drop." Lea sighed. "I know that's not much help."

"Don't worry about it. I thought it was barely possible that you might have run across the guy before. Or that he said something that might tip us off." Patrice pulled a business card from her pocket. "If you do remember anything, give me a call. You can reach me at the office during the day and at this number at night." She handed Lea the card.

They got up, and Patrice faced Lea squarely. Her expression was sober. "Just be careful around these people," she said. "We still don't know who we're dealing with. Don't trust *anyone*."

Lea was about to walk Patrice to the door when Gerard burst out of the kitchen. "Lea, there's a reporter on the phone for you! I'm not sure, but I think something has happened."

Excusing herself, Lea went to the host station to take the call. When the reporter identified himself as Kenny Mariner, Lea bristled. He had a nerve! Mariner was the one who'd written all those insinuating articles about her. Surely he didn't expect her to give him a quote.

If Mariner expected a cool reception, he gave no indication of it. His voice was breathless, and self-important.

"Ms. Sherwood, we just got word that Randy Derrough is being arrested," he said without preamble. "Can you tell us more about him? Wasn't he one of the men with Keith Whitten at your restaurant the night Whitten was killed?"

Lea's mind raced. Randy arrested? "Do you mean the police are arresting him for Keith's murder?"

"Uh, we don't have confirmation of that, but we did get a tip that sheriff's deputies are at Whitten Systems to take Derrough in. We're trying to get as much background on him as we can."

Mariner went on, and Lea tried to focus on what he was asking. She could barely follow his questions.

"Ms. Sherwood, are you there?"

"Yes," she said at last. What, if anything, should she tell him? Finally she confirmed that Randy had been with Keith the night he died but pleaded ignorance as to his business or personal life. Imagine asking *her* to divulge secrets about Randy.

Mariner hung up reluctantly when Lea refused to comment further.

In a daze, Lea walked back to Patrice and Gerard, who were waiting expectantly. "You won't believe this," she said, and summarized the call.

Patrice looked alarmed. "I'd better get down there right away."

Gerard, however, smiled broadly. *"C'est merveilleux!"* he exclaimed. "Now, perhaps, things will get back to normal."

Lea shut her eyes tight for a moment. How she hoped he was right.

Patrice had started to leave when Lea grabbed her elbow. "Wait! Let me drive you down to the Peninsula. I can't stay here, twiddling my thumbs. I've got to find out what's going on!"

"All right, but let's hurry," Patrice said impatiently.

Lea ran to her office to grab her purse and then led Patrice through the kitchen and out the back door. They got into the Renault, which was parked in its space next to the alley, and neither of them spoke until Lea had driven through the financial district and onto the freeway.

"Do you think Randy Derrough killed Keith? And Francine?" Lea asked. She applied more pressure to the gas pedal. "What would be his motive?"

"I don't know," Patrice replied after several seconds. "I can't imagine what Randy would gain from their deaths." She seemed puzzled and stared absently out the car window. It was mid-afternoon on Friday, and traffic was starting to get heavy.

Lea tried to draw her out, but Patrice resisted her efforts.

Frustrated, Lea clicked on the radio and fiddled with the tuner. Hoping that the all-talk stations had the story, she switched among them with no luck. On two separate stations, Oakland and San Francisco politicians were bickering about the design alternatives for a retrofitted Bay Bridge. Lea frowned. With one eye on the road, she punched her way through the entire band of channels. Rock and roll, blue grass, light jazz, commercials, traffic bulletins. In spite of her impatience, she smiled as a helicopter reporter advised, "A pelican is holding up traffic in the right lane of the Dumbarton Bridge. But not to worry. The California Highway Patrol is on the way to shoo him off."

Nothing about Whitten Systems. Lea sighed, turned off the radio, and stole a glance at Patrice while searching for a topic of conversation that would not be off-limits. "How did you ever get into your line of work?" Lea finally thought to ask.

Patrice roused herself. "I was a prosecutor with the U.S. attorney's office in New York and then San Francisco. And I trained in finance and investigative accounting."

"Are the others at your firm lawyers too?

"Not all of them. We actually hire all types of people. We've got pros from law enforcement, tax experts, MBAs, investigative reporters, even environmental specialists."

Lea passed a Flowers by Briana delivery van that was hogging the middle lane at 40 miles an hour. "Is the work dangerous?"

"It can be. I've been in a couple of tight spots. The worst was when I set up a sting to catch a guy stealing his employer's industrial product designs. Turns out he was selling them to a counterfeiter who made a fortune selling cheap versions. I was lucky to get out of that episode with just a few broken ribs." Patrice glanced at her watch. "My folks aren't too happy about the risks I take, but I got tired of trying cases in courtrooms. And this way I get the same satisfaction I had as a prosecutor. You know, catching the bad guys."

Lea gave her a sidelong look. "What kind of firms hire you?"

"Oh, you'd be surprised. Everyone from the blue chips to start-ups. White-collar crime is rampant. As you can imagine, the high-tech industry is a huge target for thieves. All those juicy trade secrets. Same with the biotechs and pharmaceuticals. Any firm with massive R&D can lose big time if someone steals five years worth of development. Not everyone realizes it, but corporate spying costs this country billions of dollars every year."

"I used to think foreign espionage was the big problem in the Valley," Lea said.

"Oh, it still is a killer. And the spies come from countries we consider friends as well as foes. But they're all very sophisticated these days. We've come a long way from the '70s, when agents wore sticky-soled shoes to pick up shavings on the manufacturing floor. Now they steal security codes that give them access to corporate databases and voicemail."

Lea's jaw fell.

Patrice laughed. "It's even worse when Americans get off their own turf. When our clients go abroad on business, we give them travel-sized bug detectors. Not to mention insisting that they never leave their laptops in their hotel rooms."

Lea spotted their exit, and they both fell silent as she left the freeway.

Three minutes later, they arrived at Whitten Systems. Paul, however, was not in his office, and Joy was not at her desk. Patrice marched down the hall in the direction of Randy Derrough's office, with Lea right on her heels.

22

Randy was packing his belongings into a cardboard box when Lea and Patrice reached his door. A sheriff's deputy hovered at his elbow, and Joy Nugent, Bennett Alston, and another deputy conferred in the hall.

"Did Randy confess?" Lea demanded of Joy. "Did he really kill Keith and Francine?"

Joy hesitated. She looked curiously at Patrice but didn't comment on her presence. "Randy is going to be questioned by the sheriff's office," Joy said.

"About Keith's murder?" Lea persisted.

"Go ahead, tell them, Killjoy!" Randy said, hefting the box across the threshold. "Tell them how everyone here has taken leave of their senses."

"What is going on?" Lea cried in exasperation.

"Paul sicked the dogs on me," Randy said. He set the box down at his feet. "I turned in my resignation this morning, and the next thing I knew, the authorities were crawling all over me."

"That's hardly the way I would describe what happened," Bennett said. His expression was grave.

Bennett turned to Lea and Patrice. "Randy announced he was quitting all right, but what he didn't tell us was that he was relaying proprietary information to his new employer, who happens to one of our major competitors."

Randy groaned and placed his hands on his hips. "Come on, give me a break. This trade secrets stuff is crap. I know everybody pays lip service to it, but before any product gets released, half the industry's already figured out how it works. The other half uses reverse engineering to put the pieces together once the product's out the door."

Lea stared at Randy. Patrice had sketched a scenario of corporations under siege by outside predators. Whitten Systems apparently was besieged from within.

"You're vastly oversimplifying a complex issue," Bennett said to Randy. Bennett looked put upon, as if he were trying to reason with an obstinate adolescent. "You turned over our sales records and marketing plans. And by the looks of it, you've been passing on confidential pricing data for some time, well before Keith was killed. In my book, that's theft of trade secrets."

"The sales results are mine!" Randy retorted. He stuck out his chin. "I produced them. I cultivated the clients. I developed the marketing plans. And I had to reveal them to back up my worth to a prospective employer. They reflect the caliber of work I can bring to a new firm."

"What do you mean, a new firm? You're returning to Binochet Technologies," Bennett said in disbelief. "Do you know how many questions that raises? It's not exactly unheard of in this Valley to plant an employee with a competitor and then bring him back to reveal all. And you've been here only a year, which makes that possibility all the more credible." Bennett's tone was glacial. "I don't blame Paul for informing the sheriff. I'd also say you've moved to the top of the list of murder suspects. Let's see you prove that you weren't spying for your former employer and that you didn't kill Keith when he found out."

Randy sputtered. "That's garbage! I came here a year ago in good faith. Little did I know the place was a loony bin. Trying to satisfy Keith's unrealistic expectations was bad enough. But since he and Francine were murdered...." Randy scanned the faces of those assembled, seeking support.

Lea turned away in disgust. She had always wanted to believe that Silicon Valley attracted not only the best and the brightest, but the good. The last few weeks had left her sadly disillusioned.

"Even if you didn't kill Keith—and that's a big if—do you realize you could be facing felony charges?" Bennett asked.

"Why? I haven't done anything illegal," Randy asserted. He swore under his breath. "I haven't done anything that hasn't been done dozens of times before. Hey, go to any bar in the Valley after work and you'll pick up all kinds of proprietary information. Go to any trade show. Companies give away tons of sensitive information."

The sheriff's deputy who had been in Randy's office came out carrying a small case. "We found these CDs with Whitten Systems data in Derrough's briefcase," he said to Bennett. "We'll make an inventory."

An embarrassed hush fell over the group.

"Shall we take him now?" the deputy asked Bennett.

Bennett nodded, and Lea stepped aside to let them pass.

Randy, however, bore down on her. "You can remind Paul for me of that old Chinese proverb: 'Be careful what you wish for—you may get it.' Well, Paul's succeeded. He's been trying to get rid of me ever since he came here. But he hasn't seen the last of me. Not by a long shot. I fully intend to see he pays for the way he's treated me."

Lea was astounded at Randy's bitterness. "Paul's never tried to get rid of you," she protested.

"Oh, no? He's been harassing me ever since he got here."

"That's not true!" Lea insisted as a deputy picked up the box with Randy's belongings. "You've got everything twisted."

The other officer took Randy by the arm and prodded him forward.

"Of course it's true!" Randy shouted at her over his shoulder as he was led away. "And believe me, I'll see that Paul gets what's due him!"

Bennett and Joy rushed after the deputies and Randy.

"Now what?" Lea asked gloomily. She didn't know if she was more upset by Randy's threats or by the fact that Keith's killer might still be at large.

Patrice cocked her head and stared at Lea. "I don't know yet, but this is certainly a new wrinkle. I'd say it's a perfect time to start background checks on one Randy Derrough."

Paul was on the phone when Lea returned to his office, so she headed downstairs to look for Harry. She was eager to get his take on Randy's defection.

Harry was emerging from the men's room, red toothbrush in hand, when Lea caught up with him. He greeted her testily and led the way to his office.

The instant Harry entered the room he yanked off his rumpled gray T-shirt and extracted its twin from his bottom desk drawer. "Be creative at work!" Harry cried. "Join the elite and learn the secret language of society. Become a programmer!" The pale paunch of Harry's stomach jiggled as he squirmed into the clean shirt. His eyes lit up maniacally as he grabbed his scalp and pretended to tear his hair out. "I haven't left this building in 48 hours!"

Lea laughed in spite of her dour mood. "Can I talk to you?" she asked.

Harry fingered his scraggly beard and shrugged. "I guess it'll have to wait another day for a trim."

He sat down at his desk and beckoned to Lea to take the chair across from him. "I tell you, when I first started in this business, we used to talk about the conflict between programming as personal expression—even as art form—and the compromises dictated by corporate politics and budgets. Right now, I'd be happy if I could just complete a product and maintain a little personal hygiene." He grunted. "Does that make me a burned-out baby boomer?"

"How about a cyber-cynic?" Lea suggested lightly.

"That too." Harry swiveled to his computer and called up his e-mail. "Just look at me. If I didn't check my mail three times a day, I'd drown in all the messages." He scrolled down the screen. "Uh-oh. Here's another inquiry from a headhunter. My third this week. I guess they smell blood here."

Lea felt a butterfly in her stomach. "You aren't considering any offers, are you?"

Harry flashed her a look. "Truthfully? I have been evaluating one."

"I know you and Paul are having your differences...." she began lamely.

"But I shouldn't leave him in the lurch," Harry said, completing her thought. His eyes narrowed as he turned to face her. "Don't defend Paul to me."

Lea shivered. Harry had suddenly grown cold. His jaw was set, and he had the wounded air of one used to being misunderstood. What could she say that wouldn't alienate him?

"I've tried to be loyal, Lea. If only Paul would let me decide how to design our system, we'd be able to get the product out the door on time. This is definitely a case where two heads are worse than one."

Lea bit her lip.

"Don't worry," Harry said darkly. "I haven't decided anything yet."

"I just came from Randy's office," Lea said, eager to change the subject.

Harry nodded, indicating he knew all about it.

"I can't believe anyone would hand over confidential data like that."

Harry shrugged. "I suppose it might seem outrageous. But you have to remember, the Valley runs on information leaks and job-hopping. Randy's right in a way to say he hasn't done anything new."

"Oh, please. How can you exonerate him so easily?" Marshall Schroth's voice came from the doorway, and Lea turned to see him enter the office. "Personally, I think he was here to spy on us all along."

Harry scowled as Marshall came up to his desk.

"Think about it," Marshall said. "It was a good ploy. No one would be too suspicious of a *sales* manager who'd come from a competitor. And yet Randy had access to quite a bit of our technical information." Marshall smirked. "And don't forget that our sales have been dropping. While he picked our brains, he also inflicted damage. We've lost some major customers under Randy's tenure. Who knows what he told clients in private about the performance of our software? Or our resources?"

Harry gave Marshall a sour look.

"I think Randy's behavior was anything but innocent," Marshall said. "And I think it may extend further than the theft of our trade secrets."

"You mean Keith's murder?" Lea asked. "Bennett Alston brought that up, too."

Marshall observed her shrewdly. "Certainly. If Keith had discovered what Randy was up to, he would have been livid. And Keith never allowed anyone to make a fool of him. He would have taken action to ruin Randy. Naturally, Randy would have been aware of that."

Lea listened with skepticism. Marshall was conveniently omitting the fact that he had been Randy's direct supervisor. Whatever happened to responsibility up the chain of command?

Marshall leaned proprietarily against Harry's desk. "I can tell you both that Keith spoke to me in confidence about Randy just a few days before the murder. He was rather oblique, asking veiled questions, but I see now that he had his suspicions. I also saw Keith retrieving data from Randy's computer one night."

The scenario was possible, Lea acknowledged. Joy had seen Keith at Bennett's and Francine's computers. Maybe Keith really had discovered Randy's act of betrayal.

"You know, I wondered why Randy was so nervous the day of the merger," Marshall continued. "It didn't make sense to me then—he only stood to enhance his position once we combined the two firms. Now, of course, I can see that anyone might be nervous waiting for his victim to go into paroxysms from poisoning."

"Do you suppose Keith called the emergency board meeting to get advice on how to deal with Randy?" Lea asked. "Maybe to get approval to file criminal charges?"

"Exactly," Marshall said with satisfaction, contradicting his earlier claim that the meeting was to discuss the CadSure patent infringement suit.

Harry, who apparently had heard enough, stood up. "All right, what brings you slumming to the programming department?" he asked Marshall.

The marketing director laughed and held up his hands. "It'll keep until you don't have company." He hummed as he left the room.

Once Marshall had gone, Harry exhaled audibly. "That odious son of a bitch," he said. "He knows nothing about software development, but he's always in here trying to tell me how to do my job. He prides himself on seeing 'The Big Picture' and leaving the niggling details to the worker drones. The only problem is, without the details, there is no picture." Harry's voice rose. "Ideas are a dime a dozen. The history books are full of ideas for inventions that didn't work. The difficulty is in the details. All the great systems in the world— from the Pyramids to the first personal computer—are built on details. No details: no technology. What Marshall's telling me is that *I* can sweat out the details to make things work. Then he can claim credit for it!"

Lea's eyes had grown wide as Harry had spoken. But now she nodded. He definitely had a point.

"I'm sorry, Lea," Harry said. "It's just that the guy is totally removed from reality. He doesn't realize how lucky he is. He should give thanks every day that better minds than his exist. His bloated lifestyle is based on other people's achievements. If it were up to Marshall, we'd still be living in caves and hunting woolly mammoths. Do you think Marshall could develop electricity? A cure for polio? The only thing he can create is a disturbance. All he cares about is playing the role of executive. But when he interferes with me, I feel like getting a megaphone and yelling, "Earth to Marshall. Earth to Marshall."

Paul was still busy when Lea looked in on him after leaving Harry. Her head swimming with the day's revelations, Lea wandered down the hall and into the coffee room.

Joy was seated at a table eating raspberry yogurt and talking to Dennis Zaslow, the technical writer. Joy kicked off her shoes and wriggled her toes. "It's been an insane day," she said.

"I'm glad I'm not a manager of this company," Dennis stated. "One way or another, they're disappearing at a fast clip. First Keith, then Francine, now Randy. At the current attrition rate, soon there'll be no one left to run the place."

"No one's running it now," complained a woman in a halter top and jogging shorts who was taking a bottle of water from the refrigerator. Beads of perspiration clung to her forehead. She apparently had just come in from a session on the fitness trail that circled the industrial park.

Joy elbowed her and yanked her head in Lea's direction.

"Oh, sorry," the woman said to Lea. She peered at her curiously. "You must be Lea Sherwood. I've seen your picture in the papers." She swabbed her forehead with a towel. "I only meant that with everything going on here, Paul doesn't have much opportunity for real management. He has to spend all his time putting out fires."

"Well, it's making me antsy," said a second woman who was peeling an orange over the sink. Her dark bangs brushed the top of her eyes. "I just started working here, and I'd like to think I'll still have my job in six months. The last company I worked for was a start-up in San Jose. I came here after it folded."

"Just be glad you're not being paid with stock options," Dennis said. "I had to sell 200 shares of my Whitten stock at a loss this week."

Joy yawned and stretched like a sleek panther as Dennis and the two women began discussing the office softball team.

Joy was still perfectly groomed after the events of the day, and the deep vermilion staining her lips matched the hue of her clingy silk dress.

"Do you believe that Randy?" Joy asked Lea. "He sure has a nerve threatening Paul." Joy slipped her high heels back on and flexed her calf muscles. "But then he always did have a hair-trigger temper."

Lea flashed back to the first day she had come here, when Randy had argued with Paul in his office. Randy had been quick to anger, all right. But would a person who flew off the handle so easily be apt to commit a premeditated murder? She wasn't so sure.

23

Lea licked her lips and blinked under the harsh fluorescent ceiling lights. It was 9:30 on Monday morning, and she was being questioned by the SFPD. A tape recorder whirred on the scarred wooden table where she sat opposite Inspectors Fukuhara and Talifano—who had called her two hours earlier to ask her to come in. Beige acoustic wall tiles lined the tiny, windowless interrogation room. As Lea stared at the worn sets of initials etched into her side of the table, she felt isolated from the outside world.

"Now, Miss Sherwood," said Talifano, the paunch of his stomach straining against the buttons of his shirt. "Tell us about the phone call you took from Francine Reese on the night of her death. Try to remember everything that was said."

Lea repeated the conversation as best she could. The two men observed her, poker-faced. Occasionally one of them compared her statements to a set of notes—apparently they'd been in touch with the San Ygnacio police. It was a peculiar sensation to know that someone was questioning every word she spoke. Or trying to catch her in a contradiction.

When she finished, they exchanged a look she couldn't interpret.

Talifano leaned forward. "Now tell us what the two of you talked about when Mrs. Reese visited your restaurant earlier this month."

Startled, Lea felt herself redden. *How did they know about that?* Haltingly, she tried to reconstruct their talk.

"What a load of bull!" Talifano said halfway through her account. "Come on, Miss Sherwood, you can't expect us to believe Mrs. Reese needed your help in keeping her job." He gestured impatiently, setting his bow tie askew. "The woman didn't even know you. And how could you have helped her?"

"I know," Lea agreed. "That's exactly what I told her!" She began to feel uncomfortably warm.

"You'll have to come up with a better story than that." Talifano shot his partner a look of disbelief.

"I don't know what else to tell you," Lea stammered. "It's the truth."

The inspector held her gaze. "Look. Mrs. Reese was a recently divorced woman. A single mother with a lot at stake. Maybe she really was afraid Whitten Systems would try to pin the blame on her for whatever accounting fraud was going on."

Lea was puzzled, and she waited for Talifano to continue. What was he getting at? Had the police accepted Francine's version of the story?

"Whether she was frightened for her future, or for her life, I don't know. Mrs. Reese was quite upset when she came to see us. It was our impression she knew more about Keith Whitten's murder than she was willing to divulge." Talifano paused. "But I do know she suspected you and Paul Boyd. She told us so."

Lea held her breath. Her scalp was damp with perspiration.

"As I said, the poor woman was distraught. Maybe even desperate enough to take a risk no person should ever take."

Lea was baffled. She stared at each of them in turn. "What do you mean?"

"I'm talking about blackmail, Miss Sherwood."

"Black...." Lea couldn't even say the word.

"Yes, *blackmail.*" Talifano spat it out. "I think Mrs. Reese came to your restaurant and asked you for money. You agreed, to hush her up. I believe Boyd and Mrs. Reese then agreed she should resign. After all, it would have been awkward to work together under the circumstances. Then I think you and Boyd plotted to kill her."

Lea was speechless.

"What about it, Miss Sherwood?" The detectives' eyes were pinned on her.

Lea froze.

Inspector Fukuhara cleared his throat and rubbed his chubby hands together. He spoke for the first time. "My partner assumes that's the way it happened, Ms. Sherwood. But I don't believe you're capable of murder. I think maybe you were caught in the wrong place at the wrong time. I think maybe you only suspect Paul Boyd is responsible for these deaths. Am I right?"

Lea tried to answer, but no words would come.

"In the eyes of the law, Ms. Sherwood, if you know anything about these murders—anything at all—you can be prosecuted along with Mr. Boyd if you don't come forward right now," Fukuhara added.

"But I don't know anything," Lea said. "Except that Paul and I had nothing to do with this!"

Talifano slapped his hand on the table. "Stop coddling her," he said to Fukuhara. He turned to Lea. "Miss Sherwood. You claim you arrived at the Chuck Station shortly after 8:00. But the notation in the hostess book says you were seated at 8:45. That would have given you ample time to get to Francine Reese's house, follow her to Crestline Boulevard, and crowd her off the road."

"That's not true!" Lea protested. "I waited 40 minutes for Francine at the restaurant. The hostess must know that. I was sitting right in front of her. She must remember me."

"Oh, the woman remembers you, all right. She told us you were nervous and kept checking your watch. But she insisted you waited only a few minutes for your table. She said at that hour, people hardly ever have to wait."

Lea winced. It was her word against the other woman's. "But you know my car didn't force Francine off the road," she said in a hoarse voice. "The San Ygnacio police confirmed that."

Talifano smirked. "You thought you were being clever—stealing Alston's Mercedes. Why not just admit what happened? You told Boyd about Mrs. Reese's phone call, and the two of you hightailed it out of his office together. I'm guessing as to the exact sequence of events, but I say you drove separately to Mrs. Reese's house, you in your Renault, Boyd in Alston's car. Then the two of you followed her in the Mercedes and cold-bloodedly killed her. Then Boyd dropped you off at her house, you drove to the restaurant, and Boyd headed back to his office, ditching Alston's car on the way."

"But that's impossible!"

"Why? Boyd can't confirm his whereabouts between 7:30 and 8:30."

Lea shook her head emphatically. "What you're suggesting is preposterous!"

"Hey, Miss Sherwood," Talifano said, his voice dripping with sarcasm. "It's time to tell us what really happened. Why did Mrs. Reese call you at Whitten Systems that night? Did she want more money? Was she going to expose you otherwise? Is that why you and Boyd decided she had to die?" The man's pock-marked, flaccid face was inches away from Lea's. His breath was sour against her cheek.

Lea flinched—repelled by him and his wild accusations. "But why would Paul and I kill Keith? There's no reason!" she cried.

Talifano smiled knowingly. "You've gotta be kidding. With Whitten out of the way, Boyd was named head of the merged company. Today he's more powerful than ever. I wasn't born yesterday, Miss Sherwood. I know how much money these Silicon Valley moguls make. Boyd probably calculated that it was worth the risk."

"Even if that ridiculous line of reasoning were true, why would I get involved?" Lea demanded.

"Easy. Our sources tell us your restaurant isn't doing too hot. I think the two of you agreed to pull off the job together and then split the profits."

"My business is suffering *because* Keith was killed there," Lea sputtered. "It was growing before that!"

Talifano's gaze was full of pity. "I bet you thought there'd be less risk if you did it together." He held up a hand. "You bought the poison. Boyd put it in the pills. Ironic, isn't it, that Whitten showed up at your restaurant that night? It put you in a bind."

Lea was stupefied. "Where would I be able to buy a lethal dose of clonidine?"

Talifano and Fukuhara exchanged a triumphant look. "So you know what killed him," Talifano stated.

"I ... I was told about it," Lea said. "I heard about it through someone in the media." She didn't want to drag Brooke into this. "Seriously, I wouldn't know where to obtain it."

The detective shrugged. "This is San Francisco. Anybody can buy anything here."

"But you *can't* believe we killed Keith or Francine. Or that she was blackmailing me!" Lea pleaded. "It's just not true." A cold finger of fear ran down her spine.

"Why can't I believe it? Huh? From what I hear, you were damned surprised to see Mrs. Reese show up at your restaurant. Then you were witnessed having a fight. Why would you fight with someone you never met before?" Talifano looked smug, as if to say, "Your Honor, I rest my case."

"That's insane!" Lea said desperately.

The two men didn't take their eyes off her.

Lea's head began to throb, and she shrank back against

the hard wooden seat. The room seemed to have been drained of air.

"Tell us the truth, Miss Sherwood," Talifano said in a dangerous voice.

Lea shook her head wretchedly. Beads of perspiration broke out on her forehead. She closed her eyes, overcome by humiliation, and fright.

At least they were not arresting her—yet.

24

During the next few hours, Lea merely went through the motions of running Panache. It was only when she began forgetting customers' names and rang up a bill twice that she realized she must be in a state of semi-shock.

"Go home," Sydney urged her.

"No. I'd just feel worse by myself," Lea replied.

Instead, she did what she'd always done when troubled. She set out for a walk.

She headed for the waterfront, striding at first. Breathing deeply, she inhaled the fresh air blowing in from the bay. At the Embarcadero, she squinted at the silver span of the Bay Bridge, shimmering in the sunlight. She turned left, hiking toward the wharf as the broad leaves of the Embarcadero's palm trees fluttered in the breeze. Coit Tower, alabaster against the blue sky, dominated the northern skyline.

Lea took it all in. She loved this city, and she'd always longed to run her own restaurant here. And until Keith's death, she'd thought her dreams were coming true.

She thought of her college years, when her parents had introduced her to the city's fabled restaurants. Nostalgically she recalled the magic she'd felt at their tables. Ernie's, the

Blue Fox, L'Étoile, La Mirabelle, La Bourgogne, the Golden Eagle—all now shuttered and gone. Ghosts, Lea thought. Yet they haunted her still. She felt again the excitement of entering their dining rooms, and the epiphanies she'd experienced over superb food and wine. Keenly she recalled her feelings of transcendence and the heightened possibilities of life.

Smiling now, she thought too of the many fascinating conversations, and the first stirrings of romance. Many of the happiest nights of her life had been spent in San Francisco restaurants. Her favorites had combined both an aesthetic excellence and a personal vision. Interwoven in her mind with people and events, the memories of each lingered with a special glow.

At Pier 39, Lea stopped to watch a pair of white sails as they skimmed the waves near Alcatraz. Slowly she came out of her reverie, and she realized how tired she was. But as she turned to retrace her path, she was overcome by sadness. How soon we lose the things we come to love.

That night Lea forced herself to stay calm as she greeted guests. Halfheartedly, she engaged in small talk.

Carter Weberling came in toward the end of the evening. "Lea, I heard about your session today," he said, his silver brows knitted together in a frown. "I'm so sorry."

He was a willing listener as Lea summarized the gruesome exchange.

"I don't understand it," Carter said. "I would have thought the police would be focusing on Randy Derrough by now."

"You and me both," she said. "But what about the district attorney? Isn't he going to press charges? At the very least, it looks like Randy stole trade secrets."

Carter shook his head. "The district attorney's dragging his feet."

"What else does he need?" Lea exclaimed.

"The problem is that under California criminal law, it's hard to prove actual theft of trade secrets. You practically have to catch someone red-handed. Also, a trade secret is defined as information that is technical, scientific, and of significant value. Randy's lawyer is arguing that the sales and marketing data on the CDs Randy took don't fit that description."

Lea sighed. "So he gets off without even a slap on the hand? What about filing a civil suit against him?"

"That presents its own problems. The civil definition of trade secrets is quite broad, and it does cover any data deemed to have inherent value. But there isn't much case law on the subject. It can all depend on how a court assesses value." Carter was grim. "Randy's lawyer is claiming this is just another case of a Silicon Valley firm going ballistic when an employee leaves to go to a competitor. And it's true that a lot of firms get paranoid when that happens. Many prosecute out of emotion—then their lawsuits fail for lack of proof. So to answer your question, yes, we could sue Randy, but it would be time-consuming and expensive. Plus we'd run the risk of being viewed as vindictive. With our current bad publicity, it would hardly seem the wisest course."

When Carter had gone, Lea went to her office to call Paul. She hadn't spoken to him in days, not even about seeing him at the airport. Now she dialed his home number on the Peninsula, and to her relief, he answered.

He listened carefully as she described her morning at the Hall of Justice, interrupting her at intervals to ask questions. He seemed as alarmed and baffled by the line of questioning as she had been.

Only when she'd finished her account did Lea broach the subject of Paul's recent rendezvous at the airport. Even so, she felt odd questioning him.

"Oh, he was just a guy who had a proposal for me," Paul said. "I only met with him for a few minutes." To her surprise, Paul sounded flustered.

"But you seemed to be arguing."

"Well ... I, ah, don't quite remember that."

"Why did you go to the airport to see him? If he had a pitch to make, why wouldn't he go to your office?" Lea asked, genuinely puzzled.

"Really, Lea, it was nothing. Only a small part of my day. It just happened to be convenient for me to meet him there."

She dropped the subject, not caring to harp. Yet she could tell by Paul's tone of voice that the encounter had been anything but routine. They talked for a few more minutes before saying goodnight. Then Lea stared at the phone, mystified.

Lea locked the door behind the last guests of the evening. It was only 10:40, another early night, and she'd lost money again today on the lunch and dinner services. She was preoccupied as she entered the kitchen.

"Surprise!" A chorus of voices greeted her as Sydney advanced with a towering white frosted cake. It was festooned with almonds, blackberries, and currants. Lea glanced around in amazement at a sea of beaming faces. "What's the occasion?" she asked.

"It's our sixth-month anniversary," Sydney pronounced. "We've made it this far, and we'll make it through the rest of the year," she declared.

"Here, here!" The staff cheered and clapped. Gerard, who had returned for the party, hugged her, and Sydney presented her with the cake. Lea peered at it curiously. A lone, stunted candle flickered from the uppermost layer.

"Gerard cut a candle in half to signify half a year," Sydney said to general laughter.

Tears sprang to Lea's eyes. Panache was her calm center in a chaotic world, and these people were her family. Here, with them, was where she belonged. She had to find a way to get through this crisis.

The party lasted for almost an hour, until Gerard whispered that he and Sydney wanted to take her to the Diamond Room at the top of the Pacific Park Hotel.

Lea protested, knowing how early he had to get up in the morning. But he insisted, and as soon as they had changed into civvies, Gerard and Sydney whisked Lea away.

The moment Lea stepped from the hotel's penthouse elevator, a flood of memories swept over her. She had come here with friends on special nights, and it was here that Paul had first said he loved her.

Gerard and Sydney led the way to a corner table with a panoramic view of the city and the bay. The lights of Nob Hill sparkled, fanning out to the harbor below. They ordered drinks, and Gerard proposed a toast to many happy years of working together. Sydney, in unusually high spirits, recounted anecdotes from her evidently riotous year on the British stage.

Amid the hilarity, however, Lea grew quiet, almost melancholy. She stared at a stately container ship as it wended its way out to the vast, black sea.

Try as she might, she couldn't shake the fear that the best part of her life might be behind her.

25

Lea tossed in bed and flung aside her blanket. It was just after 2:00 A.M., and she was still keyed up. Something had been nagging at her all the way home. She tried to recall precisely a comment Francine Reese had made at the restaurant. Something snide about Randy Derrough padding his expenses. Then it occurred to her. How would Francine have known?

Of course Francine would have had access to Whitten Systems' financial records. But as chief financial officer, surely she didn't waste her time processing routine expense accounts. She had a staff to do that.

Francine had alluded to Marshall's behavior, too. At the charity event, she'd remarked that he didn't cover his tracks.

Had Francine been looking through internal records? If so, what had she been seeking? And wouldn't the auditors have turned up evidence if the staff had been taking liberties? Maybe not, Lea reasoned. Patrice Holbrook had indicated that she was still verifying the big-ticket items like sales, assets, and inventory. More than likely, Francine had seen or overheard something suspicious and had checked out a hunch.

Lea was still puzzling over Francine's remarks on her drive into work. As she parked the Renault, she resolved to go to Whitten Systems that evening and look around for herself. She knew that Paul had called a board meeting for late afternoon that was expected to last well into the night. She hoped that with most of the company's employees leaving early these days, there would be few people around.

The day went by slowly, and by 6:15, Lea was tired and out of sorts. She went home to change into a sweater and slacks and then left for the Peninsula. Forty-five minutes later, she pulled into a space next to Paul's Mazda.

She got out of the car and took her time strolling to the Whitten Systems building. The warmth of the day still lingered. A ruby-throated hummingbird flitted past the white blooms of oleander trees, and a cool mist from the lawn sprinklers tickled her cheeks. She tried to plan her next step but decided to wait and see who was in the office.

In the lobby, Salvador checked her in, and Joy came to admit her.

"Paul's still in the board meeting," Joy said on their way to the second floor. "It's lasting forever, and they just asked me to call in Bennett and Marshall." She groaned. "I'll have to order dinner for everybody."

When they got to her desk, Joy glanced at her watch. "You're welcome to wait for Paul, but it could be a while." She picked up a magazine from her desk and held it out. "Be my guest."

Lea glanced at the cover, whose headlines teased: "Seven Ways to Make Your Man a Tiger in Bed," and "Is Liposuction Right for You?"

Lea smiled. "Thanks," she said, "but I think I'll go get a drink." She gestured in the direction of the coffee room.

Joy nodded absentmindedly, and Lea ventured out into the hallway, where she saw no signs of activity. It was now or never.

She decided her best bet was to try to get into the accounting office. But where precisely was it? Asking Joy would only arouse her suspicions. Dimly Lea remembered a bulletin board she had seen in the coffee room. It had been dotted with memos and game schedules for the in-house softball team. But Lea thought she had also seen an office floor plan. She padded down the hall, entered the coffee room, and spotted the floor plan posted in the top-left corner of the bulletin board. Accounting was on the first floor.

Lea took the stairs down a flight and located the office. The door, however, was firmly locked. Now what? As she considered her next step, a petite Latina in a gray and white uniform who was pushing a vacuum cleaner appeared around the corner. The woman smiled. Something about her made Lea take a chance.

"I wonder if you might let me in," she said. "I seem to have left something when I was in here earlier." Lea smiled apologetically.

The woman squinted at Lea as if trying to place her. "You are with Mr. Paul, no? I see you with Mr. Paul?"

"Yes," Lea agreed.

The woman nodded and pulled out a metal ring of clanging keys. She inserted one and swung the door open. "He good man, Mr. Paul," she said, edging past Lea and continuing on down the hall.

Lea entered the room, waited a few moments, and then checked the corridor. The cleaning woman had disappeared, and no one else was in sight. With a sigh of relief, she closed the door and locked it, then clicked on the overhead fluorescent lights. The large windowless room was suffused in a sallow glow. Luckily the solid wood door and thick carpeting, snug against the sill, should conceal the fact that the lights were on. Unfortunately, they would also prevent her from seeing or hearing anyone approach.

In the center of the room were two rows of beige metal desks; matching file cabinets lined the walls. The air conditioning had been turned off, and the room was warm. It also seemed unnaturally silent.

Fighting the urge to flee, Lea addressed herself to the task at hand. She walked to a bank of file drawers, wondering where to start. Nothing was labeled. The expense reports could be anywhere. Moving to the first row, she yanked a drawer open: dozens of manila folders, each labeled with an individual's name, were arranged alphabetically. She flipped through several. Each contained completed employment application forms, annual performance reviews, and salary history.

She skipped forward in the drawer to the Rs and located Francine Reese's file, visibly new. Lea pulled it out and carried it to the nearest desk, where she took a seat. To her surprise, the detective's report on Francine that Brooke had mentioned had been stamped with a Whitten Systems' logo and a date and placed in Francine's file.

Lea leafed through it. The investigator had collected newspaper clippings, photos, details on Francine's schooling, a résumé of her professional experience, and comments by people who knew her. Lea held up a portrait of Francine and her husband on their wedding day. An accompanying news story hailed the groom as a promising Baltimore banker and the bride as an ambitious CPA. Another story trumpeted the husband's wrath in the wake of the shooting incident. Hope turned to ashes.

Next Lea studied the comments by Francine's colleagues. Several had been guarded. Francine, they claimed, was a difficult person to know. Others were more forthcoming. "I wouldn't turn my back on her," remarked one. "Mendacious and unreliable," said another. "Sneaky, obdurate, and mean-spirited," a former boss pronounced.

In his conclusion to the report, the detective was equally blunt. "In my opinion, Francine Reese was capable of trying to kill her husband and in all probability did attempt to murder him on the night of August 5," he wrote. The husband, he went on to say, had been due to arrive at Francine's at 8:00 that night, and he rang her bell at the appointed time. A neighbor watering her lawn across the street saw him ring it twice before trying the door and finding it unlocked.

Francine, meanwhile, had insisted that she'd just entered the house through the back door when she heard a noise in the living room. She'd grabbed her gun and gone to investigate. In the unlit room, she claimed to have mistaken her husband for a prowler. But this contention was challenged by several of Francine's neighbors, who said that an earlier rainstorm had lifted and that the night was unusually clear. In fact the rays of the setting sun were said to have shone directly into Francine's living room.

Lea closed the file, feeling slightly soiled. She marveled at Keith's having hired Francine when he had known all this.

She got up and walked over to another file cabinet and found records for Whitten Systems' 401-K accounts. She flipped through the folders and spotted Randy Derrough's name. On impulse, she scanned the paperwork Randy had filled out a year ago, noting that he'd authorized the maximum 401-K withdrawal from his paycheck. Yet only recently, he had asked to borrow against the account. A sign of money troubles?

Lea inadvertently leaned against the file drawer, slamming it shut. She froze and cursed her clumsiness. She could hear the muffled sound of a vacuum cleaner in another room, and the murmur of a conversation in the hallway. She listened, holding her breath. A man laughed sharply. After a minute, the voices faded away.

Lea crossed the room and tried a new bank of files. The top row contained medical insurance records. She skipped it and tried the next tier. The folders here looked more promising—they were arranged by department. Under sales and marketing, Lea found Randy's expense file. She pulled it out, opened it, and began to read.

Randy's expense statements for the first five months of the year were arranged in reverse chronological order. Lea scrutinized the entries for May going back to January, all neatly tabulated on Whitten Systems' printed forms. Client lunches. Client dinners. Flowers for a customer's birthday. Really? Lea wondered. Or was it a personal charge instead? A two-day sales trip to Phoenix. A four-day excursion to Austin and Dallas. Car rental expenses. More lunches and dinners. Lea frowned. What had Francine been looking for?

She replaced Randy's file in the drawer and pulled out Bennett Alston's. His expenses were substantially less than Randy's—naturally, he didn't spend his time wooing clients. Lea read every entry but found nothing that provoked inquiry.

She returned Bennett's file and skipped to the back of the drawer to retrieve Marshall Schroth's folder. Strange, it was either missing or out of place. Eventually Lea located it under the Ts, as though someone had been careless in replacing it. Lea brought it back to the desk, sat down, and started scanning the entries for May. Marshall's most recent trip had been to Hong Kong, during the second week of the month, to visit Whitten Systems' regional Asia sales office.

On Monday, Tuesday, and Wednesday, according to the records, Marshall and Nigel Armbruster had entertained lavishly, taking customers out for expensive meals. Lea pulled Armbruster's file and checked his title: Regional Manager, Hong Kong.

That's odd, she thought, perusing the entries for later in the week. Marshall and Armbruster had always taken out at least two people at a time. She could see that from the column specifying the names of all persons entertained. But on Thursday, Marshall had dinner alone with an individual client, C. T. Chang. Where was Armbruster, and why would Marshall suddenly meet with clients alone?

Even more curiously, on Friday Marshall ate lunch with Sam Wong from the Hong Kong office. There was no folder for Wong, so Lea went back to the first personnel files she had seen. Wong was listed there as a sales assistant. Lea stared into space. Why would Marshall, the company's chief honcho for sales and marketing, flout corporate hierarchy to meet alone with a low-level assistant? It simply wasn't done.

Lea got up and went to the file cabinet for Nigel Armbruster's records. During the second week of May, she saw, he had left on a sales trip for Jakarta on Thursday morning. That was also odd, Lea thought. Why would he go out of town when his boss was visiting? Or had Marshall told Armbruster he'd be returning to California and then unexpectedly extended his trip?

She refiled the expense accounts and walked to another bank of cabinets. Assuming that Francine had looked through the office records, had she been looking for specific information? Or just digging at random?

The next drawer Lea tried yielded Whitten Systems' phone bills. Charges were listed by extension. Locating a list of internal phone numbers in one of the desks, Lea found Francine's extension and began to check her calls for May. Many were to out-of-state numbers. Twelve calls in all, presumably personal but charged to the company, had been placed to Boston, Baltimore, and Providence. Had Francine been looking for a new job back home to extricate herself from a tight situation here?

Next Lea studied the calls made by Bennett and Randy. Nothing seemed unusual. As she turned a page in the records, however, a block of calls to Taipei suddenly caught her eye. She checked the caller's extension against the office phone list. Keith Whitten had called the same number in Taipei on May 19, 22, 28, and 30. Each call had lasted at least 15 minutes.

Quickly Lea canvassed the other international numbers Keith had phoned. Hmmm. One to Seoul. But it was only a minute long. That made no sense. Could he have reached it by mistake? Yet Keith had only dialed the country code for Korea once. If the first call had been a wrong number, wouldn't he have tried again? Or had he simply dialed the wrong country code? Lea scanned the other foreign numbers Keith had reached. None came close to the Seoul number. It was almost as though Keith had called it just to find out what it was.

Lea flipped through more billing pages, looking for Marshall's records. She found them near the end of the May bill. She peered at a number with a San Jose area code that he had called at least four times a week. On impulse, she picked up the phone and dialed it. A recording informed her that she had reached the general offices of TYBER Semiconductor. Lea frowned. Why was Marshall regularly in touch with someone at his former employer's?

Continuing on down the page, she checked his foreign calls. Fourteen were to Hong Kong. Lea consulted the internal phone list again. Most of those calls had been to Nigel Armbruster's line, but three had been to Sam Wong. Again, what did Marshall have to discuss with the sales assistant?

It was Marshall's one call to Seoul, however, that caught her eye. It had lasted six minutes. Apart from it, the only calls Marshall had made to the Far East had been to Whitten Systems' regional office in Hong Kong. Had he called a customer in Korea? Presumably he left routine sales calls and client contact to his regional staff.

Lea went back through the billing pages, remembering Keith's odd call to Seoul. Impatiently, she scattered the sheets on the desktop, trying to relocate Keith's records. At last she found them, and the Seoul number jumped out at her. It matched the one dialed by Marshall—only Keith had called it several days after him. Lea stood back from the cabinet, more puzzled than ever.

She pulled a notepad and a pen from her purse and jotted down the number.

Suddenly a key turned in the lock and the door swung open. A cleaning woman—not the one who had let her in— began to enter the room and then stopped. She was obviously surprised to encounter Lea, and a glimmer of suspicion flickered in her eyes.

Lea tried to appear relaxed. "I'll be through in here soon," she said.

The woman nodded and gave her a slight smile. "I'll come back later," she said, closing the door. Lea heard her lock it from the hall.

Lea exhaled and realized that she'd been holding her breath. She put away her notepad and the phone bills and decided to go back to Marshall Schroth's expense account file. She sat down with it and spent the next 10 minutes studying Marshall's every movement during May.

Without warning, the doorknob rattled. Lea froze and stared at the door. A key turned slowly in the lock. Lea grabbed Marshall's file and dove under the desk.

She heard the door open and sensed someone entering the room. Whoever it was shut the door quietly behind him. Lea crouched in the narrow space, grateful that the sturdy desk was closed in front. A faint whiff of a lime-scented after-shave drifted down to her. She didn't recognize it, and she tensed, willing the man to leave. Instead, she heard the creak of a file drawer. Damn! She hadn't shut the drawer after pulling Marshall's file.

The ensuing minute of silence was oppressive. Then Lea heard the man riffling through files. Was he checking to see if his folder was missing? Lea felt as though she could hardly breathe. A cramp struck in her left calf, but she didn't dare move. She bit her lip against the pain.

Now the file drawer slammed shut, and Lea heard the man pulling out another drawer. She huddled in misery. Had the cleaning woman told him she was here? And who outside the accounting staff would have a key to this office? Had someone copied a key for his own private use?

The lime aroma reached Lea again, stronger this time. The man must be only several feet away, she realized. The pain in her calf was acute. She crouched helplessly, straining to hear every sound.

More silence. Lea's eyes were riveted on the patch of carpet next to the desk. What if he found her here? She could hardly imagine a more incriminating position.

Suddenly the man strode over and stood motionless behind the desk, two feet away. Lea nearly gasped. Surely he could hear her heart pounding! What if he looked down and saw her? What if he tried to sit down? She waited, paralyzed.

A faint series of clicks reached her ears. The man had picked up the phone and was punching in a number. Lea pressed her lips together. Her back had also started to ache. Next she heard a tapping on the desktop. The man was evidently impatient as he waited for his call to go through.

She heard him mutter a curse, but his voice was too indistinct to recognize.

He dropped the receiver heavily, giving Lea a jolt. She held herself taut, bracing for the worst. The man stepped away from the desk, then returned. Lea heard him pick up the phone again, then replace the receiver. Was he debating his next move? Lea clenched her hands into fists. A horrible thought struck her. Did he know she was there? Had he known all along? Was he calling an accomplice?

Lea strained to remain still in the cramped space. She didn't know how long she could stand the pain in her leg. She eyed the man's leather shoes, polished to a high gloss. Who was he? And what was he doing here?

Suddenly the intruder slammed his palm against the desktop, sending tremors throughout Lea's body. She stifled a scream.

Slowly, the man backed away from the desk. Was it her imagination, or could she hear him breathing? He walked away. For several moments, Lea could hear nothing. Then, abruptly, the room was plunged into darkness. Lea clenched her teeth, willing herself to remain mute. Soon, unmistakably, came the click of the door opening, then closing.

Relief flooded her. But she caught herself in time. Was he really gone? Or was it a trap? She remained motionless for what seemed like an eternity, letting her eyes adjust to the dark. Finally she felt she had no choice. She had to get up. Her body was throbbing with pain.

Warily, Lea crawled out into the open.

She managed to stand unsteadily, massaging the cramp in her leg, and began to tremble all over. She waited for a blow to fall. But as she continued to peer into the shadows, she slowly relaxed. She was alone. She fell into the chair, almost weeping from the strain.

Then she considered her tenuous position. Her mind raced. She must get out, now. But could she? What if he had gone to get a weapon? What if he were waiting on the other side of the door? In her mind Lea saw the ghastly contortion of Keith's face as he lay dying, and the mangled hulk of

Francine's car, deep in the ravine. Whoever killed the two of them would not let anyone else stand in his way.

Still shaking, Lea got up and returned Marshall's file to its proper place and closed the drawer firmly behind her. She moved to the door and pressed her ear against it. She could hear nothing. Slowly, she eased the door open and surveyed the corridor in each direction. Empty. She stepped out, pulled the door shut, and walked quickly down the hall.

26

Harry was hunched over Joy's desk eating tacos when Lea returned from the accounting office. He looked up in alarm as he caught sight of her. "Lea! What's the matter? You look like you've seen Marley's ghost."

Lea hesitated before answering. "Don't trust anyone"— Patrice Holbrook's advice—came to mind. Harry was behind the desk, and she couldn't see his shoes.

"Have you been here for a while?" she finally asked, a catch in her throat.

"No. I just got back from the board room. I was in there setting up a computer demo. Why?" Harry studied her. "Will you tell me what's going on?"

Lea tried to remain calm. She shook her head. "It's nothing, really. I was just thinking about Francine and Keith. Sometimes it hits me. You know, the violent way they both died."

Harry appeared to accept her explanation. "Oh, I know," he said. "There was no love lost between Francine and me, but I have to confess that her death shook me up. It's only natural, when someone you know dies like that."

Lea took a deep breath. "Where is everyone? Still in the meeting?"

Harry nodded. "They sure are. I just came over here to help Joy carry in the Mexican food for dinner. She ordered enough for a wake."

Lea flinched.

"Oops, wrong choice of word." Harry appraised her again. "What brings you here tonight, anyway? Can I help?"

"No," she said evasively. "I can wait until Paul's meeting breaks up." Lea felt a twinge of guilt. What would Paul say if he knew what she'd been up to?

"Well, at least have something to eat." Harry reached for a bag bearing the logo of a braying donkey. "I can vouch for Pepito's crab and avocado burritos. With salsa so hot it'll curl your toes."

Lea accepted a burrito. Now that she was out of danger—at least temporarily—she realized how hungry she was. "But hold the hot sauce," she protested. Her stomach was still unsettled.

As Lea munched, Harry polished off a family-size bag of blue corn tortilla chips and washed it all down with a Dos Equis. The hum from Joy's computer underscored the silence between them.

When Lea sniffed in Harry's direction, attempting to detect any odor of cologne, all she could smell was the spicy food.

She was trying to think of something to say when she heard a door open down the hall. Carter's voice came first, and then Paul's.

"Looks like they've wrapped up," Harry said, obviously relieved.

Paul appeared around the corner and saw Lea taking her last bite. Doubt flickered in his eyes. "Lea, what on earth are you doing here? You knew I was going to be in a meeting until all hours."

Lea stammered and was unsure of what to say. She was relieved when one of Paul's directors gripped his arm and began to say goodnight. When his board had departed, however, Paul came back to her with a curious look. "Let's go to my office," he said.

Harry mumbled goodnight to them both.

Lea rose reluctantly—fearing she would never get to see Harry's shoes—and followed Paul into his office. She sat down in one of the chairs opposite his desk.

Paul closed the door and turned to stare at Lea. "Sometimes I just don't understand you," he said. "Why did you come down here without telling me, and when you knew I'd be in a meeting all evening?"

Lea swallowed.

"Well? I'm waiting." Paul was growing annoyed.

Lea knew she had to be honest. In halting phrases, she began to tell him what she'd been doing that night.

Almost at once, Paul interrupted her. "You broke into my accounting office?" Paul looked at her as if he couldn't believe his ears.

"Well, not technically. As I said, I asked the maid…"

"You went behind my back," Paul interrupted again.

Lea squirmed. She hadn't felt so much guilt since second grade, when she'd given in to the impulse to draw a deer in red crayon on the back of Betsy Senter's white cotton blouse.

Paul, who was still standing, folded his arms across his chest.

"I'm sorry, Paul, but I couldn't see any other way," Lea said miserably. "I know it comes as a shock to you, but please hear me out. You'll be surprised at what I found."

Paul listened, irritably at first, and then with increasing incredulity as Lea recapped her evening, beginning with finding Randy's suspicious 401-K withdrawal and ending with a description of the intruder's after-shave and shoes.

"So tell me!" Lea implored. "Who was the man who followed me into the accounting office?"

Paul grimaced. "I'm not sure," he said. "With so much going on tonight, I didn't notice anybody's shoes. And as you know, my own after-shave has a tinge of lime, so I wouldn't necessarily notice it on someone else."

Lea sighed in exasperation. "Then did anyone leave the room about 40 minutes ago?"

Paul thought. "Bennett went to pull some contracts for us, and Marshall stepped out at about the same time. We asked him to track down some sales records." He paused. "Not much to go on, is there?"

"What about Harry? What was he doing?"

"Harry? I asked him to be on hand tonight to demo the new software, and I called him into the board room when we were ready." Paul paused. "Come to think of it, I had trouble locating him, and we had to wait."

They exchanged an uneasy glance.

"No, Lea. Not Harry. It couldn't be. What would be his motive?"

Lea felt another pang of guilt. Although she'd had Paul's best interests at heart, it now came back to her that she'd never told him about Harry's lunch date with Keith. In a burst of contrition, she confessed.

"Oh, my God," Paul said, stunned. He went to his desk and leaned against the corner as if for support.

Neither of them spoke for several minutes. Then Paul grabbed the phone on his desk and punched in a number. "Oh, it's you, Joy," he said in a disappointed tone. "I'm looking for Harry. Is he there?"

Paul listened for a few seconds and then dropped the receiver with a thud. "Joy said he left in a hurry about 10 minutes ago."

"Right after we came in here," Lea suggested.

Paul nodded.

"Let's not assume too much," Lea said, with more confidence than she felt. "Maybe my intuition was right, and Harry really was duped by Keith, and nothing more. Let's move on, for now, anyway."

"OK," Paul said reluctantly. "But where do we go from here?"

"What about the phone records? Who do you think Keith and Marshall could have been calling in Seoul?"

"Do you have the number?"

Lea extracted her notepad from her purse and handed it to him.

Paul peered at the number, walked over to a bookcase against the wall, and pulled out a dog-eared, foreign-language phrase book. He turned to a section and read for a few minutes before closing the book and returning it to its place. "Let's see," Paul said. "Seoul is 10 hours ahead of us, so it's about 8:30 in the morning there. The start of the work day. Maybe I can reach someone in my fractured Korean." Paul grabbed the phone again and dialed.

"What in the world?" he asked a minute later. "It's CS Global, the international trading company," he told Lea. "They have a recording in six languages," he added lamely. For the second time that night, Paul appeared to be stunned.

"Are they one of your customers?"

"No, and I can't imagine that either Marshall or Keith would personally initiate a sales call to them. They'd leave the groundwork to our Asian sales people—who know the culture and language."

"What about Marshall's meeting with Sam Wong, one of your sales assistants in Hong Kong? Could that be related?"

"I don't know what to make of Marshall's seeing Wong. Marshall's always worked directly with our Hong Kong manager, Nigel Armbruster, and I've never heard of Wong."

Lea sighed. She was more confused than ever.

"But forget that for now," Paul said, with an edge to his voice. "What really bothers me is the risk you took tonight. No wonder you didn't tell me you were coming."

Lea bit her lip. Her guilt was back, along with a measure of defensiveness.

Paul gave her a searching look. "It makes me wonder what else you haven't told me."

The strain of all she'd been through suddenly caught up with Lea, and tears flooded her eyes. She spoke before she thought. "What I haven't told *you*?" she cried. "What about all the things you've been keeping from me?"

Paul froze. "What do you mean?"

"I mean like what you found in Keith's safe, for instance."

Paul flushed. "I thought it was better if you didn't know about that if the police questioned you."

"And?" Lea demanded.

"All right, if you must know. The safe had a private detective's reports on the company's senior people. Keith commissioned them because he suspected someone was involved in shady activities. But the detective didn't turn up anything except some off-track betting by Randy, and I figured there was no point in telling the police about all that. It wouldn't have helped them, and it would have been another embarrassment for us if and when the story got leaked. When you asked me about it, I thought you'd be better off not knowing."

"All right," Lea said, both surprised and relieved at Paul's explanation. "But what about the man you secretly met at the airport last week? Who was he, really? You can't tell me he was a run-of-the-mill business associate."

Paul looked sheepish. "That's an episode I'd rather forget, but I guess I do owe you an explanation." He waved a hand. "This man who called himself Yunfei Lim phoned me at the office and said he was in town from Kowloon for a few days. He claimed to have known a detective Keith hired who could implicate someone at Whitten Systems in Keith's death. The problem was, this detective had just been killed. I told the guy to go to the San Francisco police, but he said he couldn't—that he'd acquired the information in a way that would incriminate him if he made a statement."

Lea leaned forward excitedly. "And?"

"I thought the guy sounded shady, but I did confirm with Hong Kong police that a detective by the name he'd mentioned had been found murdered. The catch was: our man on the phone wanted $5,000 in cash for his information. Well, I felt like a fool, but I talked it over with Carter and Patrice Holbrook. They felt it was a long shot, but one that we couldn't ignore. So I withdrew the money from our corporate account, and I met Mr. Lim at the international terminal at SFO. He insisted we wouldn't attract attention if we met in the lounge there."

"Not to mention giving him the opportunity to take the money and run," Lea observed.

"Exactly," Paul said unhappily. "He even instructed me to buy a certain style of briefcase so that we could unobtrusively exchange cases. I'd put the cash in mine; he'd put the documentation on Keith's killer in his. It's an old dodge, but it still works. Like I said, I felt like an idiot."

"Then what?"

"We met as planned, and he fed me a story. It was imaginative, I'll give him that. Then they called his flight, we exchanged briefcases, and he left."

"And what was his story?"

"I don't want to go into the details. Suffice it to say that none of it checked out, not even remotely. The guy was just a con man."

Lea sighed. "But why didn't you tell me that earlier?" she asked.

Paul hung his head. "I didn't want to admit to you that I'd been such a dope. I already felt bad enough that I'd helped put you in a position where you stood to lose Panache. I thought you were probably starting to hate me."

Lea was silent for a moment. Then she got up and walked over to Paul and put her arms around his neck. She gave him a long, slow kiss. "I could never hate you," she murmured, rubbing the back of his neck with her hand. "Don't you know that?"

"I wouldn't blame you," he said, wrapping his arms around her and holding her tight. "Every morning when I get up I blame myself for having gotten you into this. If I weren't involved, the police would never be after you."

27

After a fitful night's sleep, Lea got up at 7:30 the next morning. She showered, pulled on her favorite black turtleneck and a pair of slacks, and shuffled barefoot into the living room. From her windows she saw a container ship gliding out to the Golden Gate and a ferry conveying early-bird tourists to Sausalito. The sun shone intermittently through patches of fog.

Lea thought of Paul, and their leave-taking last night. She'd wanted him to come home with her, but he had stayed in his office to prepare for a trip today to New York, where he and Carter were to meet with bond analysts.

Regret tinged with uncertainty about their future welled up in her. Paul had been right to feel ambushed by her actions last night, Lea concluded. Maybe after too many years of living alone, she had become too independent. Or too set in her ways. Could she take the emotional risk of being completely open with Paul? Of fully sharing her life with him?

She slipped on her flats and went downstairs to retrieve her copy of the *Herald*, which had been placed on the table in the foyer. Dispiritedly, she carried the paper upstairs, unsure whether to even open the news sections. In the past, she'd enjoyed having breakfast and sipping a *café au lait* while reading the news, but these days she scanned the headlines apprehensively.

Lea let herself back into her apartment and fell into the ivory wing chair by the window. Steeling herself, she made it to page nine before she found a mention of the murders. Apparently a psychic from San Jose had come forward to suggest that Francine had hidden a diary in the vicinity of a Spanish mission. Lea chuckled as she imagined Francine secreting a leather-bound tome in the hollow of an old oak tree.

Poor Francine, Lea thought. Her volatile personality had left her with few friends to mourn her passing. Lea wondered what would become of Tommy, her son. Paul had told her he was still in the Bay Area, staying on with his nanny during summer vacation until his father could move him back to Baltimore. How does an 8-year-old boy ever come to terms with the murder of his mother?

As she scrutinized the photograph of an uncharacteristically smiling Francine that accompanied the news story, Lea also began to wonder what, if anything, Tommy might know about his mother's death. He must have noticed that she was upset during her last days, and he might have observed much more. Lea had known more than one precocious child of about Tommy's age.

On an impulse, Lea got up and went to her purse, where she had kept Francine's phone number and address. She dialed the number and introduced herself to Heidi Steitz, the nanny. Heidi was sympathetic to Lea's plight but reluctant to expose Tommy to questioning.

"He has good days and bad," Heidi said. "Some days, like today, you'd never suspect what he's gone through. I'd hate to upset him all over again." Only after considerable urging—and a promise from Lea to leave if Tommy became upset—did Heidi agree to let Lea meet him later that morning.

Lea called Gerard to say she'd be in after lunch, and at 10:00 she left for the Peninsula. The fog had lifted, and the sun was bright as she sped down Highway 101 toward the Valley. Inexplicably, Lea began to have flashbacks of the scene on the mountain the night Francine died.

It was shortly before 11:00 when she pulled up to Francine's house. The blue, gray, and mauve nouveau-Victorian looked just as it had on her previous visit, and aside from the potted pink begonias on the front porch that needed watering, nothing suggested that anything out of the ordinary had occurred.

Lea got out of the car, climbed the three steps to the front door, and rang the bell. She thought she heard footsteps approaching when a high-pitched "Aiyeee!" pierced the silence, followed by a crash and peals of laughter. Her heart leapt.

A woman's voice was scolding. "Tommy Reese! You stop doing that. I mean it this time!"

The door opened, and a young woman faced Lea. Her tousled, shoulder-length red hair tumbled over one eye as she smoothed a rumpled aquamarine tunic over her slim hips. She extended one hand to Lea and brushed lint off her black leggings with the other. "I'm Heidi," she said. "You must be Lea Sherwood."

"Have I come at a bad time?" Lea inquired.

"No, not at all," Heidi said, darting a reproving glance at the boy who trailed her, doubled up with laughter. "Tommy was just practicing his judo throw, with me as his projectile. He can't resist showing off since he got his orange belt."

Lea smiled at Tommy, who grinned impishly back. Tommy had Francine's fair hair and coloring, plus a smattering of freckles and a fierce cowlick. He also appeared to have Francine's nervous energy. His entire body jiggled as he shifted his weight from one foot to the other. Lea made a mental note to watch her backside.

Tommy appeared to read her thoughts. "Don't worry, Ms. Sherwood, I won't throw you," he said as he approached her. "Come on in and see my aquarium! I just added a Bandit

Angelfish to the tank, and it's way cool. Its scientific name is *Holacanthus arculatus*, and it comes from deep waters in Hawaii. Did you know it's a picky eater? It mainly eats sponges."

Tommy continued his monologue about the dietary requirements and habitat of the fish as he led the way down the hall and into a spacious living room. "See?" he said. "There he is." Tommy pointed to a black, white, and tan fish whose black bandit stripe masked his eyes. As they all watched, it cruised through a bed of quivering green algae.

"Now let me show you my rock collection!"

Heidi shook her head. "Tommy, that's enough. Ms. Sherwood is here for a special reason. To talk to us."

"I know that," he said reproachfully. "I know all about you and your restaurant," he said, turning to face Lea. "I've been begging Heidi to take me to Panache."

Lea shot Heidi an astonished glance.

"Oh, it's true," she said. "Tommy watches all the chef shows on TV, and he's very particular about what he eats. He especially loves going to restaurants."

"For lunch we're having proscuitto and fresh Black Mission figs on a bed of arugula," Tommy announced, stumbling over the pronunciation of arugula.

"Would you like to stay? We have plenty," Heidi said.

"That's very nice of you. I'd like that," Lea said. It would also be a good setting in which to raise uncomfortable questions, she thought.

Tommy raced off in the direction of what Lea presumed was the kitchen, and she and Heidi followed.

The kitchen was a foodie's dream: salmon-hued marble countertops, his-and-her island cooking centers, a wok range, convection oven, overhead racks bearing gleaming copper pots, two state-of-the-art refrigerators, and a wine cooler. Lea wondered whether Francine had ever had the time or the inclination to cook.

Tommy halted before the island and wielded an imaginary knife. With a quick chop and a grunt, he flattened his palm against the marble surface.

"What *are* you doing now?" Heidi asked him.

"Peeling bulbs of garlic, of course," he replied, flashing Lea a knowing look.

"For this I became a nanny," Heidi said with a sigh. At a counter dining area that seated six, she pulled out a high stool upholstered with a soft tiger-print fabric. "Please, Lea, have a seat. You can ask Tommy questions while I get lunch ready."

Lea perched on the stool, trying to get comfortable. The seat canted forward, and the padding was too thin. She had to admit it looked spiffy, though.

As Heidi rinsed the figs, Lea considered how to broach the topic of the murders. She glanced at Tommy, who was now clucking and beating an imaginary whisk. She exchanged a concerned glance with Heidi.

"It's all right, Ms. Sherwood," Tommy said, suddenly subdued. "Fire away. You can ask me about my mother." He laid down his imaginary whisk.

"Thank you, Tommy. I really do need to ask you both a few questions," Lea said gently. "Heidi, I guess you've been questioned already by the police?"

"Oh, yes," Heidi said. "And they treated me as if I was just another suspect, after tramping through the house as though they owned it."

"What did you tell them?"

"Not much. There wasn't much to tell at that point, except that Mrs. Reese had gotten very nervous. She jumped at the slightest thing."

"When did she start being so nervous?"

"Soon after her boss was killed. Kevin Whitten, wasn't it?"

"Keith," Lea corrected. "Did you ever ask her why?"

"A couple of times, and she just said she had a lot of worries at work. I felt badly for her, but it didn't seem to be my place to press her. She was my employer, after all."

"She started coming home from work even later than usual," Tommy interjected. "At 10:00 or even 11:00 at night. I never saw her anymore."

"She smoked more too," Heidi said. "One night at about 3:00 A.M. I came downstairs looking for her when Tommy had a nightmare, but when I saw how miserable she looked, I didn't have the heart to disturb her. She was just sitting in the den, staring off into the distance and chain smoking. The next morning I saw from the stubs that she'd smoked a whole pack." Heidi was now weaving paper-thin slices of proscuitto around morsels of figs.

"Did you ever hear her on the phone, maybe talking about what was bothering her?"

"Once," Heidi said. "She was talking to a friend of hers who works in pharmaceutical sales over in the East Bay, and she asked her how someone could acquire lethal drugs. Mrs. Reese said she was afraid that someone she knew had access to pira or pyra something."

So Francine had known about the piracetam used to poison Keith! Lea felt a *frisson* of excitement run down her spine.

"What else did she say?" Lea demanded.

"I remember she mentioned something about a mutual friend of theirs named Randy. Mrs. Reese said she was afraid he was going to leave Whitten Systems and go back to work at Binochet Technologies. And I only recall that because I'd met Randy once."

"Do you know the name of the friend she was talking to? Or the company she's with?" Lea sat on the edge of her seat.

Heidi was apologetic. "No. Just that her name is Charity. The police asked me that too. I think they may have found her name and number in Mrs. Reese's address book. They took that and some other things with them."

Lea swallowed in disappointment. "Oh. Too bad." Lea drummed her fingers on the counter.

"When did you meet Randy?" she asked, almost as an afterthought.

"About a week before Mrs. Reese died. He came over one night and had a drink with her. I let him in and then went back into the kitchen to fix dinner. He'd gone a half hour later when dinner was ready."

"Did Francine seem upset at his visit?"

"Not particularly, but it's hard to say, really. She was so tense about everything."

"Did anyone else come by the house, or did she go to meet anyone during this period?"

"Not that I remember. Not until the night she went to see you. In fact I felt kind of sorry for Mrs. Reese, because she seemed to have so few friends. There wasn't a man in her life, either, and I kind of hoped Randy might change that. Of course, he didn't seem to be her type."

Lea took a deep breath. "Do you know if she kept a diary?" She felt foolish asking, but who knew—the psychic might be on to something.

"Oh, that!" Heidi rolled her eyes. "No, not that I ever heard of."

Lea sighed. She was getting nowhere.

She glanced at Tommy, who was now sitting cross-legged on the floor with his shoulders hunched over his knees. All of his previous exuberance had evaporated.

Lea tried a different tack. "Heidi, you said you didn't have much to tell the police *then* when they questioned you. What did you mean by that?"

"Only that we just found some camcorder footage Tommy shot at Whitten Systems the Saturday before his mother died. Tommy, tell Ms. Sherwood about it," Heidi urged softly.

Tommy squirmed and stared at the floor. "I'd gotten mad at my mom because she was never home and we never did stuff together," he said, his words barely audible. "So she took me in to work with her."

"Mrs. Reese left Tommy alone in the coffee room while she went to a meeting," Heidi said. She had stopped preparing the salad and swiped at one eye with her hand. "He fooled around with the camcorder his dad had given him for a while, and he talked to a guy named Harry who came in for a Coke. But then he got bored. When he looked out the window and saw people on the fitness trail, he went downstairs and asked the guard if he could go out." Heidi opened a kitchen drawer and pulled out a tape cassette. "Here's what he shot on the trail."

Lea watched as Heidi popped the cassette into a VCR attached to the kitchen's television. She pressed a few buttons, and the screen came to life. Two breathless young women in shorts and T-shirts appeared on a dirt path bordered by tall Norfolk pines.

Lea recognized the fitness trail that bordered Whitten Systems.

The camera followed the women intermittently as they jogged along the path, stopping here and there to perform exercises. A mockingbird's song, clear at first, soon faded.

Suddenly the Whitten Systems parking lot came into view, and the camera took in a row of cars, settling by turns on a yellow Corvette Stingray, a black Maserati, and a white Jeep.

"I wanted to see the cool cars," Tommy said.

The camera had just panned back to the Stingray when the silence was broken by a man's angry voice.

Lea strained to make out his words.

"Just bribe the border patrol and get into the country any way you can, damn it! You screwed up big time on our last job. I don't have to tell you that one more mistake, and you could end up in Colma."

Then the roar of a car engine drowned out the conversation, and the camera swung to capture a vintage turquoise T-Bird. The tape ended with a shot of it peeling out of the lot.

Heidi clicked the TV off.

"Tommy, did you get to see the man who was talking?" Lea asked excitedly.

He shook his head. "Unh, unh."

"Did you see his car?"

Tommy thought for a moment. "No. I guess it wasn't cool," he said apologetically.

"Damn!" Lea said under her breath. To Heidi she said, "If only the sound was better, I might be able to recognize the voice."

Lea got up and went to kneel before Tommy. "You heard the man that day. Was it anyone you'd met at your mom's company?"

Tommy screwed up his face.

"Could it have been Harry?"

Tommy looked doubtful. "I don't know, Ms. Sherwood. I only talked to Harry for a few minutes, so I couldn't say for sure."

"I got the part about bribing a guard," Heidi said. "But what did he say about ending in coal ... coalman?"

"Colma," Lea amended. "You've never heard of it?"

Heidi looked blank.

"Around the Bay Area, it's shorthand for cemetery," Lea said. "There's a huge cemetery in Colma."

Heidi and Tommy exchanged surprised glances.

"Tommy, why didn't you show somebody what you'd shot before now?" Lea asked.

Tommy picked at the laces of his sneakers. "Right after my mom died, I kinda forgot about anything else."

Heidi began to set napkins and silverware at three places on the counter. "Tommy had no reason to link what he heard to her death," she said quietly to Lea. "And for all we know, the two may not be related."

"True enough," Lea replied. "But you know what? I'll bet you anything they are."

28

Lea was still trying to come to terms with what Tommy had overheard when she entered her office that afternoon. Halfheartedly she checked her phone messages and then went to the kitchen.

Gerard greeted her enthusiastically and was telling her about lunch when Lea lapsed back into her reverie about Tommy.

"Yoo-hoo! Is anybody home?" Gerard sang out. "I feel like I'm talking to a brick wall."

"I'm sorry. What were you saying?" Lea asked contritely.

"I was telling you that the roasted mussels in almond butter were a huge hit. We ran out halfway through the service. Same with the seared day-boat scallops with the green lentil ragout.

"That's terrific." Lea roused herself.

"I'll say. This crowd was mad for shellfish. I think I sent out only two plates of red meat—to a couple of management consultants with the Jameson Holt Group."

"Hmmm," Lea said. "That reminds me of the consultant Keith hired—Anderson Pruett—the one who hung up on me."

Gerard appraised her. "You haven't given up on him, have you? I've never known you to take no for an answer."

"I'm not sure," she replied, remembering how frightened Anderson had been and how adamantly he'd refused to talk to her. Short of storming his office, she hadn't been able to think of a way to approach him.

Gerard's question lingered in her mind as she attended to office chores during the next hour, and she was in the middle of reviewing her laundry bill when she happened to recall a conversation with Joy. She'd said she had joined a gym—and that she'd seen Anderson Pruett there. "We seem to have the same workout schedule on Monday and Wednesday evenings," Joy had said casually. Today was Wednesday. Well, why not give it a try? Lea thought. She was running out of alternatives. She called Joy and arranged to borrow her gym pass later that day.

At 4:30, Lea drove home and changed into a tank top, shorts, and running shoes—hoping to pass for a gym regular. Not too bad, she thought as she surveyed herself in her full-length bedroom mirror. Her legs and arms were pale, but still shapely.

Traffic was heavy on Highway 101, and Lea didn't reach Whitten Systems until almost 6:00. She breathed a sigh of relief that Paul was in New York—thus precluding awkward explanations—only to have a nervous moment when she saw that Joy's gym pass had a photo ID. Lea tucked the pass into the pocket of her shorts and hoped that her passing resemblance to Joy would suffice.

Kellerman's Gym, located three miles from Whitten Systems, occupied a mustard-colored stucco building wedged between a half-timbered British pub and a Salvadorian *cantina*. Lea parked in Kellerman's garage and on her way out fell into step behind two young women toting gym bags. The ash blond wore a lavender and black striped halter top that revealed impeccably toned abs. Her clingy, matching shorts left little to the imagination. The brunette strutted in a fuchsia leotard cut high across her buns. The two looked as if they'd been dispatched by central casting to film an aerobics video.

Lea straggled into Kellerman's behind the pair and waited while the women conversed with the man at the front desk. His name tag read "Sven," and he resembled a Norse god. His flaxen curls brushed the nape of his neck, and his golden chest hair protruded through the web of his sleeveless mesh shirt. The brunette preened and took the time to ask about the gym's extended summer hours.

After the women had sashayed, giggling, into the crowded fray of machines and men, Lea stepped up to the desk and gave Sven what she hoped was a winsome smile. She flashed Joy's ID, which Sven glanced at without comment.

"I'm looking for a Dr. Anderson Pruett, who's usually here on a Wednesday night," Lea said. "Have you seen him tonight by any chance?"

Sven eyed her curiously.

"He's about 42, with short dark hair and a beard, and he often wears a Cal Bears T-shirt," Lea continued, quoting from Joy's description of the consultant.

"I know the guy," Sven acknowledged, obviously unimpressed with Lea's choice in men. "He came in a little while ago. I see him over by the free weights." Sven pointed to a corner of the gym.

Lea thanked him and waded into the gym proper—a sea of testosterone and pungent aromas. She meandered past sweating, often shirtless men of all ages as they grunted and groaned. Lea had never seen so many pecs in her life. Males outnumbered females by three to one—a fact Lea was sure had escaped many Silicon Valley women. She was conscious of many sets of eyes following her.

Once past the rows of treadmills and rowing machines, Lea found a panting Anderson executing a series of curls. Veins bulged in his biceps, and his face glistened with perspiration. She hung back until he'd finished his set of reps.

"Dr. Pruett?" Lea asked as he put down his weights.

"Yes?" Anderson seemed startled at being addressed.

"I'm Lea Sherwood, owner of Panache in San Francisco. You may remember me? I was a friend of Keith Whitten's, and I've been looking into his death."

Anderson exhaled abruptly and eyed his possible means of escape. Lea, however, had positioned herself squarely between Anderson and a beefy bodybuilder who was bench pressing what appeared to be his own weight.

"Please. I need your help," Lea pleaded. "You can't imagine what it's like to be a prime murder suspect. And to have everything you've worked for placed in jeopardy."

The man regarded her warily. But Lea held his eye, and slowly Anderson's expression softened. He pulled a towel from his gym bag and mopped his face. "I'm not a terrible person, Ms. Sherwood. You caught me on a bad day before, when I was still trying to come to terms with Keith's murder. I confess I was also scared for my own hide, which I can't say I'm proud of."

"Won't you talk to me now? It's the least you can do for Keith—and the rest of us."

He sighed deeply and returned the towel to his bag. "I have to say you've got guts to pursue this. OK. Let's go somewhere we can talk."

Lea followed Anderson off the gym floor and into an alcove crowded with vending machines stocked with sugar-free granola bars, fruit juices, and three brands of sparkling spring water. She declined his offer of a drink and waited until he'd downed half a bottle of a mango and papaya juice combo. She took a chair next to him at the one small table in the room.

"Tell me how you got involved in all this," Lea said.

Anderson glanced around to make sure they were alone and pulled his chair closer to Lea's. "Keith called me one day because I know the ropes in Asia. I spend a lot of time out there for our clients. He said he suspected that one of his senior people had something going on on the side—and that it might be illegal. He also said he'd hired a Bay Area detective to poke around, but that the guy hadn't turned up anything. Keith asked that I make inquiries, starting in Taipei and Hong Kong, where some of his sales and legal people went on a regular basis."

Lea waited impatiently as Anderson took a swig of juice.

"Well, I wasn't getting very far, and Keith was antsy, so I hired a detective named Min Qian, who was based in Kowloon. He sent Keith a report saying that someone at Whitten Systems was consorting with black-market dealers. Keith didn't tell me who the guy—or gal—was. He said it was safer that way. But he did tell me what the detective suspected. Qian thought the guy was running a scam selling Whitten software off the books and pocketing the money. Naturally that made Keith insane."

Anderson stopped speaking as a man and a woman in matching white gym togs, walking hand-in-hand, entered the room. They spent a minute debating the merits of sparkling spring water flavored with lemon versus lime before compromising on veggie juice.

Anderson took up his story when they had gone. "About a week later, when I was in Taipei, I was talking to the Chinese executive who'd recommended Qian to me, and he was quite upset. He said Qian had been found dead in a back alley of Hong Kong—behind a mah-jongg parlor. He'd died of a knife wound to the back. The Hong Kong police wrote it off as one more gambling casualty, but it spooked me, I have to tell you. Then when I heard about Keith...." Anderson trailed off.

They were each lost in their thoughts for a moment.

"That must be why Keith called the emergency board meeting," Lea suggested.

"I think so," Anderson agreed. "Keith said from the start that he didn't want to go to the police. All the sordid details would have leaked out. Keith would have looked like an idiot. A CEO who couldn't control his staff. A weenie who was running for his life. So Keith must have figured he'd be protected by exposing what he knew to the board. Then they could fire the guy involved and be rid of him, knowing that he wasn't about to talk."

"But Keith must have let on what he knew to the wrong person," Lea said. Keith had never been good at hiding his feelings. "And even if Keith had intended to fire him and be done with it, whoever he suspected must have known that the Whitten board would never stop at that. With 12 directors on the board, at least one would have insisted on tipping the police to any illegal scam. So our suspect turned to murder to protect his loot—and his freedom."

Anderson nodded glumly.

"Have you told all this to the police?" Lea asked.

"I did, finally, last week. I decided that catching a murderer took precedence over Keith's concerns about his reputation. Or my own fears about possible retaliation. But they didn't seem that interested. The homicide detective I talked to—Talifano—said that my story was merely conjecture, and that he had a stronger suspect."

Lea's hands began to tremble, and she locked them firmly on the tabletop. Yeah, me, she thought.

"There's something else," she said to Anderson, recalling her conversation with Tommy. She told him about it and waited hopefully for his reaction.

Anderson shrugged. "The Far East is a big place, and the authorities have their hands full combating all sorts of illegal activity."

Lea sighed, disappointed that Tommy's story didn't suggest more to the consultant.

Anderson finished his juice and got up to go.

"Wait," Lea said. "Did you know anyone at Whitten Systems besides Keith?"

"Not to speak of," Anderson said. "I did meet his marketing guy Schroth once—only because we ran into him when we were having lunch at Bristol's around the corner from here. Keith obviously didn't want anyone to know he'd hired me. When he introduced us, he made up a story about how he might pay my firm to do a financial analysis."

Anderson picked up his gym bag. "Funny you should bring that up. I saw Schroth in here the other night. I said hello to him in passing, but he didn't seem to remember me."

"Are you sure it was him?"

"Of course. It's my business to remember names and faces. Everyone's either a potential contact or a client." Anderson laughed. "I remember thinking that Schroth seemed a little out of place."

"What do you mean? A lot of Silicon Valley executives work out here."

"Exactly. They work out. Which Schroth wasn't doing. He was just kind of strolling on one of the treadmills. Not even breaking a sweat. The whole time he seemed to be looking for somebody."

Anderson checked his watch. "Gotta run, Ms. Sherwood. I've got a business dinner in half an hour. Good luck to you, and watch yourself. I'd hate to read in the paper that anything's happened to you."

Lea smiled weakly, thanked him for his time, and watched Anderson make a dash for the showers.

On her way out, Lea stopped again at the front desk. Sven was straightening a stack of membership brochures.

"Excuse me," Lea said. "I'm wondering if perhaps you also know a man named Marshall Schroth. He was in last week."

Sven gave her a peculiar look. "Yeah, I know the guy. Why do you ask about him?" Again Sven seemed to doubt her taste in men.

"Do you know if he met anyone here? I mean, did he seem to spend more time talking to someone than actually working out?"

Sven folded his arms across his chest and looked her straight in the eye. "Look, what's this all about? I've owned this place for a year, since I bought it from the Kellermans, and I know all my members. I also know you're not Joy Nugent, but I figured if she gave you her card I'd let you in this once. I thought maybe you wanted to try out the facilities without having to put up with a sales pitch. Will you tell me what's going on?"

Lea gulped and told him who she was and why she was there.

Sven's expression softened. "And you're going to catch the bad guys yourself, Ms. Sherwood? Come on."

"Please, just tell me what Marshall Schroth was doing."

Sven ran a hand along his square jaw. "He's been in twice since he joined up. Both times he met this Asian guy, and they talked while they exercised, so to speak." Sven snorted. "They lifted a few light weights and pussyfooted around on the treadmills."

"Who was the Asian man?" Lea asked eagerly.

Sven seemed reluctant to say more.

"Please, tell me who he is."

With an air of acting against his better judgment, Sven went to a file cabinet behind the desk, opened it, and pulled out a card. He handed it to Lea.

The photograph on the card was of a man in his twenties or early thirties. A thick shock of jet black hair fell over his forehead as he looked insolently at the camera. The name he'd given was Ric Chui. Lea pulled out a pen and notepad from her purse and wrote down his home address on Balboa Avenue, and his phone number.

"Balboa isn't far from here, is it?" Lea asked. She seemed to remember having seen it on the map earlier when she'd been looking for a route to Kellerman's.

Reluctantly, Sven told her how to get there.

Lea gave him a broad smile and wished him good luck with his new business.

Sven grunted in return. "Thanks, Ms. Sherwood. And I wish you good luck in saving your skin. I don't mind telling you, I didn't like the looks of our Mr. Chui."

29

Lea nosed the Renault into a parking space across the street from 1860 Balboa Avenue. The Pacific Pearl Motel located at that address was a dingy two-story, L-shaped building with peeling gray paint and graffiti-laced balcony railings. The doors to its rooms were alternately painted pink and purple, and the letters "i" and "r" were missing from its marquee. Lea saw a disheveled man in the motel's courtyard hand another man a roll of bills. She suspected he was not buying cough drops.

This must be Chui's idea of a joke. "Damn!" Lea said aloud.

As she squirmed in her seat, considering her next move, one of the purple doors opened and a couple stepped out. The man, a middle-aged Caucasian in a gray business suit, was squiring an Asian woman, who appeared to be half his age. Her glossy dark hair flowed almost to her waist, and she wore a sheer cream-colored blouse, a teensy black skirt, and red stiletto heels with a strap across the ankles in a style Lea had once heard described as "hump-me pumps." She was tugging a bra strap into place.

Lea watched as the couple parted and the woman—girl, really—entered the dimly lit motel office. It was barely possible, Lea reasoned, that Chui did actually live here, or that he had some connection to the place. Gritting her teeth, Lea turned off the engine, got out of the car, and locked the door. She waited for a break in traffic and sprinted across the street.

The girl was smoking a long filtered cigarette and talking to the desk clerk when Lea entered the office. The clerk, a young Asian man whose dandruff made it inadvisable for him to wear the navy shirt he'd selected for the night, ignored Lea at first. Only when she'd cleared her throat a second time did he deign to turn to her.

"Excuse me," Lea said. "I hate to interrupt you, but I'm looking for a Mr. Ric Chui." She spelled the name out. "I wonder if you know him?"

The two exchanged a startled glance and immediately gave Lea their full attention. A flash of something like fear crossed the girl's face, while the man preserved his deadpan.

"Does he live here?" Lea asked when neither of them spoke.

The girl appeared on the verge of saying something, but the man shot her a warning look. "What did you say the name was?" he asked.

Lea repeated it.

"I don't think we know anybody by that name, do we, Emerald?" he said carefully.

Emerald's hair rippled as she shook her head. She raised a trembling hand to her mouth and took a deep drag on her cigarette.

"Sorry, we can't help you," the clerk said.

"Thank you," Lea said coldly to both of them.

On her way out, she brushed against yet another man in a gray business suit who was sauntering in.

B ack in the car, Lea took stock of her options. She could return home empty-handed, perhaps to lie awake most of the night trying to decipher what Anderson Pruett, and Sven, had told her. Or she could keep going.

It was now 7:45 and still quite light out. Lea started the Renault and eased it into traffic. She made a right turn onto Cabrillo Street at the next block and drove two miles toward San Benito Boulevard, where Paul had his condo. She was now in familiar territory. She and Paul had driven this woodsy stretch of road many times, and he had once pointed out the location of Marshall Schroth's house. If the inscrutable Mr. Schroth was indeed keeping secrets, what better place to look for them than at his home?

Lea drove to Marshall's and took a sharp left turn into his driveway, which wound up the hillside through a thicket of manzanita bushes. His house was perched on the hillside overlooking the surrounding valley. Built of stone and stucco and rising to three stories, it vaguely reminded Lea of a baronial country house she'd once visited on an estate in Bordeaux. Lea parked near the entrance next to a vintage Jaguar.

To the far right of the house was a paddock, where a wiry man in a short-sleeved shirt, jeans, and cowboy boots was stroking the mane of a white Arabian horse. Lea got out of the Renault and headed across the lawn in his direction.

"Hello," she said when she reached the paddock's railing. "I'm Lea Sherwood. I know Mr. Schroth from Whitten Systems."

"Are you a friend of his?" the man asked warily.

"No, I wouldn't say that," Lea replied.

Something in her voice must have given her away, because the man relaxed. "In that case, I'm Garth Stewart," he said, extending a weathered hand through the slats. She took it as Garth squinted into the setting sun, revealing deep creases in his forehead. Now that Lea could see him up close, she guessed that Garth was in his fifties—older than his dark hair and trim physique would suggest.

"I come out here to train Mr. Schroth's horses," Garth said, gesturing to stables at the rear of the house. "Isn't that right, Khaki?" he asked, nuzzling the neck of the horse, who had advanced to the railing.

"May I stroke him?" Lea asked. She had always liked horses but hadn't ridden since going to camp when she was 16.

"Go right ahead."

Lea gently raised her hand and stroked the Arabian's silky mane. The horse made a throaty sound, and Lea and Garth smiled at one another.

"I suppose you've heard about the two deaths at Whitten Systems?" Lea ventured, giving Khaki a final stroke. Something about Garth made him seem approachable.

The man nodded. "I sure have," he said. The corner of his mouth curled in what Lea took to be disgust.

"You seem to have an opinion about it all."

"Oh, I've got plenty of opinions, not that they'll do the victims any good."

"What do you mean?"

"Only that the police don't seem too anxious to dig in and solve the murders. At first they made a big fuss about investigating, because Whitten was such a prominent guy. But now they're being stonewalled by Schroth and the other rich executives at that company. I heard him tell the police the other day to leave him alone. And when you've got a dead man who can't complain and a slew of executives who don't want to be questioned, guess who wins?"

Lea nodded in agreement, and her intuition told her to probe further. "Did you know either Keith Whitten or Francine Reese?"

"Not the lady, but I did see Whitten out here one Sunday."

"Garth, if there's anything you can tell me that may be related to his death, I'd be very grateful. If you've read the papers, you probably know that I'm under suspicion," Lea said.

The trainer held her eye for a moment. "I don't mind telling you that I've never been terribly impressed by Schroth, or that I gave him notice a few days ago. I also told the police what I'm about to tell you, but to my knowledge they haven't done much about it."

"Go on," Lea said. It had gotten cooler, and she shivered in her tank top and shorts.

"Whitten came out here one Sunday afternoon, and he and Schroth had words. Whitten had never been here before, and he showed up unexpectedly with a brainstorm he wanted to discuss. Some kind of marketing campaign, he said. We were out here, getting ready to saddle up, and Whitten planted himself almost where you're standing now. He started to look around in surprise at the property, and he asked how many acres the Schroths had. I asked Schroth if he wanted me to leave, but he said no, I guess to discourage Whitten from going on. He sure never asked him into the house.

"Then Whitten said, 'How on earth can you afford this place on your salary? I know you and your wife don't have family money.' " Garth gestured up at the hills, which the summer sun and a lack of rain had rendered tawny gold. "I don't know if you realize it, but the Schroths own eight acres up here, including the land with stables back of the house, and really fine riding trails."

Lea took in the panorama. In Silicon Valley's inflated real estate prices, Marshall's spread must have cost him upwards of $7 million. Not even Keith had lived so palatially. "Then what happened?" she asked.

"Whitten started asking Schroth questions, like why he was making so many trips to the Far East. He really pressed him about that. When Whitten left, I heard Schroth say, kind of under his breath, 'You son of a bitch. You'd better mind your own business.' "

Lea tried not to let her excitement show.

"Are the Schroths at home now, do you know?"

"No. He left for a night flight to Asia about an hour ago, and she went out for the evening," Garth said.

Lea turned to gaze at Marshall's grand house. The sun had just set, and carriage lights glowed warmly at the front door. "I'd sure like to get inside," she said.

Garth gave her a long look. "I'd be happy to offer you a drink of water, or something even stronger," he said. "In fact Delores, the housekeeper, is expecting me to stop by about now."

Lea nodded her thanks, and they walked to the back door of the house, where Garth knocked twice.

After a moment, a woman with black hair, a Latin complexion, and high cheekbones appeared on the other side of the door's glass panes. She grinned expectantly at them, revealing a gold front tooth.

"There you are!" she exclaimed to Garth as she opened the door. Delores wore a short-sleeved sweater and skirt and bangle bracelets on both wrists. "I was afraid you weren't coming tonight."

Garth pecked her on the cheek and introduced Lea as an old family friend who'd stopped by to see the horses. He went to the kitchen cupboard, pulled out a tumbler, and held it up inquiringly.

"Water is fine," Lea said, glancing around the French Country kitchen. A trellis of pseudo grape vines separated the eating area from the kitchen proper, and a cocky porcelain rooster surveyed his domain from atop a cabinet.

Garth filled the glass from the tap and handed it to Lea as Delores urged them both to sit down at the bleached oak table.

Garth demurred. "I have to go put Khaki in for the night, but I'd love to have your company," he said to Delores. "Then maybe we can go out back for a walk." Garth turned to Lea. "You're driving home to the city, aren't you?"

"Yes," Lea said, taking her cue. She took several swallows of water and put her glass down on the table. "But first, would you mind if I used your rest room?"

"Of course not," Delores said. "I'll show you where it is." She took Lea by the elbow and led her out of the kitchen.

"You stay put until I come back," she called over her shoulder to Garth.

When they got to the bathroom, just off the main hallway, Lea turned and smiled at Delores. "Please, go with Garth," she said. "I'm parked right out front, and I can let myself out when I'm done." Lea gestured in the direction of the front door.

Delores smiled—obviously eager to return to Garth. "O-kee-dokey," she sang as she bustled away, her bracelets jangling.

Lea shut the bathroom door behind her and surveyed the sizeable room, whose walls were papered in a pattern depicting bluebirds and cardinals merrily building nests. The basin of the white pedestal sink bore the image of a robin clutching a squiggling worm in its beak.

After waiting a minute, Lea returned to the hall, where she did another quick survey. She guessed that all of the bedrooms were upstairs, and that if Marshall had a home office, it was on this floor.

She moved quickly, past the curving staircase, a wet bar, and the formal dining room—ostentatious with a crystal chandelier and a mural depicting bewigged French courtesans and their beaus reclining on a lawn. At the end of the hall was a room that evidently served as a den.

Lea looked each way to make sure no one was watching and entered the room. This must be Marshall's office, she decided. Etchings of the gentry riding to hounds lined a wall above a massive mahogany desk. On the opposite wall, bookshelves boasted a collection of duck decoys and dozens of books on how to succeed in business.

She went to the desk, put down her purse, and opened the top center drawer. It held nothing but note paper, stamps, pencils, and pens. In the top left-hand drawer, however, she found a slim date book. Lea sat down in the maroon leather-backed desk chair and leafed through the pages.

Eager to check out her suspicions about Marshall's recent trip to the Far East, Lea turned to the entries for the second week in May. When she came to Thursday, the 10th, a notation jumped out at her: A. Kim for dinner at 8:00 P.M. Not C. T. Chang, the client Marshall had identified on his expense account form. Who was A. Kim? And why was Marshall meeting him in secret?

The page for Friday was blank, but under Saturday Marshall had penciled in: Depart for Kimpo, 7:12 A.M. *Kimpo.* That was the airport in Seoul. Her parents had once described a layover there. Lea studied the entries for Saturday and Sunday. Marshall had scheduled several appointments on both days, flying out Sunday night for Hong Kong and hooking up with his return flight home.

Obviously he had wanted his South Korean jaunt to remain private. Not a hint of it had appeared on his expense account.

She went back to the beginning of the month and examined each page. *What on earth?* "Taipei, 8 RAMs," Marshall had written cryptically under May 3. "Pusan, 2 PROMs," she read under May 7. For May 12, one of the days he was in Seoul, Marshall had jotted down "3 SRAMs, Pyongyang."

RAMs, Lea thought. Was he referring to computer chips? RAM chips, she knew, were random-access memory chips. And PROMs were ... what? Programmable read-only memory, she decided. SRAMs, she seemed to recall, were static memory chips. Vaguely she associated them with military hardware. But what did the numerals refer to? Shipping containers? Truckloads?

Lea remembered Marshall's phone bills, and his frequent calls to TYBER Semiconductor. Was he moonlighting for the firm? Acting as an agent? None of this made any sense.

She thought back to a conversation she'd once had with Paul about the tremendous "shrinkage" in the semiconductor industry. Semiconductor chips were so tiny and lightweight that workers could easily slip a handful into their pockets. Then there were the break-ins, when huge volumes of chips got carted away. And the recent spate of kidnappings and attacks on employees, who were forced under gunpoint to admit thieves into warehouses. In other cases, thieves managed to infiltrate a company with one or more of their own security guards—or even their own technical people. Stolen chips then turned up in the gray market to be sold by middlemen, either legal or illegal.

The buyers of stolen chips were often firms who purchased in small quantities or otherwise turned to brokers when their normal distribution channels dried up—or they were people who operated on the margin.

Lea remembered too that gray market chips were often defective. Many were stolen before being subjected to a manufacturer's quality tests—which routinely rejected more than 30% of the chips produced. Lea had read of cases where bad chips even turned up in life-saving medical equipment abroad. Tough luck for the patients who died as a result.

Wearily Lea reached a hand deep into the drawer that had yielded the date book. Tucked away in the back was a tiny eel skin card case. She pulled it out and removed a handful of business cards bearing the logos of import-export firms based throughout the Far East. One was from A. Kim of Seoul and another from T. R. Yi of Pyongyang. Ordinarily she would assume the cards were those of clients, or business associates. Then it came to her. Pyongyang was the capital of North Korea. And if Marshall was doing business with Mr. Yi, it was probably illegal. The United States had trade embargoes against North Korea.

She turned Yi's card over. In Marshall's pinched handwriting was the notation: 5/12, monies due. So the clandestine trip to Seoul must have involved a meeting with the man from Pyongyang.

Suddenly Lea heard a cough behind her, and a chill ran down her spine. "Delores?" she asked as she spun around.

Marshall Schroth stood five feet from her, a compact black automatic weapon clenched in one hand. Deliberately, he released the safety.

Lea froze as Marshall lunged at her and snatched Yi's card from her hand. Marshall's eyes blazed with hatred. Belatedly, Lea recognized his after-shave.

30

"**I**...I thought you were on your way to Asia," Lea stammered.

"Evidently," Marshall said, taking in the open drawer, the scattered business cards, and Lea's purse on his desk. He walked around the desk to face her squarely. "My flight was delayed. Will you tell me what you think you're doing?"

Lea's knees began to shake. There was no bluffing her way out now. She took a deep breath and did her best to eye Marshall steadily. "I think I've finally figured out what you've been up to, Marshall, but tell me if I'm right. I'd say you're smuggling computer chips into the Far East and selling them on the black market. You're running an international smuggling ring."

Marshall's lips curled in condescension. "Yes, I suppose you could describe it that way. But I prefer to describe my business as exporting a product to legitimate dealers who in turn sell the goods at a competitive price."

"But you steal the chips," Lea challenged him.

"I have a network of suppliers who procure them outside of legal channels, yes. But enough talk. I'm afraid that now,

Ms. Sherwood, you'll have to have to pay your own price for interfering in my affairs."

Lea started as a muscular man with a buzz cut entered the room. In his hands were a tattered red bandanna and a length of cord.

"You couldn't leave well enough alone, could you?" Marshall asked. "Going through my expense accounts. Sneaking into my house. Luckily we'd worked out a plan in case you forced our hand."

Lea felt light-headed and dizzy. *Scream!* she willed herself. *It may be your only chance.* But when she opened her mouth, no sound would come.

Marshall, observing her, laughed. "It won't do you any good. There's no one to hear you."

Lea swallowed hard.

"Gag her and tie her up, Wayne," Marshall ordered the man, who was looming over Lea. Marshall rummaged in Lea's purse and pulled out her car key. "And make sure you hide her Renault until we're ready for it." He tossed the key to Wayne.

"You'll never get away with this," Lea faltered. "For one thing, you're bound to leave evidence."

Marshall smiled nastily. "Oh, I don't think so, Ms. Sherwood. Your death is going to look like a very unfortunate accident."

L ea lay prostrate on the back floor of Marshall's Lexus, where Wayne had roughly consigned her. Her hands were bound tightly behind her back, and she nearly choked on the bandana Wayne had stuffed in her mouth. The cloth felt grimy and tasted rank.

"Don't forget, Wayne's gun is on you," Lea heard Marshall say from the driver's seat. As if to underscore the point, Lea felt Wayne prod her with the barrel.

The night was still. Indigo shadows were broken intermittently by the flash of oncoming headlights. Marshall kept to a sedate pace. Once, when Wayne opened his window, a whiff of wood smoke swept over Lea. They must be traversing the back roads of the Peninsula.

Her hands throbbed in their bindings, and Lea shifted her weight. Immediately a sharp pain seared through her inner wrist. She twisted her head to see a jagged metal edge protruding from a box beneath the front seat. Biting her lip against the pain, Lea nudged her wrists up against the metal and worked them back and forth. After a minute, she tried to pull her wrists apart. The rope gave slightly.

Suddenly a loud buzzing came from the front seat. Lea started and then realized it was a cell phone.

"What?" Wayne barked. "Good job," he said a few moments later.

"That was Sam Wong," Wayne said, lowering his voice. "The chips just cleared customs in South Korea, and they're being repackaged for transshipment to the north. Sam's paid off a couple of border guards, and he expects the operation to go smoothly."

Lea heard Marshall chuckle.

"We're in on the ground floor, my friend!" Marshall said. "A population of over 2 million in Pyongyang alone, eager for the latest in technology. And with the Soviet Union out of the picture as a trading partner, the market's ours to develop."

Gradually Lea became aware of overhead lights, and of the car slowing to a halt. "Have a good night, sir," she heard a man's raspy voice call. The car started moving again. Were they crossing a guarded gate?

It wasn't long before Marshall stopped again and cut the engine. "This is it," he announced.

He stepped out and opened the rear door, inches from Lea's head. She ducked instinctively, afraid he would kick her. Instead he helped her up, keeping a tight grip on her. Wayne came around to her other side and took her arm, pinning Lea between them. Together they propelled her over a paved surface, with the muzzle of Marshall's gun grinding into her rib cage.

A ghastly vibration filled the darkness, punctuated by queer sucking and flushing sounds. The black evening sky was illuminated only by a sliver of crescent moon and a few straggling stars. Lea dimly perceived the spectral outline of tanks looming ahead, and the perimeter of a one-story building.

As they approached the structure, the vibration intensified, pulsating through her. A whirring sound was now audible against a strident whooshing, and Lea squinted to decipher the words on a sign beside the loading dock: "TYBER Semiconductor Co. Wafer Fab Operations and Deliveries."

Wafer fabrication. Why were they bringing her to a plant that made semiconductor chips?

They were now within 20 feet of the concrete building, which was bordered by acid waste tanks and low cinder-block storage sheds. Bright hazard signs glowed ominously. Diamond-shaped and divided into equal segments of red, yellow, white, and blue, they warned of reactivity, flammability, and other perils.

Marshall prodded her and guided them past another sign. "Caution. Hazardous Waste Area," it advised. The words were blazoned in English across the top and in Spanish below. Suddenly there was a roar, and a blast of cold air whacked Lea below the knees. Her legs buckled involuntarily.

Marshall laughed and yanked her upright. "If the air from the vacuum pumps freaks her out, wait till she gets inside," he said to Wayne.

They reached the rear entrance of the building, where a security guard was sitting beneath a wall-mounted camera. Hope surged through Lea.

Marshall caught her gaze and laughed again, cruelly. "Don't get excited. Wayne is a trusted employee of TYBER, and Joe here is one of ours."

Joe cracked his hairy knuckles and winked at Lea.

Marshall pushed Lea forward as Wayne signed in and ran his badge over the scanner, gaining admittance to the plant.

Inside, Lea blinked in the sudden glare of bright fluorescent lights. And when they passed a door with a tiny glass panel, she did a double take. Clean room workers in bulky, surreal white spacesuits seemed to float across the floor. It was impossible to tell if they were men or women. Lea took in the hoods, the knee-high boots, and the vinyl gloves tucked tightly into the suits. Breathing nozzles extended from the hoods and down the workers' backs.

Vaguely, she recalled reading that clean room personnel suited up not to protect themselves, but the delicate silicon chips. And that their antiseptic working area, which resembled a hospital operating room, was in fact many times cleaner. Air in a fab was constantly being channeled through a series of filters to remove pollens and other impurities, since just one speck of dust could short out the intricate layers of electronic circuitry. Ballpoint pens were also used instead of dust-prone pencils, and female workers, who comprised the majority of the workforce, were forbidden to wear makeup.

Lea squirmed. If only she could cry out!

Marshall steered her around a corner and into a narrow storage chamber. Gas cabinets with Do Not Open signs lined the walls, as did chemical monitors with sinister-looking dials. Gigantic metal exhaust ducts wound through the room, emitting an insistent hum.

Lea shook her head in frustration and tried to work her mouth around the gag. Wayne had disappeared, but Marshall was at her elbow. "I'll undo this," he said, loosening the cloth so that it slid down around her neck, "because there's something I want to ask you. But your hands stay tied." Marshall backed away from her, observing her closely. "And don't think it will do you any good to scream. With all the noise this equipment makes, the folks in there"—he inclined his head toward the clean room—"will never hear you."

Gingerly, Lea flexed her jaw muscles. "Where are we?" she asked, gazing at the monitors incredulously.

There was a long silence. Just as Lea was convinced the question had fallen on deaf ears, Marshall reluctantly said, "This area is called a chase. In a single-story fab like this, it's where chemicals get distributed into the clean room. "Those cabinets"—he gestured to the opposite wall—"contain nitrous oxide and ammonia. Oh, and watch out for the one behind you. It's full of pyrophoric silane. When exposed to air, it can burst into flames."

Lea jumped in spite of herself.

Marshall smirked. "Once when Wayne and I were discussing what we might have to do with you, he suggested giving you a dose of phosphine. It was used during World War II as a nerve gas. Then of course there's hydrofluoric acid. It attacks the calcium in your bones." Marshall waved a hand. "It's diabolical, really. It doesn't work like most acids. You don't feel a thing at first, as some poor souls in the Valley will attest. I know a guy who spilled it on himself and later lost two fingers."

Lea stared at Marshall. It took all of her resolve to remain outwardly calm.

"Of course most of the fatalities that occur in this industry are electrical," he said with an elaborate shrug. "It stands to reason. With all the high-voltage equipment, you're bound to have a few accidents."

Lea tugged at the rope binding her wrists and clenched her jaw to keep it from trembling. She scanned the room, looking for an escape route.

Marshall smiled. "Relax. It would raise too many questions if we killed you that way. You're lucky, in fact. You'll get what a lot of people pray for—a painless death."

Lea glared at him.

"Wayne is up on the roof arranging it now." Marshall craned his neck and gestured. "See the ceiling fans? Each room has fans connected to individual air handlers on the roof. We're diverting a line of nitrogen and piping it into a special room. Just for you. After Wayne shuts off the regular air flow system, the nitrogen will quickly displace the oxygen. You'll pass out in minutes, and be dead soon after," Marshall said with relish.

Sadist. He's really enjoying this, Lea thought. She swallowed hard and glanced at the hair-trigger dials on the gas detectors to either side of her. "But it looks like the gas flows are strictly monitored. Aren't there automatic shutoffs or alarms when anything gets out of whack?"

"Oh sure," Marshall said nonchalantly. "In the manufacturing areas, the shutoff system would be activated, and flow devices would divert the nitrogen. But there are a few modules in back that aren't linked to any monitors." He checked his watch. "It shouldn't be long before Wayne has the connection in place."

"And afterwards?"

"You mean after your death? Then it's back to Crestline Boulevard. You're going to emulate your friend Francine by driving off a particularly steep ridge. If your body isn't charred beyond recognition in the gas tank explosion—which it almost certainly will be—the coroner will be able to see there are no suspicious marks of struggle. Wayne was careful with your restraints. Any marks you do have might be attributed to scrapes you sustained in the accident." Marshall's look was challenging. "But enough of that. What I'd like to know is how you came to focus on my activities."

"You were careless," Lea retorted. "You called that South Korean number from the office. It caught my attention—and Keith's too. He tried it himself."

Marshall frowned. "That *was* careless of me. But my cell phone was out, and I had to reach my Korean contact right away."

He made a move toward her, as if to gag her again.

Lea forced herself to focus and not give way to panic. *Keep talking*, she told herself. And play for time.

"Tell me, Marshall, doesn't it bother you to be selling technology to North Korea? They're a major nuclear threat, and you're probably helping them build weapons that could wipe us out. We don't have trade embargoes against them for nothing."

Marshall stopped and sniggered at her. "Spare me the sanctimonious blather. Yesterday's enemies are today's legitimate business partners—just look at our trade with China and Russia. It's only a matter of time before we recognize North Korea. All I'm doing is getting in on the ground floor."

"Then why keep your legitimate job if you're such an entrepreneur?"

Marshall was gloating now. "I like having the cover. I also haven't given up on becoming president of Whitten Systems. Paul's days are numbered, and I'm the perfect choice to head the company. I'll have the recognition I deserve, and the wealth to live as I please."

Lea gave him a dubious look. "I wouldn't be so sure. You may get careless and slip up again. It's one thing to kill Keith because he was on to you and was going to inform the board. But why did you take the risk of committing a second murder?"

Marshall laughed shortly. "Francine was nosy. Just like you. I think she had some futile notion of redeeming herself after she agreed to cook the books for Keith."

"How do you know Francine was telling the truth about that?"

"Oh, I have my own means of surveillance," Marshall said airily. "I know for a fact that Keith gave her little choice. He would have fired her in an instant if she'd refused."

Lea gazed at him in disbelief. "You really don't see anything wrong with all this, do you?

Marshall laughed again. "Get real, Ms. Sherwood. This is the way of the world. Like I told Paul, there are winners and losers. I didn't invent the game, and I'm just trying to get my share. I'm not one of those little people who slave all their lives from 9 to 5 in return for a modest roof over their heads and a vacation at the beach once a year."

When Marshall wasn't looking, Lea tugged at the cords that were binding her wrists. They were still tight, but she thought she detected some slack.

She heard a noise in the hall, and then Wayne opened the door. "It's time," he said.

31

A muscle twitched in Marshall's jaw, and he removed the gun from his pocket. "Gag her," he ordered.

Wayne stepped behind Lea, stuffed the bandanna between her teeth, and secured it firmly.

Marshall motioned for Wayne to leave first and then prodded Lea to follow him. With his free hand, he picked up her purse. "For ID purposes," he said.

Now! screamed a voice within her. *Kick! Run!*

Marshall, who apparently had read her thoughts, coughed softly and curled a finger around the trigger.

Wayne led the way down several hallways, in the opposite direction of the clean room, until they reached a small, unfurnished room evidently used for storage. Boxes and crates were stacked high along two walls.

Marshall shoved her through the door and she scrambled into the room, barely able to stay on her feet.

"This is it, Ms. Sherwood. Happy eternity." Marshall gave her a long smug look. Then, with a sense of finality, he stepped back into the hall and shut the door, locking it behind him.

Through the small glass door panel, Lea saw him saunter away, talking to Wayne.

Her mind raced—she knew she had only minutes. With as much force as she could muster, she thrust her forearms apart, trying to loosen the rope bonds. Pain radiated up her arms. Yet the knots had slackened. She forced herself to try again, and again. She backed up to the door, using the doorknob for leverage. Twisting her wrists and tugging, she finally wrestled one hand free. Quickly she released the other.

Sighing with relief, she untied her gag and scanned the room. There were no windows. The only possible outlet was the glass panel in the door. It wasn't large enough to squeeze through. But if she could break it, she could breathe—and scream.

Click. A shudder of fear seized her. Lea heard thumps on the ceiling, another click, and then felt the sudden rush of the nitrogen.

She ran to the crates and hoisted one, almost reeling from the weight. She rammed a sharp corner of it into the glass, recoiled, then struck again. She staggered back, dropping the box with a crash. It was no use. The glass was as dense as a car windshield. She needed something sharper.

Desperately, she remembered her purse. Marshall had tossed it on the floor when he'd left. She grabbed it and plowed through its contents. Wallet. Address book. Comb. Pen. No sharp object. Wait!

At the bottom was a flash of metal. Hope surged through her. The gold spiral corkscrew, her gift from M. Beaulieu, gleamed as she retrieved it. Not daring to breathe, she uncapped it, aimed the tip at the center of the glass panel, and lunged.

As though shot with a bullet, the glass popped—then cracked. Lea plunged into the glass again. Digging and stabbing, she forged a ragged hole.

She screamed through the cavity for help, then shoved her mouth against the broken glass, gasping for air. She was breathing shallowly now, and growing lightheaded. She gripped the corkscrew in her right hand and squeezed it, then her arm, though the opening. She cried out as jagged glass tore her flesh.

Wincing from the pain, Lea tilted the corkscrew, straining to align its tip with the exterior lock of the door. She fought back dizziness, simultaneously twisting her arm, down and around, trying to make contact with the lock. It wouldn't work. It was too big a stretch. Lea gulped and tried to suck in more clean air. She wouldn't last much longer. Darkness began to blur the corners of her eyes.

Suddenly she heard frantic footsteps echoing in the hallway. Someone had heard the glass shatter! She rejoiced until the footfalls reached a crescendo and Marshall, panting, raced around the corner of the hall. She pulled her arm back into the room as he skidded to a stop, his face a mask of fury.

He unlocked the door, grabbed her, and pulled her free of the gas. "You bitch!" he hissed. He dug the barrel of his gun into the small of her back and shoved her forward. Lea stumbled, gasping for breath.

As if in a dream, she instinctively recoiled. Staggering, she simultaneously lifted her right foot, slamming it down on Marshall's instep, and, with her bleeding right hand, thrust the sharp corrugated tip of the corkscrew back and center.

Marshall's excruciating howl of pain resounded throughout the corridor.

Lea sprinted off, glancing back once. Marshall was writhing on the floor, clutching his groin.

She ran blindly toward what she prayed was the back door. As she reached a fork in the hallway, nausea overcame her. She stumbled again, unsure of where to turn. Left or right? The lady or the tiger?

Lea stopped to catch her breath, groping for the wall to steady herself. She struggled to recall which way they'd come. She veered left, careened down the hall, then spun to her right when she spotted an opening. Ahead of her was the clean room!

She ran toward it, her breath coming in shallow, erratic gasps. Her chest heaved as if it would burst. Suddenly strong hands seized her by the waist. They lifted and carried her, kicking, into the room Marshall called a chase. When she was back on her feet, Lea reeled to face a snarling Wayne.

"Don't let go of her!" Marshall yelled as he ran toward them.

Lea whirled and rammed Wayne under the jaw with her elbow, catching him off guard. Wayne, his arms flailing, screamed and lurched backward, into the silane gas cabinet. The keening of splintering glass reached a crescendo as Wayne's head split the case. Plumes of blue and orange flames erupted, engulfing him. A wall of heat surged toward Lea.

An alarm began to peal, all but drowning out Wayne's shrieks.

Lea bolted into the hall and raced toward the door of the clean room. Sobbing, she threw herself against it and worked the knob, but the door wouldn't budge. She pounded on the frame until she thought her fist would break, but the workers inside didn't respond.

She turned and ran toward an illuminated exit sign. It led her back the way they'd come, but no guard was in sight. She took a deep breath, yanked the back door open, and plunged out into the night.

She could see little at first, but as her eyes adjusted to the darkness, she forced herself to get her bearings. The rumble of the pumps again vibrated through her, and the hazard signs glowed eerily. Fighting back nausea, she swayed, struggling to keep her balance. She squinted at the outlines of the locked chemical sheds. Not one place to hide!

Suddenly she remembered the man who'd admitted them to the grounds. Of course! He must be posted at a guard house. But was he also on Marshall's payroll? Lea strained to remember his words. In any event, she had to chance it.

She took off, hugging the shadows at the side of the building. Blood from her wound oozed down her arm. Behind her, she heard the back door slam, and the shouts of two men. One of the voices was Marshall's.

Lea flew across the pavement, adrenaline surging through her. She ran blindly, willing her legs to go faster. Suddenly a blast split the air. Bullets whizzed past her head and shoulders, and a hail of metal pelted the ground. She raced on, chilled by the close burst of gunfire. Curses rang behind her, and Lea snapped her head around. Marshall was gaining on her.

Lungs burning, Lea bounded through the darkness. Her eyes zeroed in on the corner of the building. If only she could reach it! Another bullet whirred past. As if in a dream, Lea bolted for the corner—and rounded it.

The gatehouse now loomed ahead—the silhouettes of two men illuminated in its pale yellow light. With Lea's last ounce of strength, she sprinted toward them. The men rushed out to meet her, both yelling at once. A second later, she collapsed at their feet.

The last thing Lea heard before blacking out was the siren of an ambulance.

Epilogue

A dense fog blanketed the city the next afternoon as Lea gathered with Paul, Sydney, Gerard, and Brooke at Panache. She was calm as she described the evidence she'd relayed to the police, the all-points bulletin issued for Marshall Schroth, and his arrest at SFO hours later.

"I still wish the hospital had kept you for observation," Brooke fretted, gesturing to Lea's heavily bandaged right arm.

"I'll be fine," Lea said. She smiled reassuringly around the table, letting her gaze linger on Paul, who'd joined her in the emergency room at St. Joseph's Hospital and had not since left her side.

"I came so close to losing you," he said, his voice breaking.

She choked at the intensity of his words, and tears blurred her eyes. "We came so close to losing each other," she amended.

His puzzled frown faded into somber realization. "Yes, we did."

Sydney stood abruptly, murmuring something about making tea in the kitchen, and Gerard and Brooke jumped up to follow her.

When they'd gone, Paul took Lea's hands in his. His brow was creased, and his expression was penetrating. "You mean everything to me, and I never want to be apart from you. Do you think we can start over again?"

Lea gave him a long look—and suddenly broke into a radiant smile. She reached out to Paul as his arms encircled her.

"I know we can."